CREMORNE GARDENS

For a moment the young couple looked into each other's eyes and then their mouths met in a most delicious kiss. They sank to the ground in a close embrace and Walter's tongue made an instant, darting journey of exploration inside the pretty girl's mouth. Katie responded with avidity and did not repulse the handsome lad when his hand crept slowly, lingeringly down from her throat towards the valley between her breasts, moulding the linen blouse against her skin.

Katie gasped with joy, and the thought flashed through her mind that this must be how Tricia her cat must feel when she stroked her. Walter's hand continued its progress, insistently now, over the full twin curves of her rising breasts and the randy young girl shivered with raw, unslaked desire . . .

CREMORNE GARDENS

ANONYMOUS

 BLUE MOON BOOKS
NEW YORK

Cremorne Gardens
Copyright © 1990, 2005 by Potiphar Productions

Published by
Blue Moon Books
An Imprint of Avalon Publishing Group Incorporated
245 West 17th Street, 11th floor
New York, NY 10011-5300

First Blue Moon Books Edition 2005

First Published in 1990 by Headline Book Publishing PLC

ISBN 1-56201-497-8

9 8 7 6 5 4 3 2 1

Printed in Canada
Distributed by Publishers Group West

INTRODUCTION

It is a strange oddity of contemporary times that we do not readily associate the Victorian age with sensuality. Our picture of the Victorian decades is one of demure, downcast eyes, of maidenly blushes and tinkerings at the piano and of bewhiskered men of business standing solemnly before ornate mantelpieces.

Yet this vision is incomplete; in the great population explosion of the nineteenth century there must have been some enjoyment, however socially illicit, some revelling in the Sins of the Flesh, some private beliefs that sex was not sinful at all.

The stories contained in this book show the downside to the accepted picture of bourgeois respectability. Totally uninhibited and delightfully erotic, it was of course published privately by a group of devotees. Although written almost one hundred years ago, its frankness may well still have the power to shock as we peer beneath those swelling bodices, under the waist-coated, upright worthiness to discover an inventive appetite for sexual pleasures even in the most unlikely times and places.

How did the stories come to be written? The starting point here is found in the famous south-west London borough of Chelsea where in the eighteenth and nine-teenth century (just as in contemporary times) property developers built fine houses for the rich and influential members of society. Chelsea has always been a wealthy, upper-class area though at the same time it has also earned a slightly disreputable, raffish reputation as a haunt for artists, writers and musicians. Since the first coffee houses and restaurants opened on the Kings Road, Chelsea has always been a Mecca for the latest styles in fashion and its trendy image persists even today.

This image was well established by the 1870s when Londoners flocked to the Cremorne Gardens, perhaps the most popular of its kind in Britain. The Cremorne enjoyed an attraction for all classes of visitors. During the day, respectable middle-class folk crowded in to listen to the military bands and to take their partners for a waltz on the large floor or enjoy a meal or a glass or two of wine in one of the three restaurants.

Even that stern social critic Doctor William Acton (who believed that masturbation led to insanity) could find little fault with 'the jolly eruption of laughter that now and then came bursting through the crowd which fringed the dancing floor and roved about the adjacent sheds in search of company; but that gone by, you heard very plainly the sigh of the poplar, the surging gossip of the tulip tree and the plash of the little embowered foun-tain that served two plaster children as an endless shower-bath.'

However, as Acton sourly noted, whilst in spring and summer the clientele was sober enough during the hours of daylight, 'by dusk, as calico and merry respectability tailed off eastward by penny steamers, the setting sun brought westward Hansoms freighted with demure immorality clothed in silk and fine linen. By about ten o'clock age and innocence had seemingly all retired . . .' And as social historian Peter Quennell drily commented in his introduction to Henry Mayhew's contemporary work on the London underworld: 'the amusements (then) provided were sometimes boisterous . . . and many occasions often ended with a free fight and general panic-stricken stampede towards the safety of the Kings Road.' Alas, the current scene holds a parallel for the area is often cursed with hordes of unwanted hooligans who converge on Stamford Bridge whenever there is a major match at Chelsea Football Club's stadium.

However, one hundred years ago, any disturbances were blamed on society 'toffs' and the many members of Chelsea's bohemian artistic colony who were regular visitors to the Cremorne Gardens. Amongst those frequently seen there were Swinburne, George Bernard Shaw and Oscar Wilde, the latter being attracted perhaps by the proximity of a notorious homosexual brothel run by a mysterious Mrs Payne in The Boltons.

And of course there were was no shortage of ladies of pleasure who were on hand to partner the scores of youths who came to the Cremorne primarily to find sexual partners. Many of these young drones were scions of the aristocracy who spent their days taking morning rides down Rotten Row, enjoying huge lunches and lazy afternoons at the clubs and then dressed to dine either formally at one of the smart houses or at a fashionable restaurant, after which a carriage was called for to take them perhaps to one of the burgeoning music halls, to a Haymarket coffee house or to the Cremorne where large numbers of prostitutes gathered to find customers.

For many happy years one such lucky young man was the French born theatrical impressario Max Dalmaine (1852–1939) who spent his days in such carefree fashion, many mornings being concerned with recovering from the nights before! A second son of a wealthy Huguenot banking family from Lyons, Dalmaine was first sent to London to complete his medical studies under, of all people, the notorious Doctor Jonathan Mertley, an extraordinary rake who for many years prospered mightily in Harley Street as a specialist in 'intimate diseases' contracted by unfortunate members of fashionable London – at this time venereal infections raged through many European cities and were almost as deadly as AIDS is in our contemporary times.

Mertley was finally struck off the medical rolls for seducing his prettier female patients but was able to enjoy a comfortable lifestyle thanks to the judicious investments made on his behalf by Count Johann Gewirtz and other shrewd members of the ultra-fashionable South Hampstead set who included amongst their numbers the indefatigable collector of erotica Henry Spencer Ashbee (Pisanus Fraxi); Sir Lionel Trapes, a highly placed Treasury official and writer of much gallant literature for such popular underground magazines as *The Pearl* and *The Oyster*, two scurrillously rude publications which enjoyed great illicit popularity during the 1880s and 1890s; and Captain Terence Whitley of the Guards whose amazing capacity to satisfy girl after girl at secret sex shows at the Jim Jam Club in Soho attracted the attention of the Prince of Wales.

Perhaps not surprisingly in such company, Dalmaine abandoned his medical studies and lived a hedonistic, pleasure-filled life, staying first at his aunt's Belgrave Square mansion and then at his own apartment in Green Street, Mayfair. The handsome young Frenchman was certainly never short of money (his doting mother provided ample funds) nor indeed of suitable or unsuitable female company. He is widely believed to have shared mistresses with Prince Eddy, the somewhat unsavoury Lord Euston and with the financier Sir Ronnie Dunn, another gentleman of amazing sexual prowess whose life story begs to be told.

After the Cremorne Gardens were finally closed down (the good burghers of Chelsea managed this by buying up land for building), a group of aficionados – which included Sir Ronnie Dunn, Henry Spencer Ashbee and the young Dalmaine – formed the Cremorne Dining Society for themselves and similar robust men about town which met regularly at the aforesaid Jim Jam Club. This was a known haunt for upper class rakes where discreet privacy in luxurious surroundings was offered, and many noted orgies took place there in the late 1880s in the presence of some of the highest personages in the land. Investigative journalists of the day tried without success to infiltrate its doors but except for occasional extracts in underground magazines, little is known for sure about what took place in its finely furnished rooms.

The Cremornites (as they called themselves) flourished and began publishing at irregular intervals a club magazine in which 'The Secret Lives of Modern Girls' was first serialized in the early 1890s. Although the first episodes were written by Max Dalmaine, some scholars of minor Victorian scribes detect the hand of Sir Andrew Scott in later chapters. Connoisseurs of Victorian erotic writing will know Scott from his epic 'A Fond Memory Of Youthful Days' which first saw the light of day in the pages of *The Oyster*.

Recently, an almost complete set of The Cremornites' eponymous magazine was discovered in a refurbished old water mill near Oxford where it had lain hidden for many years. From it comes the novel published here, a work that offers an extremely interesting contrast to the accepted social mores of the admittedly fast *fin de siècle* decade.

As for our author, he was forced to change his hectic ways after his marriage to Miranda, the younger daughter of Sir Jasper Muttleberry (another stalwart of the Jim Jam and the gentleman on whom the famous eponymous rude ditty is based) in 1898. Max's parents were delighted with the match and vied with the Muttleberrys in showering the blissful bride and groom with gifts. To keep boredom from the door, Max dabbled in theatrical management and made a considerable amount of money through his own efforts, building theatres in London and in Manchester and staging popular melodramas. Later he invested heavily in the new cinematographs and the burgeoning British film industry.

Old habits died hard however, for Max was known to have enjoyed dalliances with several actresses including the famous Ethel Levey, Mrs Hugh Kenton and the extremely pretty musical comedienne Suzanne Moserre, the star of 'Nine Five Three', Dalmaine's most successful revue. Penned by Martin Wellsend and Leon D'Elstree, 'Nine Five Three' ran for more than two years at the now demolished Alhambra and Dalmaine produced one of the first advertising films ever made for the show. Alas, no copies of this three minute movie now exist although Max, a talented pianist, joined the orchestra for Suzanne Moserre's recording of her famous signature tune *A Nice Little Stroll Does You Good*, now alas also lost.

Max Dalmaine took British citizenship shortly after his marriage and left the hectic life of show business for quiet semi-retirement in Hertfordshire when in 1910 Sir Jasper (now a widower) died and left the Dalmaine family, which now included three young children, a huge inheritance of some £250,000 – well over five million pounds by today's reckoning. The Dalmaines built a splendid country home in rural Sussex and travelled extensively in Europe and in the United States where Max took a passing interest in the Hollywood movie business. But to the best of our knowledge he never again picked up a pen for The Cremornites after Sir Jasper's death – the society disbanded in the mid 1920s – or indeed for any other respectable publication. He died just before the outbreak of the World War Two.

But we can be thankful that copies of The Cremornites' magazine survived to let us delight in its naughty high spirits and also perhaps to allow us to make steps towards a truer understanding of the nature of Victorian manners and mores.

Louis Lombert
Dundee
July 1990

Cremorne
Gardens

All illusion is created when one of us reflects too well the light in the eyes of the rest.

Martin Bresslaw
Misadventures in Hades

CHAPTER ONE

'Are you actually informing me, Katie, that you are incapable of making a cup of tea?' said Lady Arkley, with a note of agitated disbelief in her voice. 'You and your sister have attended one of the most fashionable and expensive schools yet it appears that neither you nor your sister know how to perform a simple yet essential domestic chore.'

'Oh, Mother, I am so sorry,' apologised the pretty girl, sweeping long strands of blonde hair away from her face. 'I know how to serve tea from pouring in the milk and handing round the cups but as to actually making it, well, I must confess complete ignorance. Penny will be here in a minute but I don't suppose that she knows how to make tea either as we both attended Dame Bracknell's Academy for Young Ladies.

'However, if you will instruct us, I am sure that between us we will master the art,' she added, trying hard not to smile.

'My dear girl, if I knew how to do it I would not be asking you,' replied her fond Mama. 'In my day girls were kept in total ignorance of any such menial matters. However, now the modern girl spends all her time filling the surrounding air in general and her unfortunate

11

ears in particular with all the irritating iterations of all the things she would do if only she were let – yet though you feel you have the necessary qualifications to vote, for example, you cannot even perform an elementary domestic duty. In my own case this is understandable but in that of yours and of your sister's, it is quite inexplicable.

'But I must have tea, Katie. After the dreadful scene we've been through since lunch I need tea – besides all my life I've had tea at this time. If only your father were here and had not been called back to London for some stupid political business, I am sure he would have known what to do,' she wailed.

'That is the peril of being actively involved in politics, Mama,' said Katie. 'Mr Gladstone sought Papa's advice and Papa could hardly refuse such a call. Please don't fret, Mama, I think I can hear Penny coming.'

The door opened and Penelope Arkley, at eighteen Katie's younger sister by just eighteen months, stood framed in the doorway.

'I wish we were back home in Hyde Park Gardens!' she smiled, 'out here in the wilds of rural Sussex it is so difficult to summon assistance.'

'Well, I'm summoning you,' said Katie grimly. 'Mama is desperate for tea and neither she nor I know how to make it. Can you help?'

'Not really,' replied Penny cheerfully, 'after all, we both went to the same school. Actually, I am familiar with the technique but I have never had the opportunity to put it into practice.

'Rather like our attempts at making love with Andy and Edward!' she added in a conspiratorial whisper which led to both girls bursting out into a peal of laughter.

'I find nothing amusing in this dreadful situation. Such a crisis as this makes me wish that your Papa and I had never sent you to such a fashionable school as Dame Bracknell's,' moaned Lady Arkley.

'There must always be a need for perfectly useful people, Mama,' laughed Penny. 'Come now, we are at least half-way there. I would be able to make the wretched tea if I could only light the gas stove but the damned thing hasn't got a self-starter.'

'Watch your language, Penelope,' warned Lady Arkley. 'Anyway, this house is filled with every modern convenience. Even a child could run it. You don't mean to say that the average servant has more intelligence than you have?'

'It isn't a question of intelligence, Mama. If the average servant had received our kind of education she would be just as useless,' said Penny with a hint of bitterness.

'Let's not argue,' said Katie hastily to defuse the situation, for her hot-tempered young sister was continually arguing with their Mama.

'I have no intention of arguing,' said Lady Arkley majestically, rising from her chair and walking towards the door. 'When the two of you finally manage to put your heads together and make me tea you will find me sitting in the conservatory.'

As she swept out of the room, closing the door behind her with more force than was actually necessary, Penny's face went white.

'Oh heavens, Katie. I've just remembered that I was sitting on the couch in the conservatory last night.'

'So what has that to do with Mama sitting out there?'

'Ah, well, that's a little embarrassing,' said Penny, blushing in some confusion. 'But suffice it to say I have cause for concern.'

'I suppose your concern has nothing to do with a pair of frilly French knickers I found stuffed under one of the cushions on the conservatory sofa.'

The younger girl's face blanched as she put her hand to her mouth and gasped: 'My God! I must head Mama off before it is too late!'

Katie burst out laughing and gave her sister a little hug: 'Oh, don't be so silly, darling – would I have been so unsisterly to leave them there? I have already placed them under your pillow and indeed was about to tell you before you obviously recalled just where and how they had been taken off!'

'Katie, you are an absolute darling,' cried Penny, 'I would have just died if Mama had discovered my knickers on the sofa especially as she knew that I had been sitting out there last night and that I was not alone.'

'Ooh, that sounds very exciting. I would love to hear all about this naughty escapade. Hush a moment, I do believe that Mama is taking a nap. I will just check that she won't bother us for five minutes and then you can tell me all the juicy details.'

Katie slipped out of the room and padded quietly out to the conservatory where, as she had correctly assumed, her Mama was already safely gathered in the arms of Morpheus. She ran lightly back to her waiting sister and closed the door behind her.

'Now, Penny, let's hear all about it. You know that Andy is coming round soon and your risqué little tale will put me quite in the right frame of mind.'

Her sister was more than happy to oblige and tell Katie the full facts of how she lost her knickers. She said: 'Eddie and I had been to town to see a matinee performance of that marvellous new musical play at the Alhambra, ''Alexandra Widdicombe'', all about a sophisticated belle from the highest echelons of London Society who falls in love with a country bumpkin from rural Sussex.'

'Because he had the biggest, stiffest cock she had ever seen,' giggled Katie.

'Wash your mouth out with soap!' commanded Penny trying hard not to return the giggle. 'No, that's not right but in any case the story is immaterial. Now I am going to tell you the truth, the whole truth and nothing but the truth so will you promise me on your honour never to divulge the information I am about to impart to a living soul?'

'You have my word,' promised Katie eagerly.

'All right, I will trust you. Well, the truth of the matter is that Edward took me out afterwards to dine at Leon's restaurant in Goldstone Lane where all the fast theatrical crowd meet up. There was quite a gathering there as Johnny Holdershill, the handsome young scamp who has been involved with Lady Estelle Woodway if the illustrated weekly magazines are to be believed, was holding a party for Fraulein Putzie, the famous coquette from Galicia who is rumoured to have affairs not just with Bismarck and Count Gewirtz but also with the Kaiser's young son, Wilhelm.

'Indeed, this merry throng dominated the atmosphere at Leon's and Eddie asked me if I preferred to leave. But

I declined as I found it all terribly exciting and I was sitting enrapt at the witty conversation which was flying through the air. Oscar Wilde and Lord Alfred Douglas were present and I heard Lord Alfred castigate his father, the Marquis of Queensbury as being uncouth and foul-mouthed especially when commenting upon his son's companions.

' "My father is a genuine cad," said Lord Alfred with undisguised venom.'

' "Oh, I don't know about that," said Mr Wilde with a flourish, "though I admit he has a most direct way of speaking. Let me think of a few lines to describe your Papa. Ah, yes, how about:

> *Old Queensbury was a straightforward man,*
> *He did not mince his words.*
> *He spoke of all Lord Alfred's friends*
> *As buggers, shits and turds!"*

'Edward was shocked when I laughed out loud but before he could say anything, the handsome Johnny Holdershill came to sit down at our table.

' "I don't think I have had the pleasure." ' he murmured, his deep blue eyes locked into mine as I tried hard to act the demure, blushing maiden.

' "Yes you have, Johnny, but not with that most attractive young girl," called out a passing reveller. "Not yet, at any rate!"

'Edward was now obviously angry but Johnny smoothed away his wrath by a handsome apology and insisted on us joining his party. Edward was keen to decline but I was only too delighted to accept the invitation. We took our places at the long table and look, Katie, I have here the menu card which is, to say the least, somewhat different to those we are used to seeing at hunt balls and other such occasions.'

She rummaged around in her handbag and brought out the card for Katie to see. The card was printed on ivory-coloured paper decorated with a sketch by one of the guests, Mr Aubrey Beardsley showing Prince Wilhelm, naked save for a Junker military helmet, having his rampant penis sucked by an equally nude Fraulein Putzie. Johnny Holdershill had not spared any expense for the full menu was as follows:

Caviare

Tortue Claire

Sole au Vin Blanc

Riz de Veau aux Epinards

Poulet a l'Indien

Selle d'Agneau

Omelette Surprise

Glace Vanille, Fraises, Ananas, Peches

Café Turc

The Russe

'And this was all washed down by the finest wines, champagne and liqueurs,' said Penny dreamily. 'Even Edward, who as you know can be a little stuffy at times, was quite relaxed by the time the banquet was over. And who should come in just as we were finishing our last dregs of coffee but the Prince of Wales himself with Mrs Keppel!'

'Of course, we all had to stand up when HRH arrived and Lady Shawnthomas tinkled out "God Save The Queen" on the piano. Anyways, the Prince sat down a good few feet away from me and slowly he drew a coterie of men around him whilst he told some rather rude stories. There was one about a Catholic priest, a Jewish rabbi and a bacon sandwich that caused much merriment but I regret to say that I have forgotten the actual joke!'

'Never mind, Penny, do go on, it all sounds absolutely riveting,' urged her sweet sister.

'Well, to be honest, many of the ladies were rather bored and took the opportunity to powder their faces. Edward took up a position near the Prince and the original guest of honour, Anna Putzie, took the place next to me. We struck up a conversation (she speaks excellent English) and – this is quite extraordinary – I somehow divined that she was very much attracted to me sexually.'

'Goodness me! Whatever happened then?' breathed Katie.

'I will not hide anything from you. You must remember though that we had consumed considerable amounts of champagne and other fine wines and that always makes me feel sexually excited.

'To cut a long story short, we exchanged a knowing look across the table and Anna, who was wearing an extremely low-cut dress deliberately leaned forward to whisper to me: "Fraulein Penny, without a doubt you are the most attractively-built girl in this room. If you decided to become a lady of pleasure, I assure you that you are sitting on a fortune."

'I giggled at her obvious double entendre as I took the opportunity to gaze at her large ripe breasts that were barely covered by the flimsy silk of her gown (bought for her from Aspiso's that very day, she told me later, by Johnny Holdershill for the shocking sum of one hundred guineas). Her breasts swelled as she took my hand in hers and just looking at these beautiful white globes had my own titties standing erect and longing to be sucked.'

'This sounds like the fun we enjoyed with Cecilia and Francesca in the sixth form dormitory at Lady Bracknell's Academy,' said Katie with no little relish.

'It turned out to be not dissimilar,' agreed Penny. 'It all became too much to bear when under the cover of the linen tablecloth I felt a soft foot insinuate itself first against my legs and then higher and higher between them up to my groin. Sister, I was so aroused as Anna's toes rubbed around my crotch that my knickers were soon wet with the juices that were flowing freely from my pussey.

'I gasped with delight as wave after wave of a delicious sensation coursed through my body although above the table all was at least calm on the surface. I summoned up the savoir faire to softly decline the waiter's offer to refill my glass. "Come on, let us leave this chattering crowd," said Anna softly. "We can retire to my place."

' "No, no, I cannot," I said. "We are at present residing in our country home in Surrey and I must return home by midnight. Oh, Lord! We have already missed our train. What will Mama say? Perhaps I should telephone her and say we were unavoidably delayed by an unexpected royal visit. This would not exactly be an untruth, would it?" '

' "What a splendid idea, my pretty little doll. I have a Prestoncrest carriage at my disposal so make your telephone call and I will tell Grahame the coachman to be ready for us."

[Prestoncrest Carriages was a well-known company used extensively by London gentry around the turn of the century. Drivers were sworn to secrecy and many illicit romances were consummated through the availability of discreet and totally trustworthy coachmen. An unusual but effective code was used to preserve secrecy – all the gentlemen were addressed as 'Monsieur' and all the ladies as 'Mademoiselle' whilst all the coachmen were invariably known as 'Grahame'. Only a request for 'Grahame' would obtain a Prestoncrest vehicle – L.L.].

' "But what about Edward?" I objected weakly. "Shall I just leave him here?" '

' "Bah, he is busy fawning to your Prince of Wales who I assure you tells a good tale of *l'arte de faire l'amour* but is not so expert in practice, as I can testify from a most boring experience with His Royal Not So Highness. He lacks the slightest glimmering of subtlety and his idea of wooing a woman into bed goes something in the fashion of: 'I am the Prince of Wales. Would you like the honour of having me fuck you?'

' "Let us not waste time. You tell your Mama that the train has been delayed and a kind lady friend is acting as chaperone to take you and your gentleman friend back home in her carriage." '

'It all made such good sense that I readily agreed and Mama, though shocked, was nevertheless impressed when I mentioned that I was in the presence of royalty. Anyhow, let me again be brief. We dragged Eddie away from the Prince of Wales' bawdy anecdotes and as I half-expected, he fell asleep in the carriage. As he snored, Anna moved across to me and we kissed each other on the lips. Her tongue was soon in my mouth and mine in hers as she turned up my dress and, groping underneath, pulled down my wet knickers. She then broke away from our embrace and smiled in lustful anticipation. She was really very, very pretty and her teeth gleamed in the darkness like two little walls of ivory.

' "You are a real beauty," she whispered, pulling me down so that I lay across the seat. "Now, let me take these knickers right off – there, I will stuff them in your bag – and turn up your dress like so. Aaah! Feel my soft hands caress your thighs. Oh, my! What a lovely cunney you have been blessed with, you lucky girl. Such a mass of silky dark hair, and such inviting cunney lips peeping out from the hirsute forest. I cannot resist you! If only I were a man I would adore pushing my rod between these lovely nether lips."

'I blushed but did not resist as Anna's head dived between my legs and she began flicking her tongue rapidly round the edges of my mount. She passed her tongue lasciviously around my most sensitive parts, rolling her tongue around my little clitty, which was now erect and protruding between my cunney lips, and playfully nipping it with her teeth. "Oooh, I'm going to spend!" I cried as I arched my body upwards, burying Anna's face in my cunt then another delirium of pleasure surged through me and I again spent copiously all over her mouth and chin as my juices fairly spurted out from my dripping pussey. She licked and lapped, slurping greedily on the tangy rivulet that poured over her face.

' "This seems rather unfair," I gasped. "I have come off twice whilst you have yet to achieve one climax."

' "What a thoughtful girl you are," she cried. "Now just to show you that I have no bias against the male sex, would you mind very much if I pleasured myself with your good-looking boy friend?"

' "Now at all,' I assured her. "Jealousy is not one of my vices. However, I am afraid that as Eddie is deep in the land of Nod and after the amount of champagne he drank, I doubt whether he will be able to rise to the occasion."

' "Well, let us see what we can do about that," grinned Anna, running her hands over Edward's crotch. "What have we here?"

'As I had expected, Eddie did not respond to her ministrations, his eyes remaining closed and his breathing unchanged in rhythm and timbre even whilst Anna was undoing his belt and unbuttoning his fly buttons. She pulled down his trousers and drawers to expose Eddie's large yet flaccid penis to our view. "I think I have enough raw material to work with here," murmured Anna, wrapping her long fingers around his shaft and pulling down his foreskin so that the rubicund knob was uncovered. Magically, Eddie's shaft began to swell with increasing rapidity as Anna worked her hand up and down his stiffening rod. After a short while – and Eddie remained asleep – she licked her lips at the sight of his fully erect penis, the foreskin rolled all the way down and the mushroom-shaped dome gleaming with the small amount of cream that had already dribbled from the tiny hole in his knob.

'I watched with total fascination as she massaged his shaft up and down some half a dozen times and then she leaned over and took the straining shaft in her mouth, looking up cheekily to the still-sleeping boy as she sucked harder and harder. As if in a dream, I leaned forward and cupped his hairy balls in my hand. This added excitement proved too much for Eddie and his cock began to twitch and I began to feel very horney again. In a trice a thick wad of juicy cream spurted out of his shaft and shot into the back of her throat. She pulled his jerking member from her mouth and he carried on shooting his load, covering her face with sticky spunk. Anna gobbled greedily any that landed between her lips and swallowed his jism with relish.

'She squeezed his deflating prick and licked up the last vestiges of juice from the top of his cock which lay across his left thigh, shrinking like a leaking balloon. I watched his knob disappear under his foreskin as Anna asked me to help her lift Eddie into a more comfortable position so that we could readjust his clothing. We giggled like two schoolgirls while Eddie sighed and grunted yet still remained fast asleep as Grahame turned into the drive of Coppice Lodge, where Edward's family was staying for a week (just under two miles or so away from our own summer home).

'We slapped his cheeks lightly to waken our Sleeping

Beauty and this finally did the trick. His eyes opened and he mumbled: "Where am I? Who's this? Oh, I say, Penny it's you. Hallo, darling. Ah, who is this lady? Why it's Fraulein Putzie if I am not mistaken and good heavens, we're at Coppice Lodge. How on earth did we get here? Oh dear, I must have passed out at Leon's. Oh Lord, I am sorry, ladies, please forgive my inexcusable behaviour."

' "It's quite all right, Eddie," I said sweetly. "I telephoned my Mama to say I would be home late as the trains were delayed. Don't forget to back me up or we will both be in trouble! Come now, I'll walk with you to the door. Fraulein Putzie will escort me home in her Prestoncrest carriage."

' "Fine,' Edward muttered. "May I wish you goodnight, *genädiges Fraulein*. I am obliged to you for looking after Penny so well during my disgraceful absence from her side."

'Anna smiled graciously and waved goodbye as Eddie staggered to the front door. He pulled me close and whispered to me: "I shouldn't really say this but I think I should get drunk more often. I had the most marvellous dream about a beautiful woman making love to me."

'I fought back the giggles by pretending to cough and gave dear Edward a peck on his cheek. "Goodnight, Eddie. Do come over for tea tomorrow afternoon. Any hangover you have will have disappeared by then."

'When I was back in the carriage and Grahame had moved us away on the final stage of this eventful journey, I told Anna what Eddie had said and our peals of laughter must have made Grahame wonder what on earth was going on in the carriage. He let the horses trot quite

quickly to our house and although it was now very late –
about a quarter to one – both of us had now shaken off
our tiredness and were now on our second wind, as the
saying goes. I asked Anna in for a hot drink and said that
she could stay the night and she accepted the former
invitation but declined the latter, saying that Grahame
would have take her back to HRH whatever the hour or
the Prince would sulk for the whole of the following day.
Not wishing to be the cause of friction, I did not press her
further on this, for as we all know, the Prince is a terribly
difficult man when he imagines that he has been even
slightly crossed.

'So we bade each other a fond farewell and Anna
promised upon her honour that she would contact me on
her next visit to London and that I would be invited to
one of Lord Fletcher's soirees and meet the Prince of
Wales. I crept indoors through the back door which
Mama had instructed be kept open for me and closed it
quietly behind me. I was now past tiredness and indeed
felt quite spry again.'

As she paused for breath Katie said: 'This all sounds
frightfully exciting, sister, though you have still not
explained how you came to lose your knickers in the
conservatory.'

'Be patient, Katie, and all will be explained,' Penny
continued. 'As I locked the door behind me I heard a
noise emanating from the direction of the conservatory.
Who could be up at this unearthly hour? I grabbed hold
of a rolling pin that Cook had left on the kitchen table
and ventured forward to discover if a burglar was trying
to effect an entry.'

Katie was now on the edge of her seat. 'Golly, I must

have slept right through all this,' she exclaimed. 'And was someone trying to effect an entry?'

'Not exactly, although I must admit that an entry was effected a little later in the proceedings! What happened next was that I peered into the conservatory from the lounge to see the shadow of a man silhouetted against the window, leaning over one of the boxes of plants. "Who's there?" I hissed which startled the man perceptively. He straightened up and faced me and no doubt to our joint relief we immediately recognised each other.'

'Heavens above, Penny, who on earth was this nocturnal visitor?'

'No visitor as such, Katie, for it was none other than Bob Goggin, our shy young gardener. "Bob Goggin, what on earth are you doing up at this time of night?" I said weakly, letting the rolling pin which I had raised in case of trouble fall down by my side. "Oh dear, Miss Penny, I do hope I have not frightened you," said the well-built youth. "But Lady Arkley asked me to stay up until you arrived home and whilst I was waiting I thought I would water some of the plants in the conservatory. I was so engrossed in what I was doing that I did not hear you come in."

' "I thought you were a burglar, Bob," I said. "You know that the notorious Greenford gang have been active around here recently."

' "I am so sorry if I frightened you, Miss Penny," he replied. "I do apologise most profusely."

' "That's all right, there are no bones broken although there might have been if I had attacked you with this rolling pin! Tell me, what could you find to do at this time of night?"

' "Well, I decided to water the plants. You see the weather has been very good over the last few days and you should never water whilst the sun is shining directly on plants as leaves cook, discolour and wither. And you have to be especially careful with conservatory plants and fruit. My Uncle Felix worked for eight years as deputy head gardener to Lord John Rolle, under the direction of James Barnes who was famous for his pineapples, and he taught me the value of methodical watering arrangements. So I was simply following Uncle Felix's advice when we frightened each other to death just now!''

' "We certainly did, didn't we? I tell you what, Bob, let's calm our nerves with a little of my Papa's special cognac.''

'I brushed aside his protestations and within twenty minutes Bob had lost his shyness and soon I was to lose something else!''

'Penny!' gasped her sister. 'Surely you don't mean that a mere gardener has plucked your cherry!'

'Well, only in a manner of speaking,' admitted Penny, her cheeks colouring as she raised a hand to her mouth to cover a giggle. 'I cannot believe that Andrew and yourself do nothing but read poetry aloud to each other when you are alone. I am sure that Andy is as passionate as Edward and I know that we share a love of matters pertaining to *l'amour*. Certain boy friends have enjoyed viewing my naked breasts and a privileged few have also seen me totally nude, whilst an even smaller number have caressed my titties and played with my pussey, inserting and withdrawing their fingers until I have coated their hands with my love juices.

'And I am not ashamed to admit that I have handled some members in my time and have brought boys to climax by manipulating their shafts until the white cream has shot out of their pricks like miniature fountains. Oh, do not look so shocked, sister, as I am sure that you have experienced such heavenly joys.

'Anyway, after a while, Bob and I were sitting side by side quite intimately on the sofa and it seemed to be the most natural thing in the world to lean over and kiss him on the lips. He trembled with emotion and threw his arms around me, saying: "Oh, Miss Penny, if only you knew how much I have adored you from afar. My heart turns over every time I think of you and my whole body has been aching for such a kiss."

' "How lovely, Bob," I said, nibbling his ear. "Tell me, have you put a watering can spout in your trousers or indeed are you really pleased to see me?" For an answer, the handsome youth threw his arms around me in a passionate embrace. We may have thought Bob Goggin a shy lad, Katie but I can tell you that hardly before you could say Jack Robinson he had unbuttoned my dress and was caressing my bare breasts. He squeezed them lightly and began to play with my nipples which were now like two stiff little stalks against the palms of his hands. By this time, I had no qualms about letting my hand fall over the huge bulge in the front of his trousers and I stroked the hard shaft I could feel throbbing under my soft touch. He rained kisses on my face and neck and I responded wildly as he suddenly pulled away and said: "Darling Penny, I do so want to fuck you. You will let me won't you, I do so want you. But despite my lowly position I hope I can still act honourably and walk away if you say 'No'."

'I think it was this last noble phrase that led me to decide that Bob's pego would be the first to penetrate my pussey. You recall the words of our somewhat radical tutor Mrs Titchfield that she saw more gentlemanly behaviour amongst the young artisans building the new library at Cambridge than amongst the aristocratic undergraduates who supposedly studied inside it. Why cannot men understand that gentle honesty will win more minds and bodies than roughness and force?

'However, I digress – the appealing look on Bob's face was simply irresistible. I pulled him back to me and crushed his chest to mine as our lips met in a lovely wet kiss. I was almost fainting from the excitement of the moment and I felt a strange tingling in my tummy that spread like a warmth down to my cunney. I clung to him more tightly as he whispered that he, too, had never before enjoyed the full delights of fucking. How splendid, flashed the thought through my mind, that both our virginities would be lost in the passion of our love-making.

'I was ready to make the decision that I knew I could never undo. I clung even more tightly to him, pressing my firm breasts against his chest. I was ready and wanted to know above all what it meant to be taken by a man, especially by such a handsome, sweet-natured boy as Bob.

' "Oh, Bob," I sighed as he swept me into his arms and laid me down gently on the sofa. Now even though his own young passion was at a peak he treated me with utmost gentleness, slowly unbuttoning my dress and kissing me deeply and passionately as he slipped off my knickers and the rest of my underwear. He then hastily shed his own clothes and for the very first time a totally naked young man was exposed to my gaze. I admired the silkiness of his hair, the curvature of his chest which was as smooth and hairless as my own, the shape of his strong arms and as he turned to put down his shoes, the suppleness of his white bottom.

'But then as he turned my eyes fastened upon the *pièce de résistance*, his absolutely gigantic penis, as erect as could be, the stiff truncheon standing up against his flat belly . . . Oh, my dearest Katie, my blood was up and nothing in the world could have prevented me taking hold of this huge monster in my hands. I pulled down the foreskin to reveal the smooth ruby knob which throbbed in my hands and as I gently stroked it I could feel the thick veins running along its length, the shaft so thick that I could barely grasp it. A piercing hot sensation welled up between my legs as my pussey began to ooze its juices and I needed dear Bob's massive organ inside me.

'Our two naked bodied crashed together as we rolled onto the sofa in sheer ecstasy and, grasping his lovely cock, guided the rubicund mushroom knob to the portals of delight. He first gave a gentle push and with only a little discomfort, pushed an inch of his pego between my cunney lips. I shuddered in exquisite agony and dear Bob asked anxiously if he should withdraw but I begged him to continue. I stretched my legs to the widest extremity and then, aaaah! His gorgeous penis was no longer battering at the gate but had pushed forward into the realms of absolute bliss. My maidenhead was now completely broken (though riding Captain Radlett's horses and our secret little dormitory games had already weakened the hymen to a great degree) and I quivered as my ardent lover thrust in and out of my willing, wet nest.

'Bob too was similarly affected by emotion as his swollen staff entered my juicy cunney. Every nerve in my body thrilled with exquisite rapture as Bob's simple instinct led him to thrust forward, pull back, thrust forward, pull back in a heavenly rhythm. I heaved up to meet his thrusts, winding my legs around him so that his heavy, hairy balls banged against my bum as he buried that delightful shaft in me to the very hilt. We rolled, we gasped, we wanted to scream but were afraid that we should wake up other members of the household and be discovered.

'All too soon, however, I felt his cock tremble and almost immediately my cunney was drenched with a coating of frothy spunk as with every throb of Bob's huge shaft, spasm after spasm of creamy juice, as white as liquid starch, shot into my womb and my own peak of pleasure arrived very soon afterwards just as his cock was beginning to shrink into semi-flaccidity and my now saturated pussey sent shudders of delight all over my body as my own juices mixed with those of my first lover.

'Bob rolled off me and collapsed on the floor. I slid down to be next to him and he cradled my head in his strong arms. I smoothed my hand over his tummy and into the mass of dark pubic hair. I looked with interest at his thick cock which was no longer erect but was hanging over his right thigh looking full and heavy despite disgorging all that lovely love juice inside me. I gently squeezed Bob's pole and at once his magnificent tool sprung up into full erection, uncapping the delicious-looking purple head.

'I felt the full length of his shaft again (I later measured it with your tape measure, sister, and erect it topped seven and a half inches!) and marvelled at its thickness, so wide that my hand could barely encompass it. Was it simply Nature that led me to fancy taking this giant lollipop in my mouth? Whether or no, I must admit that my head swooped downwards and I opened my lips and sucked greedily on the hot, velvety flesh, dwelling around the ridge and then up and down the shaft, closing my eyes as I pumped his prick, keeping my lips taut on his length, kissing, sucking and licking until I felt that he would explode in my mouth. I hastily withdrew as I did not wish Bob to spend too quickly and the lovely lad sensed this and concentrated upon tweaking my titties with his palms which I found led to the most arousing and enjoyable sensations.

'But Bob's staff stood so ready, so erect, so swollen that I just could not resist popping it back inside my mouth and I took as much of his shaft as I could and again I felt the juices boil up inside his hairy ballsack. This time the lusty young man just had to spend and it was my sheer joy to coax the spunk out from him. From the tiny jerks of his shaft I knew that his moment of truth was at hand but I made no attempt to disengage as he came copiously, squirting jet after jet of tangy, frothy sperm into my mouth which I swallowed with genuine relish. This was the first time I had ever swallowed spunk and though for a moment I was dissuaded, I let myself cross the Rubicon and was far from disappointed with the outcome.

'Ah, sister, you doubtless recall the wise words of Dr Nicklee's little book *The Facts of Life for Young Ladies* that we smuggled into Dame Bracknell's Academy – I believe I can recite them from memory: "First love can be idyllic – or rapturous. Which way the coin falls will depend on the circumstances, upon the partner concerned and to a very great extent upon ourselves. For all animals copulate but only homo sapiens is capable of extending physical need into an act of love. This ability sets us apart from the lower species, although it is surely an unfortunate fact that far too few people recognise and develop this unique talent with which we are all blessed.''

'I was naive, shy and perhaps even slightly bewildered by what had taken place between Bob Goggin and myself but I count myself fortunate that I made the first journey down the highways of *l'amour* with a caring, romantic, and gentle lover who only wished to ensure that the pleasure we experienced was shared and that I was never forced to partake in anything about which I had any misgivings.

'So I thanked Bob in all sincerity for his manly love-making though I was concerned that his lovely prick, now forlornly drooping downwards, had not been exercised too hard. He gently wiped my still-pouting nether-lips and his own affair with my knickers, telling me that he would always treasure the memory of our virgin love that had been surrendered so gallantly.'

There was a little pause as Katie expelled her breath and said: 'Oh, Penny, what an amazing tale! I do so envy you your night of passion and I am so pleased that it was I who found your missing knickers which obviously you had forgotten, in your tired condition, to collect and bring upstairs. Never fear, sweet sister, your secret shall remain with me for ever!'

The girls embraced and upon hearing a noise from the direction of the conservatory, decided to beard the lion, or in this case the lioness in her den and went to see whether their fond Mama was still in an angry mood.

Lady Arkley's temper had not been mellowed by her nap. 'It really is too bad,' she complained bitterly as the girls entered the room. 'Formbey, Connie and Mrs Beaconsfield all giving in their notices this morning without so much as a by-your-leave.'

'But just why did they walk out in such a fashion?' asked Penny. 'I knew that the servants had left us but whatever made them do so?'

'I don't know, Penelope, I just do not know at all,' replied Lady Arkley irritably. 'All I can tell you is that at twelve o'clock Formbey marched into this room followed by Connie and Mrs Beaconsfield and Connie was hanging onto Formbey's arm.'

'Sounds like an advertisement for an Epyptian cigarette,' murmured Katie.

'Or an illustration for a book about an American chain gang,' muttered Penny.

Lady Arkley glared at her daughters and continued: 'If you will permit me to finish the tale without any further interruption – without offering a word of apology for leaving us three women in this terrible predicament, Formbey said that he and the others, having opened our little summer residence, could not bear to spend the summer away from London and had decided to go back there this afternoon.

'I begged them to change their minds but to no avail. I even offered to increase their wages substantially – another eight pounds a year I offered Formbey, a liberality that borders upon foolishness – and I said they could have two more half holidays per annum. But their minds were set and I could not move them. I would not be surprised if Lady Hutchinson is not behind all this as she has long since coveted the services of Mrs Beaconsfield, especially after eating her Upside Down cake.'

'What a predicament!' said Katie. 'The kitchen is in chaos and the house is full of food that nobody knows how to cook. What on earth is to become of us?'

'Well we won't starve,' declared Penny. 'Bob Goggin knows how to cook, so there is no cause for concern.'

'Goggin the gardener?' exclaimed Lady Arkley. 'How on earth are you possessed of such knowledge? I beg to differ about whether or no there is cause for concern.'

Penny flushed but thought quickly to extract herself from the awkward situation. 'Y-e-e-s, how indeed do I know that? Isn't it funny how ephemeral information remains glued to the brain, though in this case it is indeed fortunate that I have remembered this scrap of trivial knowledge. Ah, yes, one day last week I was sitting in the garden, it was last Wednesday, Mama, you recall what a spendidly sunshiney day we enjoyed, yes, that's it, I was sitting in the garden watching Goggin weeding the flower beds and I asked him if Mrs Beaconsfield was looking after him as she was well-known for her culinary prowess. And he said that she was a marvellous cook but that he too knew his way round a kitchen as his mother had been in service as a cook.'

'I do not approve of your partaking in conversations with the servants,' said Lady Arkley coldly. 'Although I suppose that in this case the information obtained will be of use. However, Goggin will not return until this evening and we still have to solve the immediate problem of my need for tea.'

'Look, I'm not going to be beaten by all this,' said Katie suddenly. 'Come on, Penny, let's run down to Mister Maher's bookstore in the village. There is bound to be a little cookery *book* that will explain how to use the gas stove and refresh our memory about how to make a nice cup of tea.'

'That sounds like a jolly idea.' said Penny. 'Mama, we will be back in half an hour or so. Can you wait until we return?'

'I have little option but so to do.' replied Lady Arkley. 'I applaud your initiative and indeed I had thought of that solution myself but was waiting to see if one of my daughters had the *nous* to think of it herself.'

To the girls' credit, neither of them contradicted their Mama and somehow they stifled their giggles as they put on their hats and coats and made their way briskly to the village bookshop.

CHAPTER TWO

With the aid of Miss Fletcher's *Domestic Economy* purchased for one shilling and sixpence at the village bookshop, Katie and Penny were able, after one or two unsuccessful trial runs, to light the gas stove, boil the kettle and make their Mama the cup of tea she craved. They even managed to cut a loaf of bread and butter the slices as well as dividing a slab of Mrs Beaconsfield's famous Upside Down cake they found in the larder.

The servants might have walked out but the beds had been made, the house cleaned and Mrs Beaconsfield had cooked enough to provide a cold collation for supper that evening and luncheon the following day.

But what Katie did not and indeed could not have known was that she was seen and admired by Walter Stanton, a bright young spark who was browsing in the bookshop looking for a light novel with which to pass away the afternoon. Wally was staying in the village just a mile or so from the Arkley residence on a duty visit to his Uncle, the crusty old General Stanton who made Wally an annual allowance to supplement the relatively small amount provided by his worthy parents who alas had lost a great deal of cash through unwise speculation in Hudson's railway stock.

Walter was twenty-two years of age and supposedly spent his time in London studying as an articled clerk at Godfrey and Co, solicitors to the gentry, but the temptations of the capital city took their toll and one of the reasons why he did not begrudge the few days spent with his Uncle in the country was that here at least there were no gardens of pleasure such as The Cremorne where a young man could both be parted from his cash and joined in relationships which might be difficult out of which to disengage.

But, for a young man of Walter Stanton's spirit, the attractions of female flesh were never far from his thoughts. And when he glanced up from the book he was leafing through and saw the lovely Katie, her blonde hair tumbling down her shoulders, her pretty face with those large blue eyes, sparkling white teeth and charming dimples, he was irretrievably drawn as metal is to a magnet.

'Egad, what a stunner!' murmured Walter to himself as he looked upon Katie's merry face with unconcealed delight. To his eyes, the sweet girl was the very beau ideal of feminine beauty and after Katie and Penny had left the shop Walter hastened to the cash desk and purchased the novel he had been reading.

'That will be two shillings, sir.' said Mr Maher, wrapping the book in a brown paper bag.

'Oh, er, could you wrap it in coloured paper?' said Walter with a flash of inspiration.

'Certainly, sir, although that will cost an extra two pence.' said the bookseller. 'I hope you don't mind the small extra charge but in Beerstone's shop down the road coloured paper costs even more and they don't stock the range that we do.'

'No, no, don't worry, I don't mind the cost,' said Walter. 'But tell me, who are those two attractive girls who just left the premises?'

'Oh, you mean Lady Arkley's daughters, Miss Katie and Miss Penny. Miss Katie is the blonde-haired girl and I think that she is a year or two older than her sister.'

'Do they live near my Uncle, General Stanton?' Walter enquired, exchanging coins for the neatly-wrapped parcel.

'Oh, yes, not too far away, sir. Walk along the High Street for half a mile or so and then turn left into Titchfield Street and then right up Healy's Hill. It's probably less than a mile in all.'

After thanking the kind bookseller for his information Walter hurried home. At first he was minded to run after the sisters and present his compliments but he wisely decided to go home and change first and think of a suitable reason for his visiting their home. Such a reason was not hard to find and he smiled happily as he walked briskly back to Stanton Lodge where the General was snorting grumpily over a copy of *The Times*, a glass of whisky and soda on a table besides him.

'That you, Walter?' shouted the General who was inclined to deafness.

'Yes, I'm back, Uncle, but unless you have any objection I shall be going out again shortly.'

'Are you now? I thought you came to keep me company, young feller-me-lad. Where are you off to?'

'I shan't be long, Uncle,' said Walter, trying to keep a note of convivial civility in his voice. 'One of our neighbours left a *book* she had purchased at Mahers and I thought I would walk down the road and return it to her.'

'Well, can't a servant take it round?' fretted the General. 'I want you to meet Colonel Bailstone and his niece who are dining with us tonight.'

'I won't be long,' promised his nephew. 'Don't worry, Uncle, I shall be back in good time.'

'Well see that you are,' said General Stanton, returning to the pages of his newspaper.

Walter rushed upstairs and ran a brisk if cool bath. He dried himself well and decided to shave for the second time that day. He was a handsome young rogue who was somewhat sallow in complexion with a dark growth of hair that often seemed to elude the strictest attempts at shaving. Certainly, he needed to run a razor over his face which he did carefully, for appearing before this delicious girl with a face covered in cuts was something he wished to avoid. He splashed on some *eau de cologne* – unlike many Englishmen he thoroughly approved of the Continental practice of masculine toiletries which perhaps accounted for his many successes with the fair sex. He changed into fresh clothes and after bidding his Uncle goodbye, set forth at a good stride to the Arkley residence, in happy anticipation of seeing the stunning Miss Katie again.

Young Walter – or Wally as he was known to his friends – walked as quickly as he could to *chez* Arkley. He did not run as the sun was now shining quite fiercely and he did not want to perspire. By the time he had reached his destination the girls had laid out a splendid tea for their Mama and partaken of the feast they had prepared. They were engaged in deciding how best to clean the cutlery and plates they had used when Walter rang the front door bell.

'Please answer the bell, somebody,' called out Lady Arkley. 'And remember, unless it is Reverend Tagholm or somebody important I am not at home.'

Katie marched out and opened the door herself. 'Good afternoon, Miss Arkley,' said the bold Wally, raising his hat. 'My name is Walter Stanton and I am staying with my Uncle, General Stanton at his home just down the hill.

'I do hope you will forgive my forwardness in speaking to you without an introduction but I saw you and your sister in Maher's bookshop this afternoon and I thought you might like to read this jolly little novel which I can recommend.'

Katie smiled and her dimples looked so kissable to the smitten Walter that he could scarcely keep his hands to his sides after passing the package wrapped in the coloured paper which had cost him an extra two pence to this lovely creature who stood before him.

'That is very kind of you, Mr Stanton,' said Katie. 'However, I regret that I cannot accept a present from a total stranger.'

'Oh, Miss Arkley, I do understand – but then if we were formally introduced I would no longer be a total stranger and then perhaps you could accept my little gift.'

'Yes, I suppose there is logic in your argument – but unfortunately there is no-one to introduce us.'

'Oh yes there is,' broke in the cheerful voice of her young sister. 'Actually, although we have never met, Mr Stanton, I have been introduced to your Uncle, the General, by my mother with whom he is acquainted. Let me do the honours, starting perhaps with myself – I am Penelope Arkley and you are . . .'

'Walter Stanton, Miss Arkley, at your service,' murmured Wally gratefully.

'Very well. Mr Walter Stanton, I have the honour to introduce my sister Miss Katherine Arkley, but as my Mama has met your Uncle, do call us Penny and Kate.'

'And do call me Wally,' said the happy young man. 'Now, Katie, please do me the honour of accepting this little gift of a novel to while away a pleasant morning or two.'

'Thank you, Wally, I look forward to reading it. Look, do come in, we are in a bit of a mess just now as the servants have suddenly decamped but if you don't mind coming through into the kitchen for a moment whilst we clean up after tea –'

'It will be my pleasure. Do let me assist you,' said Walter. 'I live quite simply in town and am used to doing many of my own chores, which is perhaps as should be for an impoverished articled solicitor's clerk.'

'Golly, can you cook?' said Penny admiringly. 'How terribly clever you must be.'

'I can make a very passable omelette and prepare straightforward dishes like steak and chips,' said Walter modestly. 'I have a daily charwoman who comes in every morning but generally speaking I look after myself. Now, do let me help you with anything you need doing.'

It is strange how women of all ages and classes can divine when a man is interested either in themselves or another of the fair sex. Penny knew immediately of Walter's passion for her sister from the manner of his speech, how his words were spoken in her direction and in the way he looked as often as possible at Katie without staring in a vulgar fashion.

'If you two will excuse me, I have a slight headache coming on,' fibbed Penny. 'I hope you will not mind too much if I retired from the fray and went upstairs for a nap. Anyhow, you know the saying, too many cooks spoil the broth.' She almost spoiled the speech by adding 'and two is company but three is a crowd' but managed to restrain herself with a charming little giggle, closing the door behind her before either Katie or Walter could challenge her.

'That was very, very nice of your sister to leave us.' said Walter. 'She knew that we wanted to be by ourselves.'

Katie's pretty face coloured up as she looked down demurely at the floor.

'Now you must know what I mean,' continued Walter. 'Penny knows that I would love to be properly acquainted with you, Katie. I do hope you will let me be your friend.'

'You can be my friend if you will help me wash up,' said Katie quickly as she heard footsteps outside. 'And I do hope you can make as good an impression upon my Mama as you have done with Penny and myself, for otherwise all your words will count for nothing.'

'Never fear,' said Walter grandly as Lady Arkley entered the room. Luckily, Lady Arkley was in a mellow mood having partaken of tea and was easily flattered into accepting Walter into the family circle after he explained his relationship to General Stanton and that yes, indeed, he was one of the Gloucestershire Stantons and that on his mother's side he was a Hackney.

'Lady Arkley, I would be grateful if I could obtain your permission to take Katherine for a short walk after we have finished our domestic chores,' said the cunning Walter with his most practised dazzling smile.

'Certainly, Mr Stanton, it will do you both good. Do not forget to give the General my kindest regards when you return home,' said Lady Arkley graciously as she swept majestically out of the kitchen.

'Thank you, Lady Arkley,' said Walter happily to her disappearing back. 'Thank you very much indeed.'

And Katie, too, smiled with genuine delight.

So not long after this conversation Katie and Walter went off for a quiet stroll and came to a pretty stream where they sat down on the mossy bank to chat. But alas, just as Katie was taking off her shoe to take a pebble out of the heel, she saw a beetle on her leg which startled her and she dropped her shoe into the stream.

'Don't fret, Katie,' said Walter as he leaped up and cleverly fished out the dainty little shoe with the aid of a stick.

'Did ever Jove's tree drop such fruit?' he quoted as Katie hopped towards him.

Walter polished the patent leather inside and out with his handkerchief and offered it to her with a flourish. Katie sat down on the ground and, dimpling in the most distracting manner (there should be a law against that, thought Walter), said: 'Thank you so much, Walter, you really do seem to be my knight errant.'

'Don't put it on yet, Katie,' he said carefully. 'The shoe is still a little damp, so let's sit down here and rest for a few moments. Oh, I would so like to stay the evening with you but my dratted Uncle has invited guests to dine with us tonight so I shall have to take my leave of you within the hour.'

They chatted pleasantly about this and that until Katie's shoe was dry and then they set off home. But as the couple crossed Farmer Dawson's meadow they heard a muffled roar and saw a creature with tossing horns and waving tail making for them, head down, eyes flashing. Katie gave a shriek but luckily they happened to be near a pair of low bars and Walter had not been a college athlete for nothing. He swung Katie over the bars and jumped after her.

But she, not knowing in her fright where she was nor what she was doing, supposing also that the mad creature would still pursue her, flung herself bodily in his arms, crying: 'Walter! Walter! Save me!'

The young rascal needed no second invitation and proceeded to save her in the usual way by holding her close to his supple frame and kissing her boldly on the mouth, murmuring: 'You are safe, my darling. Not a hair of your precious head shall be hurt.'

'But what was it, Walter – I cannot help being so scared. Was it a dangerous bull?'

Walter looked up and saw the animal trotting off in the distance. It was that rare yet entirely possible thing – a sportive cow.

'Is he gone?' breathed Katie from his chest.

'Yes, the cow has gone and won't come back, darling.' smiled Walter. 'But you'd better not move just in case I'm wrong!'

'A cow?' exclaimed Katie. 'Oh Walter, I feel so ashamed. What a silly girl I've been, making all that fuss.'

'No, no, no,' said Walter quietly. 'I shall always be eternally grateful to the beast for enabling me to hold you in my arms in this lovely fashion.'

For a moment, they looked into each other's eyes as Katie lifted up her pretty face and then their mouths met in a most delicious kiss. They sank to the ground, clutching each other as Walter's tongue made an instant, darting journey of exploration inside the pretty girl's mouth. She responded with avidity and did not repulse the handsome lad when his hand came up and touched her throat before moving slowly, lingeringly down towards the valley between her breasts, moulding the linen blouse against her skin.

Katie gasped with joy and the thought flashed through her mind that this must be how Tricia her cat must feel when she stroked her. His hand continued its journey, insistently, now, over the full twin curves of her rising breasts and she shivered with raw, unslaked desire.

'Oh, you are so beautiful,' murmured Walter as he eased her down on the dry grass and leaned over her. She hardly felt his swift fingers unbutton her blouse and slip the straps of her chemise down from her shoulders. He slid his palms over her breasts, feeling the rosy red nipples pouting hard against his hands. He dared venture further, moving his hand along her leg and under her skirt until he reached her thighs.

'Ah! Oh! Oh! Walter, don't!' she gasped, contracting her thighs around his fingers.

'I cannot resist you,' whispered Walter, smothering her with a renewed burst of kisses, thrusting the velvet tip of his tongue between her soft lips.

Katie sighed and relaxed her grip around his hand which proceeded to unbutton her drawers and work its way onto her mount of silky golden hair. Very soon, almost to her surprise, the lovely girl found that somehow Walter had slipped off all her clothes and she was lying quite naked on the grassy knoll as Walter's tongue explored her breasts, lingering over each nipple in turn as his fingers found their way through the triangle of golden hair nestling between her thighs. His wicked fingers stroked, probed and caressed her pussey which now dampened with her love juices and she cried out with pleasure at the joy it afforded her.

'Katie, Katie, feel here the staff of desire impatient to enter the divine lips of love between your thighs,' he whispered in her ear, pulling her half-resisting hand to the bulge in the front of his trousers. Now as aroused as he, Katie slid her hand to feel his stiff member as he wrenched off his belt and unbuttoned his fly. She assisted him to pull down his trousers and underpants in one fell swoop and she grasped his rampant penis. As his hand continued to plunge in and out between the lips of her pliant pussey, Katie jerked her hand up and down on the hot, velvet skin of Walter's swollen shaft, faster and faster until seconds later the white love juice gushed out of the purple bulb in a swift little fountain and a shuddering orgasm of pleasure flowed through his quivering body.

His lips remained glued to hers as her hand held his gushing rod in a convulsive grasp whilst his fingers continued to play with her clitty and cunney until Walter felt his hand deluged with her warm, juicy spend, spurting over his hand in loving sympathy.

'Katie, my darling! I must kiss your sweet pussey and taste the nectar of love!' exclaimed Walter, snatching his lips from hers and burying his face between her unresisting thighs. He licked up the luscious love juice that poured from her pussey lips and then his tongue found its way further till it tickled her sensitive little clitty which rose up to meet the welcome intruder. Katie moaned with passion as she twisted her legs over his head, squeezing it between her firm thighs in an ecstasy of delight.

'Mr Pego is now coming to meet you, darling,' panted Walter, his penis rising majestically upward as he went back to work titillating Katie's stiff little clitty, inserting a finger in her beautifully wrinkled little bum hole, which worked her up to new paroxysms of desire. She now clutched at his rampant prick and rolled her tongue round the uncovered purple dome, licking and lapping in an acme of erotic enjoyment. She spent again in a second luscious flood whilst she felt his shaft swell and throb until with a shudder he sent a hot stream of creamy sperm into her mouth and she unthinkingly swallowed the veritable jet of love juice which had burst from Walter's excited engine of love.

They both nearly fainted from the excess of their emotions and lay quite exhausted for a few moments till Walter felt her sweet lips again sucking his still-erect cock.

'Oh, Katie, I must now position myself for the *coup de grâce*, the real stroke of love,' he said, his eyes shining brightly with desire as he parted the pretty girl's quivering thighs.

At first Katie made no resistance but then she struggled free and wriggled away from him. 'No, no, Walter, I am not ready yet for this. Please, please do not force me!' urged the lovely girl, covering her gorgeous naked body with her dress.

'You must forgive me, Walter, I got carried away but I will only make love when the time is right for me in both mind and body. Oh, my love, I do feel very much for you. Will you respect my feelings?'

Katie need not have worried her pretty little head about Walter's passion. For he was, after all, a gentleman who had been schooled at Nottsgrove Academy where the progressive views of the headmaster Doctor Simon White stressed the absolute necessity of always obeying your partner's wishes. 'When a girl says no she means no,' Doctor White declared to his Sixth Form again and again. 'Any man who forces a girl to submit to any intimacy to which she is not a willing partner deserves to have his testicles removed!'

So Walter immediately took a pace backwards and said: 'Of course I respect your feelings, Katie. I hope I always have and always will. Come, let us get dressed. Perhaps I may persuade you to change your mind at a another time and place.'

'If anyone will, you will, Walter,' said the grateful girl. 'I only wish all men were as kind and understanding as you. You aren't angry with me, are you?'

'No, no, of course not,' smiled Walter, kissing her on the tip of her elegant little nose. 'How could I be angry with such a beautiful creature like you?'

'Oh, Walter, you really are the nicest man I have ever met!'

They kissed again as they said their goodbyes and Walter made Katie promise that she would go out for another walk with him the next evening. She agreed and they waved farewell as Kate walked back home alone (as she had told Walter that she preferred to do) and the love-sick young man set off for Stanton Lodge. He looked at his pocket watch and noted that he was in good time – which was as well, for as he reached the road back to his Uncle's house he noticed a dark brown piece of leather lying on the grass. He picked it up and discovered that it was a pocket diary.

It was obviously a private diary, as opposed to one that simply recorded appointments, but Walter felt not unreasonably that he had to peer inside if for no other reason to see who was the owner. He looked at the inside page and read the name 'Connie Chumbley' – a name that meant nothing to him although Katie could have enlightened him. For Connie was, until that morning, the Arkley family's maid and was one of the infamous trio – the other members being Formbey the butler and Mrs Beaconsfield the cook – who had walked out on Lady Arkley earlier that day.

The temptation to read the diary was too much for Walter and he had time on his hands before going back home and dressing for dinner. And when he found out almost immediately that he possessed the intimate diary of a young girl, wild horses would not have moved him from the wooden seat that had been thoughtfully placed at a pretty spot for pedestrians by a kindly old gentleman some five years previously.

Walter soon discovered by skimming through the first few paragraphs that Connie had been in service in India with Katie's uncle, Lord Daniel Arkley, and she had written of an encounter with a young lieutenant in the British Army in south India. Late one warm afternoon she had decided to wander down to the beach. His eyes widened and his heart began to beat a little faster as he read on:

*   *   *

'I drank in the solitude of the loveliness of it all. Though the sea sparkled benevolently, the golden-coloured sand somehow told me of being harried by the endless ebb and flow of storm-roused tides. Suddenly I was transfixed as an elephant apparently emerged from the shadows of a sandy grove. With some relief I realised that it was made from stone but the consummate skill of those Indian rock masons of long ago had for a moment scared me stiff!

'I turned away and yet another shock awaited me – there in the azure blue sea swimming lazily towards me was young Lieutenant Randolph Barnett of the Royal West Kents. Lieutenant Barnett was a liaison officer between the military authorities and the local Maharajah and as such had been summoned to several meeting with Lord Arkley. I had waited upon him and whilst passing round the tea and biscuits, I could not help but admire his handsome face, slim body and gracious manner.

' "Hello, there, I know you," he called out. "It's young Connie, Lord Arkley's maid, isn't it? Come on in for a dip, the water's warm yet so refreshing."

'I blushed but of course was quite delighted that the handsome young man had remembered me. "I can't come in, Lieutenant Barnett," I called back. "I don't have a bathing costume or a towel with me."

' "Don't worry about that," he replied. "I have a towel and as for a bathing costume, you don't need one. Come on in and swim without anything on – it's far, far nicer, Connie, I do assure you. Look, I haven't any clothes on! It feels so free to swim in the nude, do try it and you'll never want to put your costume on again!"

'I could hardly believe my ears but as if to prove that
he was telling the truth, Lieutenant Barnett swam
towards me until the water was too shallow to stay hori-
zontal. He scrambled to his feet and to my astonishment
I saw that the good-looking rogue had spoken naught
but the truth! He paddled through the water towards me
unashamedly naked and oh, diary! he looked a real
Adonis, so well muscled in a manly fashion yet his face
was totally smooth and free from any blemish. I admired
the strength of his broad chest and the flatness of his
belly. And of course I could not resist taking a demure
look at the fine-looking penis that dangled saucily
between his legs.

' "Come now, Connie, I promise you that you will
enjoy yourself." urged my new companion.

'Suddenly a quotation from the book of sayings by the
wise Indian sage Mustapha Pharte which I had been
studying the previous evening came into my mind: "In
our wild and dangerous world we must drink deeply
from the cup of sensual joy lest it be suddenly dashed
from our lips." In other words, enjoy yourself whilst
you can, I thought and so I nodded my assent and kicked
off my shoes. I unbuttoned my blouse and allowed
Randolph (as he insisted I called him) to undo my skirt
which I let fall onto the soft sand. I shrugged off my slips
and pulled down my drawers leaving my naked body free
to his gaze.

' "Gad, what a beautiful girl you are, Connie," he
murmured, and I noticed that his cock twitched slightly
as he spoke. "Can you swim? Yes? Good, let's strike out
and then make for that deserted little cove over on our
left. I've left my towel there together with a hamper."

'We stayed in the water for a quarter of an hour or so and I had to admit to Randolph that his comments about the joys of swimming in the nude were absolutely true – I did indeed revel in the glories of a sense of total freedom. I let myself wallow in a kind of sensuous joy, floating on my back and letting the gentle waves wash over me. Then I swam to Randolph's little cove and dabbed myself dry with the towel. It was hardly necessary to do so as the warm sun evaporated the moisture from my skin. Randolph had swum back for my clothes which he brought over to this pretty place which was hidden from general view. Randolph had prepared a fine feast of sandwiches and cake and had even brought a bottle of wine packed in crushed ice which was very welcome indeed.

'We lay naked on the sand and somehow it seemed the most natural thing in the world to be in Randolph's strong arms and exchanging the most passionate of kisses. My blood was now up and as our mouths crushed together I put my tongue in his mouth and explored the top half between teeth and lips with a long probing kiss. His hands descended to my full breasts and he squeezed my hard little nipples and my own left hand was suddenly pulled down to meet Randolph's rising shaft which fairly leaped into my grasp.

'My body was now on fire with unslaked desire – I whispered my wish to Randolph who smiled gently and murmured back "it will be my pleasure" as I lay back and opened my legs in preparation. I positioned Randolph on his knees in front of me so that he would have full view of my furry bush and pouting cunney lips. I took his hand and placed it on my already-dampening mound. His fingers splayed my outer lips and the fingers of his other hand ran down the length of my crack. I gently pushed the finger in as my hips rose up to meet the welcome visitor. Now I felt his lips part my cunney lips and I was soon in raptures as he found my excitable little clitty which sent waves of passion spilling all over me. My pussey was now spending freely under the voluptuous titillations of his velvety tongue. Aaah, the sweet memories of the moment make me ache with desire for another afternoon of love-making with dear randy Randolph!

'I clasped my legs around his head as he continued to lick and lap on my engorged clitty and I screamed with unalloyed joy as I reached the peak of pleasure. I released Randolph's head from between my thighs and pushed him firmly down on his back so that I could repay him for the joy he had given me. He had no protectives with him so I could not allow him to fuck me. However, I was determined to thrill him in another way that I knew he would find almost as exciting!

'He obeyed with alacrity my command to lie still and I smoothed my hand over his flat stomach and into the curly mass of pubic hair. I licked my lips with gusto when I looked at his thick shaft which was not fully erect but had that lovely, full, heavy look about it. I gently squeezed this huge pole and immediately his cock stood up in full erection, uncapping the delicious-looking purple knob. I grasped his shaft again, marvelling at the width of the monster – even bigger than that of Sir Leon Standlake, the scourge of every servant girl in Belgravia – and I could scarcely enclose it with my hand. My head now swooped down and I began to kiss and lick the red mushroom dome with my tongue. Then I began to suck greedily on this delicious-looking sweetmeat, dwelling around the ridge, up the underside and sucking up as much as the shaft as possible into my mouth. I pumped his prick firmly, keeping my lips taut on his length, kissing, sucking, licking and lapping as I took him fully into my mouth in long, rolling sucks. I continued to suck furiously until I felt the juices boil up inside that hot, hard shaft and then I knew he was about to spend which he did in long powerful squirts that I swallowed eagerly, milking his rod of every last drop of white love-juice.

'To my amazement his shaft remained semi-erect and after I had rubbed it up and down for a minute or so it swelled up again as stiff as could be!

' ''Goodness gracious, Randolph,'' I giggled. ''You certainly have extraordinary powers of recovery.''

' ''I know,'' sighed the young rascal. ''If only I could place my staff in your c-''

I put my hand to his lips and murmured that today was too dangerous for a bareback ride but that next week he might be able to aim his charger at a wet and willing target. Still holding his magnificently thick tool, I sank down to the sand for a second helping as I kissed the ruby knob and then opened my lips to take it in my mouth. I sucked gently this time around, rolling my tongue over his knob, savouring the tangy taste of his juices. My tongue ran down his length and then ran back to the top to catch a sticky drip of spend that had formed around the 'eye'. I ran my lips around his noble cock, closing my lips firmly around the shaft as I squeezed his balls care-fully to heighten his enjoyment.

This caused Randolph to spend almost at once, sending a second stream of salty hot spunk down my throat. I swallowed to the final burning drops, smacking my lips with total abandon as, at last, Randolph's stand began to wilt and his shaft shrank down to its normal size.

"Come on, Randolph," I said. "We must get dressed before we are discovered." We scrambled into our clothes and to my surprise I noticed that Randolph had been wearing his revolver belt.

' "Do you always wear a gun?" I asked.

Randolph chuckled and said: "I'm glad it was you and not I that said 'gun', Connie.

' "Why?" I said with some puzzlement.

' "We don't use that word in the Army," he explained. "A pistol is a pistol, a revolver is a revolver and a rifle is a rifle. If a soldier says 'gun' instead of the noun of correct terminology, after morning drill he has to stand naked in the barrack square and with one hand holding, say, his pistol and the other holding his prick is forced to recite:

> *This is my pistol*
> *This is my gun*
> *This is for fighting*
> *And this is for fun*

Needless to say, not many recruits make this mistake more than once!"

I laughed and we made our way back to Randolph's barracks where he showed me all round the camp and then entertained me to an early supper in his rooms. Later he drove me back to Lord Arkley's and I was hard put to keep my resolve not to let his stalwart pego enter its desired haven that night.'

Walter closed the diary and breathed heavily. Reading this erotic tale had excited him almost to a frenzy. His hand grasped his shaft which was as hard as a rock and threatened to burst out from the stretched material of his trousers. He took several deep breaths and forced himself into a calmer train of thought. He stuffed the diary into his pocket before marching purposefully back to Stanton Lodge, idly wondering whether General Bailstone's niece would be of an age and of a kind that he would find attractive.

He arrived back in good time and after a brisk wash changed into evening dress.

Luckily the General was in better humour as he had received a telephone call from London in which his close friend Mr Roy St Clair had informed him that the tip they had received from their Club's head waiter had in fact 'turned up' – for as forecast the filly Amhurst Park had won the third race at Goodwood at odds of twelve to one. So the ten pound wager struck with the Cavalry Club's bookmaker would yield a handsome profit of one hundred and twenty pounds.

'Help yourself to a whisky and soda, my boy,' said General Stanton genially when Walter appeared in the drawing room. 'I don't expect Colonel Bailstone and his niece for another ten minutes or so. Sit yourself down and enjoy your drink.'

And the blessing of good fortune would have appeared to continue to hover over Stanton Lodge that evening, settling this time over young Wally's head for, to his absolute delight, Colonel Bailstone's niece, Louisa, turned out to be an extremely pretty girl of just eighteen years of age, as lithe and lovely as a fawn with masses of tawny brown hair and with a fine sense of mischief that sparkled in her large brown eyes.

On the other hand, Colonel Bailstone was a pompous old bore who liked nothing better than listening to the sound of his own voice. He was of a corpulent build and years of 'lifting the elbow', as the modern colloquialism has it, had no doubt added inches to his portly waistline as well as causing his face to flush a bright shade of red after only a glass or so of General Stanton's Bollinger '87 champagne.

The two old Army martinets were snorting their anger over a letter in *The Times* that day about the need to alleviate the sufferings of the poor.

'Just listen to this idiot,' grunted Colonel Bailstone, picking up the newspaper and reading aloud from the letter which had roused his ire.' I can't believe that *The Times* would even deign publish such rot, Frederick, but it's all here in black and white – let me quote: "A way must be found of helping those thrifty working people who show no apparent evidence of dire want. At present it would appear that worthy working people who by industry and thrift have raised themselves above the brink of abject pauperism can make no further claim for assistance to lift the veil of greater want.

' "In addition of course we must also acknowledge the sad fact that people quickly forget that more than sympathy is needed to relieve those poor souls who have been brought to misfortune often through no fault of their own. There are far too many who in their professed detestation of roguery, supposed or real, forget that by a wholesale condemnation of charity and so-called demoralisation, they are running the risk of driving honest men to despair and peaceful folk to violence. Indeed, it may be wondered whether these comfortable wealthy people are in fact secret supporters of the Socialists for it is surely only in such interests that misery, hunger and social unrest should increase – I am, Sir, Yours Faithfully, Reverend T H Cooney, Vicar of Nayland, Colchester, Essex.'' So now we have padres writing this subversive kind of nonsense in *The Times* of all places – what is this country coming to?'

General Stanton nodded his agreement: 'I can't imagine what the twentieth century has in store for us. All we need to do is return to the good old military maxim of having a few people to give the orders and the rest to obey 'em, eh?'

'You dictatorial old fool,' muttered the delicious Louisa to Walter which startled the lad so much that he choked on a mouthful of apple flan.

'What did you say, Louisa?' snapped her uncle, fixing a gimlet eye upon her.

'Louisa asked me if we had any fish in our garden pool,' said Walter with commendable speed of thought.

General Stanton was a little hard of hearing but Louisa's uncle stared grimly at the young couple before deciding that it would be politic on this occasion to give his niece the benefit of the doubt.

Louisa sensed it was time to retreat in good order, to use an appropriate military metaphor and said: 'If you gentlemen would like to take your cigars and brandy in here, I will retire to the lounge. Would you mind if I took the opportunity of practising on your piano, General Stanton? I am due to play at a charity concert next Wednesday evening at the Wigmore Hall in London.'

'Of course, my dear, feel free. We will join you there later and perhaps we could be entertained by a short recital,' said General Stanton. 'Your Uncle and I will join you in about half an hour.'

'With your permission, sir, I will escort Miss Bailstone to the lounge and take coffee with her there,' said Walter hopefully, rising from his seat.

'As you wish, my boy,' replied the General amiably, waving the young couple away as Cheetham the butler placed silver decanters of port and brandy upon the gleaming white tablecloth.

Once they were outside and Walter had closed the door, Louisa giggled and said: '*Tirez le rideau, la farce est jouée*!' Walter looked blankly for a moment and then returned her smile. 'That's Rabelais isn't it? Pull down the curtain the comedy is over.' he translated.

'Quite correct, and thank you so much for saving my bacon with your quick thinking just now. I really must learn to curb my tongue but Uncle, though a sweet man in many ways, is such an old reactionary when it comes to matters of social affairs that I just cannot keep quiet when he spouts such nonsense.'

'Are you a student of political economy?' asked Walter.

'Only in an amateur way,' dimpled the delicious girl. 'At the college I attend, Dame Bracknell's Academy for Young Ladies, we were taught by a daughter of Mrs Shackleton, the famous campaigner for women's rights and she has all the zeal of her mother when it comes to obtaining women such fundamental rights as the right to vote.'

'I haven't thought too much about votes for women,' Walter admitted. 'But of course all logic demands that men and women enjoy equal rights. After all, why should Dame Bracknell, for example, not be allowed to vote whilst her blacksmith may well possess the franchise?'

'Precisely, Walter,' she added. 'and I must tell you that in my opinion it is the Socialists who are showing us the way ahead, and soon the working people of this country will possess the full power of government through elective institutions to embody in law their rightful economic and social desires.'

Walter hardly heard her words, so dazzled was he by her pretty face and long hair which was worn simply, framing her attractive features and forming a level fringe on her forehead.

In the lounge, where Cheetham had set a pot of coffee bubbling cheerfully under a tiny gas light, Walter asked Louisa if he could turn the pages of her music.

'That's very kind of you, Walter,' she said, passing her tongue over her upper lip in a most sensuous fashion. 'But I was thinking of playing on some other instrument rather than General Stanton's piano.'

'Some other instrument, Louisa,' said the puzzled Walter,' – such as what?'

'How about the little piccolo down there?' said Louisa boldly. 'Gracious, it's more like a clarinet! Wally, have you something stuffed in your pocket or are you just glad to see me?'

Walter could not believe the evidence of his eyes and ears! But here was this lovely creature fondling his erect pego with one hand and unbuttoning her creamy Italian linen blouse with the other. The girl sensed his amazement and whispered: 'There is something else we learned in the Sixth Form at Dame Bracknell's Academy, Walter, best expressed perhaps in this little rhyme:

We may live without verses, music and art,
We may live without conscience and live without
heart,
We may live without friends, we may live without
luck,
But life's mere existence without a good fuck!

'This is a motto which the girls in my little circle there took to heart and with the aid of Doctor Coley's little book *The Young People's Guide to Procreation* to ensure the obtainment of the fullest joys without any accidents, we have discovered a very happy mode of living.'

Walter gulped and said: 'Do you mean you believe in free love?'

'Well, we don't charge for it nor do we expect to make payment to our partners,' said the delightful girl, stepping out of her drawers so that she stood completely nude in front of him. 'And of course we only pleasure ourselves with boys who we believe can match our standards in hygiene, ability and, above all, discretion.'

He stared in wonder and then with unabashed lust at her exquisitely-formed uptilted breasts each crowned by a rosy red nipple set in a large rounded areola, and her smooth white-skinned tummy below which twinkled a curly mass of fine brown hair.

Without further words they sank down to the floor, entwined in each other's arms, exchanging the most ardent of kisses as the hot-blooded Louisa unbuttoned Walter's trousers, releasing his straining shaft which sprang up like a flagpole between his thighs. She encircled his rigid member with her hand and planted a wet kiss on top of the uncovered red knob.

'My God, I didn't lock the door! Suppose someone comes in!' gasped Walter.

'No-one will come in, darling,' she whispered. 'I will confess to you however that covert intercourse does give me an added thrill. What a snub to the established order to enjoy the raw heat of ecstasy whilst everyone else is carrying on boring and being bored, totally oblivious to the intimacies taking place right under their silly noses!'

'If this is Socialism, I shall make a donation to the Party first thing tomorrow morning,' promised Walter.

'Never mind about a donation tomorrow, let us see if you can spend tonight,' said Louisa, diving down to wrap her lips around the swollen head of his rigid pole, taking as much of him as she could into her mouth. Her warm breath and moist mouth sent chills racing up and down his spine and her tongue slithering around his tingling rod soon brought him to the brink of orgasm. Louisa's delectable palating brought his truncheon past the point of no return and, as Walter began to spend, she gripped the base of his shaft, sucking him harder and harder until he felt his testicles hardening and he gasped a warning that his climax was near.

'I'm going to spend, Louisa!' he cried out, his penis jerking in and out of the sweet prison of her wet mouth.

But she made no move to extract his throbbing shaft

from between her lips. She grasped his firm, muscular cheeks of his bottom, moving him backwards and forwards until with a final juddering throb he spurted a copious stream of spunk into her willing mouth. She swallowed his emission joyfully, smacking her lips as he quivered with convulsions of delight as they finished by wrapping their arms around each other and sealed their delight with a loving kiss.

Unlike earlier in the evening, Mr Pego could not be encouraged to remain at attention for there are limits to the stamina even of the most well-hung young gentlemen such as Walter. However, this did not preclude him from repaying his amorosa as she leaned back on the carpet with a cushion behind her head and another cushion stuffed underneath her delectable little bum. She spread her legs invitingly, affording Walter a bird's eye view of her silky-haired quim. His hands stroked her bare thighs and he moved higher to stroke her moist mons veneris, purring with sheer delight as he rubbed her furry little pussey.

She leaned forward to position Walter's head between her legs and he buried it in the hairs of her brown motte that covered her moist crack. It was delicious, divine. His heartbeat quickened with erotic excitement as his tongue raked her erect little clitoris then slipped down to probe inside her. Almost of their own volition her legs splayed even wider, bent at the knees as she sought to open herself even more to his questing tongue. He slurped lustily as he drew her cunney lips into his mouth, delighting in the taste of her flesh which he found clean and sweet to his tongue. Her hips thrust up in urgency, moaning and panting her pleasure as Walter lapped up the juices that were flowing freely from her cunney.

He was in the seventh heaven of delight as the unique feminine odour assailed his nose and he frantically attacked with his tongue the erect little clitty that trembled and twitched at his electric touch. This set Louisa off on her final journey to the highest hills of delight. She jerked her hips upwards as her stiff clitty was drawn further and further forward between his lips and her hands went down to clasp his head, pressing his mouth even more tightly against her. Her legs, folded across his shoulders, trembled as she cried: 'Walter, Walter, here I come! I can't stop now! Aaah! Aaah! Aaah!' She, too, spent profusely all over Walter's mouth and chin as she swam in a veritable sea of lubricity until she sank back exhausted and satiated by the delightful experience.

'What a superb *hors d'oeuvres* – now for the entrée!' enthused Louisa as, slowly at first, she gently stroked the underside of Walter's stiffening penis, allowing her fingers to trace a path around it and underneath his hairy ballsack which made his entire frame tingle with gratification. After a while she closed her finger and thumb around the shaft, sliding them along its length and easing down the foreskin, baring his purple knob as her head bobbed down and, like a lizard, her tongue slid around his rigid rod until it stood up firmly to attention.

As soon as it reached its fullest extent Louisa climbed on top of him with her knees on either side of his muscular trunk. The thick pile of the Turkish carpet acted as a mattress as she rubbed her pussey across the uncovered knob of his straining member. She smiled as she took hold of his prick and guided it slowly inside her. Walter could feel her cunney muscles contract and relax as she rocked up and down on his shaft, moving backwards and forwards in rhythm whilst Walter cupped her firm, uptilted breasts, flicking the rosy little nipples between his fingers and rubbing them against the palms of his hands.

Louisa bounced, shook and ground her hips and leaned first forwards and then right back so that his shaft was sliding deep in and then almost falling out – but never quite! Now their orgasms approached and the delectable girl drove down hard, spearing herself on his glistening cock as wave after wave of nervous spasms shot through her. Each spasm tightened her cunney muscles and then Walter began to jerk underneath her, thrusting up his hips to meet her pushes as their climaxes arrived simultaneously. Their hoarse cries of joy rang out as Walter pumped jets of salty spunk into her dark secret warmth whilst, with an immense shudder, Louisa's climax flowed and gradually subsided as her own love juices dribbled down the sides of her thighs.

She rolled off him and they lay panting with exhaustion until Louisa said: 'Walter, be a dear and pour some coffee. I think we both need a drink to revive us!'

'But of course, my love. What a terrible host I am not to have offered you something beforehand,' said Walter, rising to his feet and padding naked to the sideboard.

'I have no complaints about what I've eaten and drunk tonight,' murmured Louisa naughtily. 'But whilst you are up there, hadn't you better put on some clothes. After all, you know how traditional our two old uncles are about dressing for dinner!'

'Damnation, we'd better hurry!' exclaimed Walter, putting down his coffee cup and sorting through the pile of clothes for his underclothes.

They both dressed hastily and sat down on the couch to await the arrival of their avuncular fellow diners. Strangely, they waited in vain until Walter looked at his pocket watch and said: 'Do you know, it's almost an hour since we left the old boys. I think we'd better see what's going on.'

'Don't disturb them, perhaps they are in the middle of one of those interminable conversations about the Crimean campaigns,' advised Louisa, brushing the hair away from her eyes as they walked slowly back to the dining room.

So Walter opened the dining room door – which was well away from the top of the table where dinner had been served – just a fraction and they popped their heads around just to see what was going on. Their mouths fell open when they saw that their uncles were engaged in activity with Nancy, the plump young kitchenmaid, which had little to do with military matters!

The table had been cleared but it was not empty, for lying across it, stark naked and flat on his back was Colonel Bailstone. His chest was covered with matted grey hair and his corpulent belly, without the restrictions imposed by a belt, sagged all over the place. But his member stood up smartly enough, a thick, twitching truncheon which was being manipulated with an expert hand by Nancy who was dressed, or rather half-undressed in her black maid's uniform. The Colonel, assisted no doubt by General Stanton, had undone all her top buttons and her large breasts were free of any covering and stood out naked and mouth-wateringly ripe for a touch of lips or fingers.

Nancy continued to rub her hand up and down his enormous shaft whilst the Colonel fondled her breasts. General Stanton muttered: 'A manoeuvre from the rear will win the battle,' as he undid the remaining buttons on the back of Nancy's blouse and slipped it off her. Her skirt and underdrawers soon followed along with the General's shirt, belt and trousers. He grunted with the effort of joining the pair already on the table but he made it without too much difficulty, panting 'Steady, the Buffs,' as he placed his hands on Nancy's bum cheeks. She had rich, sumptuous buttocks and as he prised open her legs the General and the prying eyes at the door were treated to a tantalising glimpse of her furry pussey, a soft delicate purse waiting to be filled. She raised her buttocks slightly, showing herself wet and open, spread like a flower, inviting the General to plunge himself into her.

'Come on, sir, I'm ready for inspection.' cried Nancy but the General shook his head as he held his turgid penis and said apologetically: 'Sorry m' dear, my unit has surrendered without a fight. Gad, if I were twenty years younger!'

At the door, Louisa tapped Walter on the shoulder and said: 'Wally, in the name of social justice it is bounden upon you to fuck that poor girl immediately. Why should she not enjoy the same pleasures chance to find a suitable lover and is forced to make do with two old buffoons.'

'Do you really think I should?' said Walter whose bulging trousers showed how stimulated he had been by the wanton exhibition that was taking place on the dining-room table.

'Without any doubt,' said Louisa firmly. 'Go and do your duty at once.'

He needed no second bidding as he boldly marched

forward and shucked off his clothes saying: 'Here comes the cavalry, Nancy!' as he leaped onto the rather crowded table behind her. She took one hand away from pumping Colonel Bailstone's tool and reached for Walter's rock hard shaft to guide it between her luscious bum cheeks. He was soon buried in her throbbing sheath as she thrust her bottom to and fro and Walter passed his hand round her waist to handle her luxuriously-covered mount quite freely, slipping two fingers inside to join his prick for her added enjoyment.

This was all too much for Colonel Bailstone who with a groan spent over Nancy's hand as she wriggled with glee for now she could concentrate on the velvety spear that was piercing her so engagingly from behind. She turned her head and exclaimed: 'Why Master Walter, fancy finding you here. Ooh! Ooh! Ooh! That's lovely, lovely. Now finish me off, sir, as I'm about to spend.'

She wriggled and worked her bottom cleverly so that Walter could embed even more of his thrusting shaft as her cunney magically expanded to receive it. How her bottom cheeks rotated as Walter's prick rammed in and out and his balls banged against her arse. Nancy screamed with happiness as Walter crashed down hard, pouring his frothy seed inside her in a tremendous gush just as her own explosion sent her over the edge into Nirvana.

Louisa had now walked into the room and on seeing her, the two uncles hastily pulled on their trousers, fumbling with red-faced embarrassment. However, the girl's eyes were fixed upon Walter and Nancy who had collapsed in a heap on the table.

With sublime coolness Louisa said that she hoped the

copious libations of the love-making would not irretrievably stain the fine cotton tablecloth.

'Oh no, miss, I find that a few dabs of Doctor Weston's Elixir will remove most stains from any material,' said Nancy, pulling on her drawers.

'Good heavens, I take a spoonful of Doctor Weston's Elixir to ease a cough,' said Walter.

'And I use it on my roses to keep the greenfly at bay,' confessed Colonel Bailstone, who may have held ridiculously reactionary political opinions but who possessed the saving grace of a sense of humour, which showed as he led the burst of laughter that followed his remark.

The party broke up shortly afterwards and nothing was mentioned then or ever afterwards about the goings-on in either the lounge or dining-room. Fortunately Cheetham had dozed off in the kitchen and was totally unaware as to what had taken place at Stanton Lodge – which was just as well for there are no bigger gossips than butlers.

Walter fell asleep that night almost as soon as his head touched the pillow, leaving the book he had purchased secretly at Hottens(*) *An Introduction To The French Art of Fucking* by A Gentleman Much Experienced In

---

* John Camden Hotten kept a small discreet bookshop in Piccadilly during the later Victorian decades. He specialised in gallant literature and enjoyed the custom of the cognoscenti, making a considerable fortune from importing books and prints from the Continent.

Hotten paid liberal amounts for police 'protection' and when Scotland Yard finally moved against him he had sufficient warning to lease his Belgravia home to a regular customer, Sir Lionel Trapes, and take his considerable bank balance to Europe where he settled first in Berlin and later in Cannes where he died in 1902 at the ripe old age of ninety-one.

These Arts unread. But before he drifted into the arms of Morpheus he suddenly thought of Katie Arkley for whose favours earlier that day he would have almost cheerfully laid down his life. He had been unfaithful to his would-be love not once but twice! He could not help smiling as John Gay's lines entered his mind:

> *How happy I could be with either*
> *Were t'other dear charmer away!*

I behaved like a cad, he told himself and resolved to continue wooing the lovely Katie at the first opportunity that presented itself. He closed his eyes and fell into a deep sleep, no doubt sated with all the pleasures that had been so freely and unexpectedly lavished upon him.

CHAPTER THREE

Having left Walter and his partners sleeping peacefully
(and, for the time being, in separate beds), we must now
retrace the paths of those peripheral yet important personages without whom this narrative could never have
been written. We refer, dear readers, to Lady Arkley's
disaffected servants, Formbey the butler, Mrs
Beaconsfield the cook and Connie the maid with whom
we have already made a passing acquaintance. You may
recall dear friends that Lady Arkley made a grim accusa-
tion that Mrs Beaconsfield had probably been seduced by
an offer from Lady Hutchinson who had long coveted her
services after consuming three slices of Mrs
Beaconsfield's noted Upside Down cake.

The truth, however, lay elsewhere for Lady
Hutchinson was totally guiltless of any such underhand
behaviour. Incidentally, it ill-behoved Lady Arkley to
point the finger at any other London hostess. It was an
open secret in London Society that Lady Arkley herself
had obtained Mrs Beaconsfield for her household by
offering six pounds a year more than the Honourable Mrs
Jeremy Austin had been paying this excellent cook. But
whilst we record these matters to enable the facts of Lady
Hutchinson's innocence and Lady Arkley's tantrum of

ill-temper to be more widely known, we must not digress and now return post-haste to our narrative.

After standing firm and refusing to be browbeaten by the formidable Lady Arkley, the three servants took the train to London and near Paddington Station sat down in a clean little cafe and ordered themselves a nice pot of tea and a plate of tomato and cucumber sandwiches.

'Well, I don't know about you ladies, but I feel like a prisoner who has just been released from jail. I know we won't obtain any references from Lady Arkley but I don't think anyone who knows her will be surprised that we walked out on the old cow,' said Mr Formbey, a tall, slim man in his early thirties who had led the walk-out by the staff.

'She really was too difficult for my liking,' said Mrs Beaconsfield. 'Well, George, I'm off down to Pimlico to stay with my sister for a couple of weeks whilst I look around for another job.'

'I have already obtained employment with a foreign gentleman,' said Mr Formbey, taking a letter from his inside jacket pocket. 'Aspiso's Agency offered me a position within a week of receiving my letter requesting a list of prospective employers. It will be only a temporary post of just six week's duration but it is very well-paid for they are looking for a man who can be trusted to be discreet. Mr Edwards adds that the work will bring me into contact with many titled personages which is always useful for a man in my position.'

'You might find yourself waiting upon The Prince of Wales and Mrs Keppel!' laughed Mrs Beaconsfield.

'How do you know that I have not done so already?' grinned the butler. 'But even if I had, I would never mention it to a soul. My lips are as sealed on the subject of my employers as are those of a Romish priest concerning those who enter the confessional.'

'You two can laugh but I'm still more than a little worried about the future. I don't know why I let you both talk me into leaving,' fretted Connie. 'After all, good, experienced butlers and cooks are always in demand but young servants like me are all too easy to come by.'

'Now Connie, don't worry,' said Mrs Beaconsfield, 'George has promised you a position in his new household. And if by any chance he can't keep his promise, I'm sure I won't have too much difficulty finding you something myself.

'Meanwhile, my sister has plenty of room and I really do want you to stay with me as it's too far to go to Cumberland to see your old Dad just for a few days. You can send him a letter telling him all your news.'

'It's very kind of you, Mrs Beaconsfield,' said Connie, perking up as the cook refilled their tea cups. 'So long as I won't be in your way.'

'Far from it, it will be our pleasure. Grace hasn't seen many visitors since she had the 'flu back in the spring. It's taken her so long to shake off too!'

'Well, you must let me pay my way,' said Connie.

'We'll talk about that later, dear. I'm not short and Grace has a gentleman friend in the force, a P C Fulham if you please, who looks after her well enough, though she is in constant demand to cook dinners for young hostesses. Still, it's nice of you to offer, Connie, though I don't see Grace accepting a penny for one minute.'

'So many cooks and policemen end up as married

couples,' ruminated the butler, 'perhaps your sister will become Mrs Fulham.'

'Ah, if only Grace and her bloke could get together – but you see, he is already married although they haven't lived together for eight years. I sometimes wonder whether divorce shouldn't be made easier for ordinary folk.

'Anyhow, Connie and I had better be making our way out to Maida Vale. It isn't far, Connie, so you know what – I bet you've never been in a hansom cab, have you? Well, let's go back to the station and pick one up there. I don't fancy lugging these cases up on a bus. George, here's our address, 22 Plattsgrove Street, Maida Vale. Do write to Connie as soon as you have a job for her.'

'Or indeed for you, Mrs B,' said Mr Formbey, shaking hands with the two ladies. 'Let's keep in touch come what may. We make a good team and we all get on well together. Perhaps we should hire ourselves out as a trio!'

The two ladies were seen off in their cab by the good-natured butler who had planned to stay the night in Mrs Shawn's Private Guest House in Bloomsbury. He also decided to treat himself to the luxury of a cab and within fifteen minutes was presenting himself at Mrs Shawn's front door in Tavistock Street.

'Why, hallo, Mr Formbey, how nice to see you,' said Mrs Shawn as she welcomed him inside. She was a buxom lady of about five and thirty who had been left a widow for some years, her husband having passed away with tragic suddenness. Fortunately the late Mr Shawn had taken out a substantial insurance policy and with the proceeds she had opened a small private hotel for respectable commercial and other passing travellers.

'I'll just unpack and then I have to go to Great Titchfield Street and pop into Aspiso's Agency. But I'll be back in time for supper,' said the butler.

'It's liver and bacon tonight, Mr Formbey. That's one of your favourites if I remember correctly.'

'Sounds delicious,' said her new lodger. 'I must go now but I'll be back by six o'clock at the very latest.'

At the Aspiso Domestic Agency Mr Edwards gave him full details of his new post which sounded from the usual terms of employment. 'Count Gewirtz is a wealthy Central European nobleman, Mr Formbey. He is extremely well connected in this country and when in London is always asked to dine with the Prince of Wales.'

The agent paused and took a deep breath before continuing. 'Now, Mr Formbey, as I may have hinted in my letter, I must stress the delicate nature of this unusual appointment. The Count is a man of, ah, let us say robust inclinations and has several friends of a similar ilk, some being amongst the very highest in the land. Whatever you see or hear in the Count's employ must remain strictly confidential. Don't even tell me about anything afterwards! I don't want to alarm you but on a previous visit years ago one of his servants – not a person supplied by this agency I hasten to add – tried to blackmail the Count by taking a photograph of him with a lady at a time when no-one would want to be viewed. The man was last seen in the hold of a ship bound for the Argentine, so I am sure you will well understand the need for complete and utter discretion.'

'That poses no problem for me, Mr Edwards,' said the butler. 'I did spend some time in the service of Sir Ronnie

Dunn, a well-known gentleman about town who is known to enjoy a somewhat bizarre style of living.'

'Well you will know what to expect then, I suppose. I've been a little negative perhaps, so I should add that Count Gewirtz is known to be a most generous employer. In addition to your wages, which for six weeks work will be about the equivalent of six months in the employ of a more typical household, the Count has an endearing habit of giving each member of his staff a five pound note when he leaves London for home.

'So the job is yours, Mr Formbey, if you want it and I wish you the very best of luck. Mind, I don't suppose you know of a really good cook, do you? I was hoping to tempt Mrs Koone away from Professor Harrow but the old boy has suddenly proposed to her! Not that I blame him as her *canard à l'orange* is said by many to rival that of Escoffier. However, this has left me with a problem of who to send to Count Gewirtz on Friday.'

'You're in luck, Mr Edwards, have I got a cook for you! My colleague Mrs Beaconsfield gave in her notice to Lady Arkley at the same time as I resigned.'

'Beaconsfield, Mrs Beaconsfield,' said Mr Edwards thoughtfully. 'Not Hetty Beaconsfield of Upside Down cake fame. Your old friend Sir Ronnie is supposed to have offered five hundred guineas for the recipe!'

'The very same,' said Mr Formbey with pride. 'And we are both very fond of a young parlourmaid, Connie Chumbley, who would complete a trio of staff for the Count. Could she join us?'

'By all means,' said Mr Edwards genially. 'I'll send over two maids for the kitchen and scullery.'

'What about a coachman?'

'Count Gewirtz doesn't keep a carriage in London so we'll use Grahame from Prestoncrest. You have their telephone number and address? Good, tell them to have carriages on stand-by day and night and that all bills should be sent to my office. You can make your own arrangements with household suppliers but be sure to use the very, very best fruiterer you can find. The Count is especially fond of fruit and likes to have a fresh basket daily in the drawing room. Tell all your people to send their accounts to me for prompt payment.'

'So we start on Friday and can expect the Count to arrive by Saturday afternoon?' said Mr Formbey. 'I'll contact Mrs Beaconsfield and Connie Chumbley and tell them the good news. Don't worry Mr Edwards, they will be pleased to work with me again. I presume they should write to you about their wages, Mr Edwards. They will be paid by you at the end of six weeks like me? Splendid, I'll telephone you from the house on Friday. Oh, goodness me, I quite forgot to ask you which house Count Gewirtz has rented.'

'It's not rented, Mr Formbey,' said the agent. 'He is so rich that he bought 46 Green Street, Mayfair three years ago even though he rarely spends much time over here. I've had the house kept clean and tidy and all the china, selver and linen will be sent over from the warehouse where they are stored when the Count is out of the country.'

Mr Formbey was duly impressed and he assured Mr Edwards that Count Gewirtz would be well satisfied with the house servants whilst he stayed in London especially if Mrs Beaconsfield and Connie Chumbley would make up the team.

'If he really takes to you, there may be an exciting

bonus,' concluded Mr Edwards. 'The last butler but one so took the Count's fancy that he paid for a round trip to New York for the man and a friend with all hotel expenses paid. What do think about that?'

That evening at supper with Mrs Shawn he recounted the conversation about the eccentric European aristocrat. 'If he gives me a trip for two to America, I'll take you along, Betty,' he told the attractive landlady.

'I'll hold you to that, George,' replied Mrs Shawn roguishly, pouring the last of a bottle of beer into the butler's glass.

'No, I mean it, I really do,' he insisted. 'I'm sure you can always find a manager to lock after this place.'

'Let's drink to it,' said Mrs Shawn, opening another bottle of beer. 'Here's to our American trip!'

There being no other guests at present – three lodgers having moved out that day and none being expected before noon on the morrow – the happy pair were able to enjoy the freedom of the house for the two servant girls lived in their own rooms on the top attic floor. So they spent a jolly evening and went upstairs to bed together at half past ten, just a tiny bit worse for wear from the beer and brandy nightcaps which Mrs Shawn had generously provided.

'What a pleasant evening, George. I do hope you will be able to stay with me again after you finish with Count Gewirtz,' said Betty, opening her bedroom door with only the tiniest hint of unsteadiness.

'Seems a pity to end the evening here,' said Mr Formbey a trifle thickly. 'Especially as we could save on the gas lamps and bed linen if we shared a room.'

'Now, now, you naughty man, you mustn't tempt me,'

said Mrs Shawn as she gave him a goodnight kiss on the cheek and closed the door behind her.

Mr Formbey's bedroom was next to hers and he sat on his bed somewhat disconsolantly. He pulled off his shirt and hung it up in the wardrobe. He looked at the faded painting of a bowl of fruit on the dividing wall between his bedroom and Mrs Shawn's and decided that the picture was hanging at a lopsided angle. As he was a man who liked things "just so", he decided to adjust the frame but as he did so he noticed that the lopsided picture had concealed a peephole into Mrs Shawn's boudoir!

Here was an unexpected bonus, not as rich perhaps as a trip to America but a bird in hand was worth two in the bush, he said silently as he peered through the cunningly made gap which had been carefully drilled and hidden by the previous occupant.

His eyes almost popped out of their sockets as Mrs Shawn came into view wearing only a flimsy transparent nightgown. She sat on the bed and, to the butler's unalloyed joy, drew her nightdress up to her navel, exposing a thick bush of black hair that covered her cunney. She sighed and then began to rub her fingers against her crack which protruded from the mossy thatch. She found her clitty and gently frigged it with two fingers and he could see the little soldier stand out quite clearly. Her busy fingers worked nervously for a moment or two as her face flushed and her ample bosom begin to heave with emotion. Then all of a sudden she fell back on the bed in the act of spending, her legs wide open, allowing him to see clearly the glistening wetness around her pussey.

He told her later that this erotic sight was more than flesh and blood could stand. He moved quickly to open and close his door softly and to open hers as gently as possible so as not to frighten the dear lady.

She lay exhausted on the bed recovering from the effects of her spending but her head shot up when she saw that she was no longer alone.

'George, what are you doing here?' she gulped.

'Betty, I must admit that I saw you enjoying yourself just now. It's a great game but much better played two-handed than solitaire,' he said, placing his hands on her knees.

She looked up at him with an odd smile as he continued: 'Betty, there is something you must do for me right away.'

'What's that?' she asked.

'Take my prick out of my trousers. I've had a boner on for the last five minutes and these trousers are killing me.'

'I'd much rather it was killing me,' she said, unbuttoning his trousers and taking his not inconsiderable weapon in her hands.

'That's quite a cock you have there,' she said admiringly, capping and uncapping the reddish mushroomed head as she pulled up and down on his shaft.

'There's eight and three quarters of an inch in your hand,' said the butler proudly as she leaned forward to implant a wet kiss on his straining knob.

'Let me honour His Hugeness with a twenty tonguelick sucking,' said Mrs Shawn, opening her lips to slip the ruby knob inside her mouth. She worked on the knob with her tongue, easing her lips forward to take in a little more of the shaft. She circled the base with her hand and began to work the hot, plush velvety skin up and down, bobbing her head in rhythm as she sucked away lustily on his engorged staff.

'Careful, Betty, or I'll come too quickly,' groaned the panting Mr Formbey. 'Let's move to the bed and enjoy some rumpty-dumpty.'

She gave his cock a final kiss and obeyed him. In an inkling they were entwined upon the soft mattress with George Formbey's head ducking down beneath Mrs Shawn's ample thighs. She opened her legs wide as the butler lifted up her hips and held her pussey tightly against his mouth. He thrust his tongue between her nether lips and she cried out with delight as his hands slid under her to clutch the globular *rondeurs* of her backside. He licked with slow and persistent strokes, kissing and sucking her cunney, rubbing his soft, moist lips against her dampening crack, mingling his saliva with her juices that were starting to flow.

He grabbed a pillow and inserted it under her back so that her thighs and cunney were positioned at an excellent angle for the arrival of his charger. He then moved between her legs, nudging her knees a little further apart and took his truncheon in his hand, squeezing the shaft which capped and uncapped the purple helmet. Carefully, he guided the crown into her dripping wetness and began to piston in and out of her pussey at a slow yet steady pace. He cupped her ample breasts in his hands, pinching her nipples between his thumb and finger.

Mrs Shawn closed her eyes and savoured the feelings of arousal that rippled through her senses. His cock sluiced in and out, causing her the most divine raptures and her tight cunney clutched at his embedded penis as with a soft gurgle they entered the last lap in the race. Their movements quickened and the butler's cock drove in and out of her pussey at ever-increasing speed until he exploded and melted into her as he first reached his climax, spilling spasm after spasm of milky-white sperm into her vitals while she shuddered into her explosive spend, her saturated cunney sending delicious waves of pleasure all over her body.

Mr Formbey rolled off the panting lady and lay on his back panting with exhaustion.

'You're a marvellous screw, Betty.' he said admiringly, wiping a bead of perspiration from his brow.

'You're not so bad yourself, George,' she replied. 'Though I don't want you to think that I have enjoyed all that many men since poor Cecil passed away 'cos I haven't, more's the pity.'

'What a waste, what a waste,' murmured Mr Formbey, letting his hand stray through her sopping cunney hairs until his palm pressed against her pussey.

'There are not that many men I really fancy,' continued Mrs Shawn.

'The last gentleman lodger I would have liked in my bed surprisingly turned out to be a bum-boy.'

'Good heavens! What a dreadful misfortune!'

'Well, he was a travelling salesman for a publisher and you know what a randy lot they are. It was just my bad luck to pick a nancy boy.'

'So you must have been feeling very frustrated,' observed Mr Formbey.

'Yes, indeed. Fortunately, I procured an excellent dildoe from Tom Goldberg's Military Equipment Emporium in Tottenham Court Road. Not many people know that the Army is supplying home comforts such as these to wives when their menfolk are sent abroad to defend the flag.

'Such is the number and length of various colonial skirmishes these days that it is increasingly the lot of the soldier's wife to be alone for months on end. And when they return they are often, through sickness or fatigue, unable to resume their marital pleasures for quite some time. If you add those to the number like myself tragically widowed – though Cecil, of course was a civilian – you will understand that there is a great demand for an effective substitute for the male member.'

'Yes, I do see your point. But fancy having the dildoes on sale in a general store. Surely they should only be on sale in specialised shops?'

'There are such shops like Nickley's in Dyott Street.'

'Nickley's? Surely he is a horologist,' said the puzzled butler.

'No, no, George, he sells dildoes.'

'But he only has clocks and watches on display.'

'Well, what on earth do you expect him to put in his window?' asked Mrs Shawn quizzically and the couple dissolved into peals of laughter.

The next day at 22 Plattsgrove Street, Maida Vale, Mrs Beaconsfield read Mr Formbey's letter inviting her and Connie to begin work at Count Gewirtz's Mayfair house for just six weeks but at a rate of remuneration which the cook could hardly believe.

'Grace, where's Connie?' she asked her sister who came into the kitchen carrying a bowl of flowers which P C Fulham had brought with him the previous night when he had been a guest at dinner.

'I've sent her down to the shops as we need some carrots and onions for the Irish Stew tonight.'

'Irish Stew? That's one of my favourites although Lady Arkley could not abide lamb and I could only make it infrequently there. But what do you think of this, love?'

She passed Grace Mr Formbey's letter and her sister burst out into a peal of laughter.

'What's so funny, Grace?' said Mrs Beaconsfield.

'Oh, Hetty, this is a remarkable coincidence. Unless I have misread his note, you are being invited to work for one Count Gewirtz, are you not?'

'Let's have a look, yes, that's right – G,e,w,i,r,t,z. Why do you ask?'

'Oh, Hetty, don't you remember last night Peter was talking about his new beat next week in Mayfair? He said he was picked to be part of a special patrol the station has been ordered to make up for the visit of a very important foreign gentleman.'

'And this gentleman's name –'

' – is Count Johann Gewirtz!' said her sister with a curious smile.

'That's a coincidence right, enough, Grace but what's so amusing?'

'Well, Inspector Rogers told them that this chap's a bit of a lad.'

'A bit of a lad? What, you mean with ladies?'

'I should say! It seems that every time he comes to London all the toffs sends their wives out of town and try to lock up their daughters!'

'Crikey, is he as bad as that? I don't want to take a job where I'm always having to keep my hand on my ha'penny.'

'No, no, Hetty, he never bothers with the servants –

well, he's always on the prowl but if you say 'no' he won't drive you mad. But Inspector Rogers told the boys that Count Gewirtz has a different woman almost every night and that the toffs call him 'the gobbling Galician'. Do you reckon you can handle him?'

'Only if I'm in the mood,' said Mrs Beaconsfield and the sisters exchanged a naughty little cackle. 'I'd better warn Connie if she decides she wants to take the job – which I'm sure she will.'

And Mrs Beaconsfield's prognostication proved absolutely correct as Connie jumped at the chance to work in Mayfair, especially with Mr Formbey and Mrs Beaconsfield who she already knew to be congenial workmates.

After dinner that night Connie asked the two sisters if they had any objection to her going out to the music hall. 'I met this girl at the greengrocers,' she explained. 'She is a companion to some old biddy up in Kilburn and, whilst waiting in the shop, we struck up a conversation. Pearl doesn't have very many nights off and has no friends living round here and she was saying how lonely she finds it in London. I said I would meet her at the Kilburn Theatre this evening so long as you don't mind.'

'Mind? Not at all, lovie, you go off and enjoy yourself,' said Grace. 'Are you all right for cash or can I lend you a few bob?'

'No, no, I'm fine thank you. I have almost twelve shillings in my purse and Mrs Beaconsfield is kindly holding two pound notes for me in her post office book.'

'All right, dear. You won't spend more than three bob or so, I wouldn't have thought.'

'Hold on, Grace,' said Mrs Beaconsfield. 'Connie, you

should really put the boat out tonight with your friend. After all, it's not every day you land a job which pays six month's money for just six week's work. Perhaps you and this young lady should find a couple of nice young men and crack open a bottle of champagne!'

'I'll settle for a trip to Kilburn,' laughed Connie. 'I have the key, remember, so don't wait up for me tonight.'

So, later that day Connie bathed and changed to meet her new friend Pearl at the Kilburn Empire. She caught a penny omnibus up the road and was there in good time. Whilst she was waiting, however, to her surprise a doorman came up to her and asked if she was 'Miss Connie' as he had a message for such a lady.

'Your friend telephoned the theatre to say that unfortunately she would not be able to be here for another half an hour and that perhaps you could see the show on another night. She said she hoped you would go round to see her at number twelve, Ronald Square which is just round the corner,' explained the friendly doorman.

Connie thanked the man for his trouble and decided that she would take up the offer of a visit to Pearl. It would not be as exciting as a visit to the theatre but as she was still excited about the news of the new job, all in all, she did not feel too disappointed.

Ronald Square was not situated in perhaps the most fashionable part of London but the houses were of solidly-built design. The back gardens were a little small but the inhabitants (many of whom were somewhat elderly) were free to use a railed oval of grass fringed with evergreens which sat in the middle of the square. It made a lovely patch of greenery and, as the gates were kept locked and the spiked railings were high enough to thwart stray urchins, residents enjoyed the peaceful surroundings of this private enclave.

The night was still very warm when Connie knocked on the door of number twelve. Pearl answered the door herself and apologised immediately for having to change their engagement. She was an extraordinarily attractive girl of about twenty-two years of age – of dark complexion, rather slender of figure with languid hazel eyes. Her lips were a succulent shade of red and revealed sparkling white teeth when she smiled.

'I have a bottle of wine here on a tray, Connie, along with two glasses,' she whispered. 'Lady Pokingham is asleep right now but as the slightest sound wakes her up, let's go out into the Square. I have a key to open the gates.'

Although the light was now fading, the weather was still warm and uncomfortably sticky as it can often be on a hot summer's night in London. The two girls sat on the chairbed Pearl had carried out earlier that day for Lady Pokingham but which she had neglected to bring back.

The girls chatted away happily and almost before they knew it the bottle was empty. Perhaps it was the combination of the drink together with the heat and the excitement of the day that made Connie feel so tired.

'You look exhausted, Connie,' said Pearl. 'Put your head on my shoulder and take a little nap.'

That seemed a good idea and Connie complied. She felt totally relaxed and made no attempt to stop the other girl who was stroking her sides and fondling her breasts in a most intimate fashion.

'What on earth are you doing, Pearl?' she asked drowsily.

'Just relax, my love, just relax and let me take off some

of these unnecessary clothes that are making us so uncomfortable.'

Connie let herself be undressed and made only a token protest as she was laid down on the bed and her underdrawers pulled off to leave her totally naked. Pearl then began to disrobe and exposed her beautiful bosom, ornamented with dark nipples, as she lay down besides Connie.

She kissed Connie's shoulder and murmured: 'Don't worry, no-one can see us and no-one will hear us for no-one uses the Square gardens after dark.'

Connie offered no resistance as Pearl began to explore her rounded, firm breasts which she cradled in her hands, teasing, caressing and kissing. Connie closed her eyes, letting her head fall back as she felt Pearl's lips close on her nipple and begin to suck, tenderly at first and then more hungrily. Her hand then moved between Connie's legs where she began a stroking that was more tender yet arousing than the action of any man that she had yet encountered. She slipped her long fingers into Connie's dampening pussey, moving them deliciously inside as the heel of her hand rubbed the clitty which was as hard as a little walnut.

Connie's hands gripped her back, pressing their slippery bodies together. Pearl moved her head downwards to the pleasure patch of silky dark hair at the base of the trembling girl's belly and with a sudden dart plunged her pointed tongue in and out of the hairy mound in which she buried her face. Her tongue revelled in the wet smoothness, licking, flicking and sucking as one arm went round Connie's waist and the other downwards to her own pussey which was now almost equally aroused, quickening her fingers to meet the pace of Connie's culmination.

'Oooh! Aaah!' moaned Connie as her body tensed towards her release. Pearl's tongue gave one final sweep of the sopping tunnel walls and Connie began to spend. Her hips bucked violently, her back rippling and then from her twitching pussey gushed a fine, creamy emission that flooded Pearl's mouth with its milky essence as they brought themselves to that delicious state of annihilation which causes the soul to dissolve in an ocean of bliss.

The two girls rested for five minutes and then Connie asked if they could continue their little joust indoors for by this time the sun had completely disappeared and the night air was beginning to chill their naked bodies.

'Can we continue elsewhere?' she enquired anxiously of her newly found tribade.

'Most certainly,' Pearl replied, pulling on her dress. 'And I can provide an even better environment for our play if a little plan I have concocted comes to fruition. With luck, I shall be able to leave Lady Pokingham's house and we can go on elsewhere to visit a very nice Scottish gentleman who lives just round the corner. My friend Claire has promised me that she can stay with Lady Pokingham from eight o'clock as she has a novel to read and does not mind staying in tonight.'

The girls quickly finished dressing and, as good as her word, Pearl's friend arrived just after eight o'clock to keep watch over the still dozing Lady Pokingham.

'Where are we going now?' asked Connie as they turned out of Ronald Square into Chester Street. 'You say we are to meet a very nice Scottish gentleman – but is he expecting you and even if he is, won't I be playing gooseberry?'

Pearl laughed and shook her mane of tawny brown

hair: 'No, no, Connie. Mr John Gibson of Edinburgh is known to all as a most hospitable fellow and is always pleased to see new people – especially if they are young, fair and feminine like you!'

'Who is this man?' asked Connie, still rightly concerned about entering the house of a total stranger.

'Oh, he owns some property on somewhere called Princes Street,' said Pearl carelessly. 'But he travels down to London as frequently as possible to indulge his hobbies.'

'What are those, Pearl?'

'Choreography and copulation – but not always together and not necessarily in that order,' answered the pert little minx with a knowing smile as they opened the gate to Mr Gibson's house.

'John rents this place from Lady Gaffney by the week as he can only come up to London once every two months or so,' she added, ringing the front door bell.

Mr Gibson opened the door himself and welcomed the girls most warmly. He was a handsome young man, slight of build with merry eyes, a winning smile and a pleasant, cheery manner which made Connie feel at home straightaway.

'How delightful to meet you, Connie,' said Mr Gibson. 'It is especially grand to meet a friend of Pearl's tonight as I received another expected visitor tonight, my cousin Bruce from Aberdeen. He is upstairs just now but will join us in a few moments. Meanwhile, may I offer you ladies a glass of champagne?'

The offer was politely accepted and Pearl asked him whether he had seen any new ballets whilst he was in town.

'Alas, no, but did you know that I went to Russia earlier

this year and saw some magnificent dancing in Petrograd?
I was there at the behest of the Duchess of Midlothian who
required my services of a gentleman in waiting when she
travelled there for the wedding of Grand Duke Schmockle
of Carpentia to the Czar's niece, Princess Natasha. What
a cluster of Central and Eastern nobility was gathered for
the nuptials!'

'You didn't by chance meet a Count Gewirtz of Galicia
there?' asked Connie.

'I most certainly did! My goodness, there isn't a major
social event in the world where he is not present. Actually,
I think he is related on his father's side to the Grand Duke
though I wouldn't swear to it without first consulting the
Almenach de Gotha!

Connie smiled shyly and said: 'I am hardly liable to be
acquainted with any noble gentleman. In fact, I will be
working in the Count's house next week when he arrives in
London.'

'He's coming to London, is he? That's splendid news
indeed, which I am very pleased to hear. We must fill up
our glasses and drink a bumper to our absent friend. He
stays in Green Street doesn't he? Right, I'll be round there
next Monday before I take the night sleeper back to
Scotland if I can re-arrange my present appointments.

'You see, ladies, I took a wager with the old devil for
five hundred guineas that Scotland would beat England in
the international football match at Crystal Palace – and I
haven't seen him since to get my money as we trounced the
Sassenachs by three goals to one! Now I'm not saying that
the Count has been avoiding settling the bet but we did
exchange cards and I've heard nothing from him!

'Connie, if I get my winnings from him, I insist on your

accepting ten per cent commission for your invaluable information,' he added.

Before Connie could thank him for his kind words, John's cousin, Bruce, came in and both girls were impressed by the handsome looks of the powerfully-built man to whom they were introduced by John Gibson.

'Bruce, I have the honour to present Miss Connie Chumbley and Miss Pearl Bailey,' said our host. 'Ladies, Mr Bruce McGraw, the Laird of North Fife.'

We both looked admiringly at the healthy, fresh-complexioned blond gentleman who was attired in full Highland dress. Bruce McGraw was also blessed with a ready wit and his amused, intelligent conversation made the evening an extremely enjoyable one for all concerned. However, the liberal quaffing of champagne after the wine they had consumed at Roland Square affected the girls much in the manner as Mrs Shawn's nightcap, twenty-four hours earlier, had enlivened her evening with her amorous butler.

If truth be told, by half past ten the passions of the two lusty Scotchmen were ready to be reciprocated by the two equally attractive girls. To be chronologically exact, one could state that the physical proceedings that then took place at around that time began with a bold comment from Pearl who suddenly said: 'I wonder if Bruce could enlighten me about a matter that has been on my mind for the last hour or so. Tell me, just what is worn under the kilt?'

'What is worn under the kilt!' echoed Bruce jovially. 'Why, Pearl, absolutely nothing is worn – if you want to see for yourself you will discover that what's there is all in good working condition!'

The pretty girl impudently walked over to sit on Bruce's lap and holding him round the waist for balance, leaned down to let her hand dive down to feel for herself whether Bruce was telling the truth.

'Ah, I see what you mean,' she gasped. 'Bruce, would you stand up for a moment, please? Connie and I would like to see this Scottish staff in all its naked glory.'

He politely propelled them both upright and, at her bidding, sat down again. But this time she did not resume her seat but briskly flipped his kilt back to reveal a substantial Caledonian cock in full erection. She lightly fingered this enormous plunger before grasping it firmly and asking Connie if she shared the opinion that Bruce possessed one of the most beautifully-shaped instruments she had ever seen.

'Feel this velvety warm shaft, Connie,' urged Pearl. 'Oooh, is it not as smooth as polished ivory? And this curly crop of crisp light hair sets off this magnificent pole so nicely and its little hairy pouch underneath, would you not agree?'

'Let me see for myself,' said Connie, dropping to her knees and placing her hand round the thick shaft. 'Yes, I think this must be one of the prime candidates for the title of Cock of the North.

'And South, West and East as well.' she added, pulling down his foreskin to reveal to the assembled company a wide mushroomed-shaped knob.

There was room for both the girls to encircle their hands round its ample girth and they eagerly performed an indoor version of Tossing the Caber to the great delight of the young Laird as the soft hands were replaced as if previously planned by two sweet faces lowered in unison and two tongues licked out to tickle his member to almost unbearable heights of pleasure. Pearl reached down to squeeze his ballsack gently, whilst the girl's questing lips met at the moist uncovered red head of his gigantic erection. Tongue touched tongue as they jostled to suck upon these engorged flesh but this delicious stimulation was too much for even the most hardened man to bear and, with a tidal rush, a stream of spunk burst from Bruce's shaft, jetting into mouths, over lips and into the air. Their hands stroked and scratched lightly along the blue, distended vein as he spent fully in a juddering ecstasy of relief.

'Oh dear, now look what we've done,' giggled Pearl. 'I do hope that I can raise our Scottish soldier into another rousing action.'

'You won't find the task too difficult,' said Bruce, laying her hand on his semi-limp organ. His prognosis proved to be accurate for, by dint of some sensual stroking, she primed his weapon up to the fully cocked position. Then she plunged her hand beneath her skirt to lubricate the source of her passion and make ready for the fray. She unbuttoned her skirt and pulled down her drawers for comfort before climbing onto Bruce's lap and lowering herself carefully but easily upon his straining sword.

She began to ride him with style, maintaining a steady rhythm up and down on his ramrod. As she breathlessly plunged down, he lifted his hips to meet her and the two spectators were treated to the tantalising sight of Pearl riding now almost completely out of control as she rubbed her swollen button of a clitty along the top of Bruce's slippery, distended member. Pearl bucked even harder up and down on the gleaming shaft and then suddenly cried: 'The Campbells are coming!' as a great tremor swept through her body. Bruce, too, was grunting out what Connie took to be a Gaelic oath as he reached the summit of Ben Nevis, shooting a generous measure of Highland Cream inside her sensitive pussey.

The effect of watching this exciting exhibition was naturally to stimulate the pair who had a grandstand view of the prurient activity. John Gibson had let his hand stray beneath Connie's legs and the girl had seized it and rubbed it back and forth across her aching pussey in her agitation.

'Let us repay the compliment to our friends here and execute my favourite version of Bonnie Prince Charlie's Jig-a-Jig,' he cried out, tearing off his trousers. He revealed a machine less thick perhaps than that of his cousin but of a goodly length which did not displease Connie who vigorously rubbed it to full erection before, aided by the still nude Pearl, she slipped as quickly as possible out of her clothes.

Connie stepped out of her drawers to display with pride her beautiful young body to John Gibson who stood open-mouthed in silent appreciation of her firm jutting breasts and as she twirled around in a dainty pirouette, her chubby, dimpled bum cheeks.

'Well, are you satisfied, sir, or do you wish to return the merchandise to the manufacturer?' pouted the lovely Connie, smoothing her hands provocatively down her sleek thighs.

He found his voice again as he muttered: 'Och no, lassie. I'm just drinking in your beauty. Connie, my wee love, we must fornicate without delay or I shall simply expire out of sheer frustration.'

As he struggled to tear off his clothes Connie teased him further, sliding her hand slowly across her furry pubic mound, rubbing her thumb in a series of fast tapping movements against her stiffening clitty which was now peeping out of its shell between her cunney lips.

As soon as John was naked, Connie pulled him down onto the thick carpet and soon she was stroking his veined Scottish gamecock whilst his hands moved over her body with practised ease. He moved his lips from her pretty mouth to those luscious rose-tipped breasts and began noisily slurping and licking from one hard dark nipple to the other. She moaned softly and begged her Midlothian gallant to kiss his way further down to her dampening pussey. She obeyed with alacrity as he lapped her tasty juices, licking every inch of her cunney lips, sucking them into his mouth before sliding his tongue into her tight, wet hole. Connie moaned again and her hips squirmed against the carpet.

He moved up slightly now, closing his lips over the swollen nub of her clitty and Connie's hips then began to move even faster. The more he lapped and sucked her love button, the more her muscular mons veneris squirmed under his probing tongue. Then her body went perfectly motionless for long, breathless seconds. She did not move a muscle until first her foot started to vibrate, and then her leg and afterwards her entire body trembled as his wicked tongue continued to flick into her and then, with a great wail, her first contraction exploded like a volcanic eruption. Again and again the orgasmic pulses jerked her body convulsively as her head rolled from side to side and her belly rippled with each seizure. The throbbing finally slowed and decreased in intensity leaving her lovely body satiated by the tidal waves of passion.

'That was marvellous, John! No-one has ever tongued me to a spend before. Your technique cannot be bettered. Now let me see what I can do for you,' said the grateful girl.

She gave his stiff shaft an encouraging rub using both hands and when his prick was as hard as iron she fondled his heavy balls with one hand and peeled back his foreskin fully with the other. She opened her mouth and sticking out her little pink tongue, lapped all around the purple knob and sucked lustily on his straining sap until she felt he was on the verge of a spend. She took her mouth away from the twitching cock.

'I want you to bury that fine claymore in my pussey,' she murmured in his ear.

Who was he to argue? He pulled himself on top of her as she guided his prick home with trembling hands. 'Hard and fast now, John, that's what I want,' she breathed. He nodded and began eagerly to thrust in and out of her sopping muff as quickly and as firmly as he could. Their bodies slapped together as she met each thrust with one of her own. His shaft was being bathed in loving wet warmth as her pussey rubbed his flesh every way from Land's End to John O'Groats. All his senses were now in thrall to her soft clinging pussey and soon, all too soon, he felt the familiar tingle in the head of his tool, spreading downwards to his rapidly moving balls which swung against her wriggling bum cheeks.

'I'm ready, John, I'm ready for your juicy spend. Fill me up, I want it all!' she hissed through clenched teeth.

Just seconds later his body stiffened as, with a low cry of 'Hoots!', he shot wad after wad of white love juice deep inside her vitals and, as his jism splashed inside her,

Connie's fingernails clawed his back and she came again, screaming out her joy, their bodies threshing together in wild abandon.

They clung tightly together until his flow slowed and his chastened, shrinking length slipped from its wet embrace. She kissed it happily and sucked the last dribble of spunk from the tiny 'eye' until they collapsed in a happy tangle of arms and legs.

This erotic exhibition set Pearl's tribadistic feelings aflame and licking her lips she slid to the floor and wriggled deftly under Connie so that her legs were extended between the girl's arms and her face came immediately under her pussey.

'I'm retiring for the moment,' announced John Gibson, as he climbed to his feet and padded across to the decanter of brandy.

'Try and stay still, darling,' grunted Pearl as Connie, with a wriggle of her hips, felt the upwards insinuation of the tribade's tongue between the pouting lips of her cunney. The two gentlemen had all under their delighted gaze. The top of Pearl's head was towards them as were Connie's plump bum cheeks and their saplings swelled in unison as they saw Connie's downy nest being delicately kissed and tongued by the flickering tongue between Pearl's lips that gradually gathered speed all round the sweet slit like a warm snake.

'Ooooh! Ooooh! Ah!' cried Connie. 'Get your tongue working round my clitty for I am dying to spend. Ooh, that is nice! Ah! I must, Oh! Oh! There!' With a great shuddering she clamped her graceful thighs against Pearl's neck with her knees hooked over her shoulders and spurted her warm, trickling tribute in a fine salty rain over her tongue. Her bottom bounced a little and then she sighed and relaxed her legs whilst Pearl continued to nuzzle into her musky grotto.

By now Bruce's red-headed champion was looking ready to burst as he caressed it in his hand until it was stiff and hard as marble and it stood high in all its manly glory. As if sensing his need, Pearl clambered to her knees and pushed the splendid orbs of her bottom out behind her. She continued to kiss and nibble Connie's sated cunney but she pulled her bum cheeks apart in an open invitation to one of the gentlemen to offer her satisfaction.

Bruce McGraw needed but a second to place himself behind the lovely girl. He moistened his knob with a little champagne and worked his shaft between those luscious bum cheeks until he found the wrinkled rosette that lay between them. He attacked his target with vigour but not too quickly, as he had no desire to hurt the dear girl. So he thrust forward carefully and slid back with equal care in and out of her succulent tunnel – and he was so pleased to tell from the wriggling of her arse how much she was enjoying his injection that he threw his arms around her waist when he was finally firmly ensconced and frigged her pussey with his fingers for her additional pleasure.

Penny continued to work her wicked tongue in and around Connie's soaking pussey but John Gibson cleverly found the means of enlarging the trio into a quartet by kneeling on a cushion next to Connie, who at once pulled his corpulent shaft close to her mouth. She was kissed, licked and sucked the bulbous head so energetically that her voluptuous mouth was soon filled with his copious ejaculation and her lips were greased with his creamy essence which she gulped down so quickly that she could not prevent a tiny burp escaping from her lips.

'Now, now,' said Bruce McGraw. 'Remember what Nanny used to say – each mouthful should be thoroughly chewed before it is swallowed.'

'No time for that,' replied Connie. 'Besides I am coming again!'

She was as good as her word as Bruce and Pearl joined her in a three-way scream of ecstasy. Connie's warm fluids flowed for the second time into Pearl's mouth; Bruce McGraw flooded Pearl's nether orifice with a stream of creamy spunk whilst her cunney juices drenched Bruce's fingers which were working in and out of her sopping pussey.

John Gibson then suggested a variation on a particular mode of intercourse favoured by the gentry in Kirkudbrightshire which involved two girls, one man, a dildoe and a feather duster but the house was short of the necessary *godemiché* and, in any case, time was pressing on both Connie and Pearl who were concerned about returning home.

'Don't be concerned,' declared John Gibson. 'I'm a subscriber to Prestoncrest's Carriage service so I'll telephone for a driver to come round as soon as possible.'

Whilst he was busy on the telephone, Bruce McCraw poured the last of the champagne and handed glasses to the girls. 'I think I should mark the end of this delightful evening with a poem that I shall compose for one of those rude magazines that John buys from Hotten's bookshop.

'Can you simply make up verse without prior thought?' asked Connie, who enjoyed reading good poetry.

'That I can,' said Bruce proudly,' I have no wish to

boast but the Inverness Courier compared my work to that of the great William McGonagall, poet and tragedian to Her Majesty.

'Ah, the Muse is upon me:

> My Connie is a lover gay
> She is so very funny,
> Tonight we came to sport and play
> She led me to her cunney.
> So I drew out my sturdy prick
> Right in her hand I placed it,
> And quoth 'twould be a jolly trick
> If in her mouth she'd taste it.
>
> She kissed its bright and rosy head
> And then began to suck it;
> Her mossy crack I felt and said
> 'My love, it's time to breach it.'
> Her smiling eyes showed their assent
> On the floor I laid her gasping,
> My stalwart shaft showed my intent
> Of what we both were wanting.
>
> Och, when yon truncheon waves in fun,
> Sweet lassie do not grieve him,
> Just spread your legs and heave your bum,
> For soon you'll enter heaven!
> I love you lass, I love you so,
> Though you can be so flighty
> When the moonlight flits across your tits –'

'It's enough to tempt the Almighty!' finished John

Gibson who brought in a fresh bottle of champagne for the foursome to finish whilst the ladies waited for the carriage. Pearl and Connie heartily applauded this most worthy rendition and the party drank each other's health in a most convivial fashion whilst Bruce penned his poem to send the next day to the editor of *The Oyster*. As luck would have it, a Prestoncrest driver had telephoned his headquarters from West Hampstead after taking Reverend and Mrs Jackson back home from the Atheneum so the party had to wait only ten minutes for 'Grahame' to arrive at Chester Street.

After exchanging their fond farewells, the two Scottish gentlemen escorted the girls to the front gate. 'The fare's on my account, Jimmy – I mean, Grahame,' called out John Gibson to the coachman. 'Take the first lady back to Roland Square and then on to 22, Plattsgrove Street, Maida Vale as quickly as possible.

'And put five shillings on the bill for yourself,' he added, giving lie to the old canard about the so-called miserliness of our Caledonian cousins.

Nevertheless, it was well past midnight when Connie slipped her key into the lock of the front door. She knew that Mrs Beaconsfield was an inveterate early riser and usually went to bed by eleven o'clock at the latest. And she had no desire to wake her generous hostess Grace, who in all probability was also safely ensconced in the arms of Morpheus. So she took off her shoes and was about to creep upstairs when she was startled to hear sounds emanating from behind the closed door of the drawing room.

There was a tiny light showing under the door and at first the thought flashed through Connie's mind that she may have come across an unwelcome guest who had turned up a gas lamp to rummage through the room for valuables. Only the other day she had read in the local newspaper how the police had warned householders that a plague of housebreakers had seemed to have descended upon the neighbourhood.

So on tip-toe she made her way into the kitchen and grabbed a rolling pin that had been left on the table – for the thought of anyone robbing her kind benefactor made her blood boil and at that moment nothing would have given her greater satisfaction than to execute retribution upon the nocturnal prowler. With commendable courage she slowly opened the drawing-room door to confront the intruder . . .

But in an instant she realised to her exquisite embarrassment that the only intruder was that of the pego of a handsome gentleman which was – by invitation – slewing in and out of the welcoming pussey of Mrs Beaconsfield who was sprawled nude on the large sofa with the equally naked gentleman between her legs, his lean bottom cheeks pumping up and down as the couple rocked in time with their amorous exertions.

Mrs Beaconsfield let out a little scream when she was Connie who hastily blurted out her apologies: 'Oh dear, I'm so sorry, I heard a noise and thought there might be a burglar.'

'Don't be sorry, my love, better to be safe than sorry,' said Mrs Beaconsfield. 'Connie, this is Inspector Glenton Rogers from Paddington. Glen, this is Connie Chumbley who is staying with us till next week.'

'Pleased to meet you.' said Inspector Rogers cordially, not for a moment changing his rhythmic coupling.

'Will you excuse us a minute whilst we finish our fucking?'

'Do take a seat, Connie,' panted Mrs Beaconsfield. 'Glen wants to speak to you about Count Gewirtz. Now Glen, let's build up some steam. Let me feel the hardness of your truncheon!'

'My pleasure, Hetty, but let's change positions,' grunted the burly police officer. He abruptly took out his glistening stiff shaft and turned her over face downwards. He reached across for a soft cushion and inserted it under her belly so that her hips and plump bum cheeks were raised up in the air. He moved between her legs, nudging her knees apart and took his thick member in his hand, capping and uncapping the ruby helmet. 'Are you ready?' he asked, and receiving a quick nob of assent, he then carefully guided the gleaming knob slowly into the soft, wet folds of her pussey from behind and began again to mate in a slow, regular rhythm.

Connie embarrassment now turned to excited interest as the Inspector bent forward so that his hairy chest brushed against Hetty Beaconsfield's back. He reached under her and took hold of her globular breasts, holding them in thrall as he continued to pump in and out of her juicy cunney. Her plump bottom slapped enticingly against his strong thighs as she fitted easily into the rhythm he had established, now forcefully pounding away at her fleshy white bum. Connie relished the sight of his veined member see-sawing in and out of her willing cunney, above which the little wrinkled rosebud of her bumhole quivered and winked with each stroke.

Hetty Beaconsfield reached behind her to caress his big ballsack as she rocked to and fro, her head thrown back and her hair billowing from side to side. Sensing the time had come, Inspector Rogers croaked: 'Hetty, I'm on the last lap!' His torso went rigid as he spilled a flood of pearly jism into her womb. Hetty yelped with glee as her own orgasm thrilled through body as the Inspector gave a last drawn-out thrust, collapsing on top of the delighted cook who manoeuvred her body into a comfortable position whilst they recovered from their heady joust.

'I hope we haven't shocked you, Connie,' said Mrs Beaconsfield, wiping her face with the towel she had laid across the sofa to prevent any staining of the sofa. 'I can't believe that a pretty girl like you hasn't enjoyed a bit of slap and tickle in her time.

'Oh, yes,' said Connie, who had now regained her composure even though she felt a little strange sitting down clothed with the two naked lovers. 'Why, tonight, my friend and I met up with two very nice Scottish gentlemen and I must confess that we played some naughty indoor Highland Games.'

'What, all four of you?' said Inspector Rogers. 'Hold on, let me get a notebook and take down the details.'

'Why, will they be used in evidence against me?' asked Connie anxiously.

'Oh, no, nothing like that. It'll just be fun reading my notes when I've nothing better to do,' replied the laughing policeman.

Connie looked a little shocked but Mrs Beaconsfield said: 'Now, now Glen, don't frighten the poor girl.

'Mind you, Connie, like many youngsters you probably only think that once you're forty you lose the urge. Nothing could be further from the truth. Still, I'm glad you've already lost your cherry. Virginity can be a burden but the problem is best tackled between the ages of eighteen and twenty. After that, the disease can become chronic. Just be careful and you won't go wrong.'

'That's sound advice, Hetty,' added the beaming Inspector Rogers. 'And just to prove it, Connie, how do you fancy a little how d'you do in the strong arms of the law?'

'That could be very nice,' said Connie whose blood was up. 'But only if Mrs Beaconsfield has no objection.'

'Go on, lovie, enjoy yourself. Share and share alike, that's my motto. Besides it will be good preparation for what I expect will happen most nights next week at Count Gewirtz.'

Inspector Rogers paused for a moment but then said: 'Oh, yes, our foreign friend, we must talk about him – but first things first.' And without further ado he covered Connie's mouth with a burning kiss and pulled her down on the sofa, whilst at the same time slipping his hand under her skirts to rub his hand against her pussey and rousing all her warming passions. She moaned with pleasure as the jovial officer unlaced her drawers and pulled them down to her ankles. He tenderly opened the yielding lips of her pussey, sliding his fingers into the dainty passage that was already moistening to a delicious wetness. As he frigged the trembling girl with one, two and then three fingers she took hold of his sizeable truncheon with both hands and lowering her pretty mop of curls, bent forward to receive the fiery red dome between her pouting lips. She waggled her tongue over the uncovered knob, her soft projectile rolling over and over the smooth, hot helmet which she licked and lapped to the joint pleasure of them both.

Mrs Beaconsfield thoughtfully placed two plumped up cushions under Connie's bottom. Inspector Rogers was now on his knees with his shaft now being lustily sucked by the sweet girl who took hold of his balls in her hands – but alas, this proved too exciting for the policeman's pego and with a groan he plunged his tool as far forward as Connie could allow. The pearly liquid gushed out, flooding her mouth with his copious effusion.

'What a splendid sucking!' wheezed the Inspector, sitting down on the floor, his chest heaving with the exertion of the orgasm.

'You were a bit quick, Glen,' commented Mrs Beaconsfield.

'No, no, the fault was mine,' Connie insisted. 'I should not have held his ballsack whilst sucking his shaft. This always leads men to spend swiftly but as I have already enjoyed the delights of a Celtic cock tonight, I don't really want to spoil the evening with a bout of over-indulgence.'

'Quite right too,' said Mrs Beaconsfield. 'I like a nice fat whopper like Glen's to get my teeth into but so few men can hold back long enough till I'm ready to spend.'

Connie nodded her head in agreement and said: 'I do know what you mean. I so enjoy caressing the uncapped knob and drawing out the tangy lubricant from the balls. It is so exciting to my senses when a boy squirts out his spunk into my mouth. And I do love the taste. I cannot think of any other liquid that tastes so fine and clean.'

'Here, come on, girls, enough of all that smutty talk. It's all wasted on me, for sure, as I won't be able to raise another stand for an hour or so at least,' protested the police officer.

'Very well, Glenton Rogers. I'll get dressed and I suggest you do the same. Then I'll put the kettle on whilst you tell Connie about Count Gewirtz,' said Mrs Beaconsfield.

'Oh dear, I hope there is nothing wrong as I would like to earn all that money Mr Formbey said we would get if we worked for this gentleman,' said Connie, suddenly worried that her new job was at risk.

Inspector Rogers soothed her fears immediately by saying that there was no bar to her employment with the extraordinary Galician aristocrat. 'But the point is, Connie, that we've been asked to check that all the servants working in the house can be trusted,' he said.

'It's not their financial honesty we're worried about primarily, it's their wagging tongue. You see, some very important ladies and gentlemen indeed may well be invited by the Count for one of his peculiar parties,' he continued. 'You may recognise some of the guests or you may not – but whether you do or not, afterwards you must never reveal the identity of who visited the house. I know Hetty here is discreet and she assures me that Mr Formbey and yourself can also be trusted to keep secrets.'

Connie was a little taken aback. 'Well, of course, I'll keep my mouth shut,' she said. 'But if all this takes the attention of the police, we must be talking of some very important people.'

'Amongst the highest in the land, my girl, the very highest,' leered the lecherous copper, licking his lips as Connie wiped her hairy mound with a handkerchief before pulling up her drawers.

'It could be a very exciting week for us, Mrs Beaconsfield,' said the young parlourmaid. 'I am really looking forward to it.'

CHAPTER FOUR

We will leave Connie, Mrs Beaconsfield and Mr Formbey in eager expectation of the excitement of working in the service of the eccentric Count Gewirtz and return to our two sweet sisters, Penny and Katie Arkley, and their respective would-be lovers, Messrs Goggin and Stanton.

On the same day as the events just described in the previous chapter of this history, both our lovely young heroines woke up to some excellent news. A telegram had arrived from Sir Paul Arkley, their fond papa, stating that his business with the Prime Minister had now finished and that the family should come back to London for an important social event.

Even Lady Arkley was in a good mood as, at Walter's request, General Stanton had sent round Mutkin, his former batman who he now employed as a valet, to assist with any chores the Arkley ladies might need doing – and packing their suitcases was work perfectly suited to Muktin's liking!

After he had finished, Katie and Lady Arkley decided to take a short constitutional, leaving behind Penny who pleaded the excuse of a slight headache. When her mother and sister had left and she was all alone, the beautiful nymphet went upstairs to compose a *billet doux* to her sweetheart, Bob Goggin, who was busy in the garden, toiling over Lady Arkley's little Italian garden which was that dame's pride and joy.

Penny dared not venture out in case her Mama decided to take her walk nearby as Lady Arkley had given her younger daughter strict instructions that she was no longer to exchange even the time of day with the good-looking gardener. If Penny were to disobey, Lady Arkley threatened, Bob Goggin's employment would be instantly terminated.

So she decided that the best way she could communicate with him was via a *billet doux* which Katie could pass to him. She reached for pen and paper and, with an impudent grin, she determined to write to Bob about all the joys he might experience when they would next meet.

Licking her lips, Penny pictured her dear lad's face (and tool!) when he would open the envelope and to his surprise find a steamy love letter inside it.

She thought for a moment or two and then undressed completely except for her garter belt and stockings so she could catch the mood in which to write the following letter to her beloved:

Dear Bob,

You may have guessed by now that Mama has forbidden me to talk to you. So we must arrange to meet again through messages passed via my sister. Katie is a sport and will play the telegraph girl to the best of her ability.

Mama, Katie and I are off to London this afternoon and I believe that you will be coming back tomorrow. There must be a great deal of work for you back in Hyde

Park Gardens as old Fagan does nothing these days but mow the lawn and water the plants.

If Thursday is your day off as usual, let's meet at the bandstand in Hyde Park and find somewhere to stroll. I'll be there at twelve o'clock.

Oh, Bob, what I would give to have your hands freely roaming across my body as they did that night in the conservatory. I am sitting here quite naked and I am moving my hands slowly across my breasts, cupping their firmness and rolling my palms over the upright little red stalky nipples that rise up to greet them.

Dear Bob! I am moaning your name softly as I close my eyes and slowly slip my fingers down into my silky pubic mound. With hand I am fondling my breasts as my finger finds the wetness of my passion tunnel and excites the heat and the juice that will soon ooze from me. As I part the lips of my pouting pussey I feel the soft folds of skin and think of how I adored the touch of your fingers and lips down there.

My hands are now both busy, forming circles over my aroused clitty, pressing my mons veneris until I can feel the waves of pleasure mounting inside my very core. I am squeezing my fingers with the muscles of my cunney – I wish my fingers were elsewhere, preferably raking your back as your raging stiff staff pumped in and out of my eager crack.

My left thumb is now slipping inside my slit though it is but a poor substitute for your thick cock. Ah, though I cannot have your rock hard rammer I do have in my jewellery box a well fashioned dildoe from Madame Nettleton's Pottery. It is part of a matching set of basin, ewer, chamber pot, soap dish and dildoe given to me by my sister Katie for a birthday gift last April. Mama is of course ignorant as to the existence of the finely modelled godemiché, the tip of which is now nudging its head between my nether lips. As I push it in I think of how you would push yourself into me, in and out, in and out of my welcoming cunney, slowly dipping into me at first and then moving harder and faster just as I am moving my dildoe now.

Where are you, Bob? What are you doing now? Is your pego swelling straighter and harder, being propelled to new heights by my lewd letter? My juices are flowing freely, dripping onto my thigh. Now I am lifting my titties and pressing my firm breasts together so by bending my head I can lick my nippies and run my tongue back and forth between them. My dildoe is slipping in and out of my cunney at a great speed and I can feel the waves of orgasm overwhelming me . . . aaah, if only your head was between my legs and your prodding tongue was licking and lapping at my engorged little love button. Oh! oh! oh! I am spending! There! My juices are dripping over my thigh . . .

What a wonderful time we had in the conservatory, Bob, and how marvellous it will be to repeat and enlarge upon that performance. I shall fill the time until we meet again by remembering those special moments with you. Then I shall think of the lovely times we will have in the future.

All My Love,
Penny

Whilst she was writing this exciting letter she actually did find the dildoe presented to her not however by her loving sister, if truth be told, but by Miss Nottsgrove, the games mistress at Dame Bracknell's Academy and practising tribade who seduced all the pretty girls in the fifth form.

She sealed the letter and after her Mama and Katie had returned from their walk she took the opportunity when Lady Arkley retired to her room of buttonholing her sister and persuading her to pass the letter to Bob Goggin in the garden.

'Look, I've got a much better idea. I'll keep Mama occupied whilst you pop down and see Bob yourself.' said Katie.

'Are you sure you can keep Mama away for ten minutes?' asked Penny anxiously.

'I will guarantee it,' said Katie with a smile. 'Off you go and enjoy yourself.'

Katie blew a kiss of gratitude and walked out quietly through the back door and looked around for Bob who was nowhere to be seen. Where could he be? she wondered and then she realised that he could be taking a rest in the wooden shed which was situated at the bottom of the garden. She skipped down to the shed and opened the door and, to her delight, there was Bob sitting on a garden chair in a well-worn cotton shirt and a pair of shorts. He had taken off his socks and thick gardeners' boots and was soaking his feet in a bowl of warm water.

'Hallo, Penny, I didn't expect to see you. Lady Arkley has warned me that if she sees us together I'll be fired,' he said.

'Don't worry, Bob, Katie is keeping Mama at bay. Look, I can't stay long but here's a letter you can read when you have a minute or so to spare. Goodness, what's the matter with your feet?'

'Oh, it's nothing much. I've been standing so long though that I just like to rest and relax with my feet in a bowl of nice clean water. I was just about to take off my shirt as there's some darning to be done and I'm not very able with my needle.'

'You make up for it in other ways,' laughed Penny, unbuttoning his shirt. 'Come on, off with it and I'll do all the necessary repairs if you'll just give me a needle and thread.'

Bob took off his shirt and Penny admired the golden tan which he had acquired since the beginning of the exceptionally sunny weather three weeks or so before. She squeezed herself next to Bob and busied herself sewing up his shirt. They were sitting so close together that each could feel the other's tensed-up nerves and erratic breathing.

'There, that should do the trick,' said Penny, bringing her lips down to bite off the thread.

'Thank you so much,' Bob said gratefully, kissing her gently on the cheek. She returned his kiss – but on the lips – and suddenly they were clasping each other in a rough, hasty embrace, their mouths devouring each other as they tumbled off the chair onto the rug, tearing at their clothes in a frenzy of lust as if Lady Arkley might walk in any moment and they had to make love in record time.

Penny reached down and pulled Bob's shorts down as he lifted his trunk so that they fell to his ankles. He kicked them off and she clasped her hand round his stiff hardness. She delicately fingered the large bulbous knob before she extended her tongue and began lapping and licking all round the plum-coloured helmet. She circled her tongue all round the dome and, without using her hands, sucked in four inches of his wonderful velvety cosh which seemed to grow even harder in her mouth as she sucked up and down, varying the intensity and timing. She took his hardness right out of her mouth and looked cheekily up at his face. Bob's eyes were closed and he was breathing heavily so she giggled and returned to her sweet labours. She gave the glans a long, swirling lick and then plunged her mouth down again, giving the ridge round the head a teasing brush with her teeth.

Bob moaned as she wriggled out of her drawers and swung round so that her naked bottom and pussey were directly over his face. She lowered herself gently upon him, parting her labia so that he could repay in equal measure the exquisite palating her little pink tongue was giving to his swollen dick.

The lad's hands trembled as he parted her pussey lips gently before kissing and sucking on her sweet, moist flesh. He began to roll his tongue all around her cunney whilst she was bent over him, working on his thick, hard shaft, running her teeth gently up the length and then sucking in his smooth, hot knob, flicking her tongue teasingly over its slitted end. He now withdrew his tongue and slid two fingers into her open wetness, sliding his fingers up and down as she cried out with joy – the first senses of a spend began to tingle in her veins. She grasped his love pole with both hands and rubbed them up and down over the massive shaft until the temptation to replace his willing digits with a genuine sinewy penis became too great.

She leaped off his fingers and moved her soaking pussey down over his throbbing, twitching prick, sitting with her luscious buttocks towards him while she rode a St George with delightful vigour. He grasped her bum cheeks with both hands and squeezed them rhythmically as she pushed up and down, contracting her powerful vaginal muscles with every down movement to their joint delight.

Now she reached between his legs and took his balls in one hand and began palpitating them, running her fingers back to the perineum, that most sensitive of areas and then forward again to his hairy ballsack, scraping the testes lightly with her fingernails so that they writhed in her hand.

Bob began jamming his rod up to meet her downward thrusts and his powerful urgency was so strong that Penny lowered herself comfortably above him, her pussey simply hovering over Bob's prancing pego as the tides of approaching orgasm overtook them. She felt his shaft twitch and contract and then send a mighty stream of frothy sperm shooting up inside her cunney. There was so much jism that her pussey overflowed and a stream of love juice ran down his quivering cock while Penny too, spent, sending further rivulets of love juice over his soaking shaft.

She levered herself off his softening weapon and, turning round, licked every drop of pearly liquid off his balls and belly.

'That's much better than weeding, isn't it?' she giggled. 'But now I had better take back my letter as I promised you that which we have just enjoyed as a delight to come.'

'Oh, no, no, please let me keep it. I shall read it and reread it and every time I shall think of how much I enjoyed our lovemaking and how exciting it will be to anticipate a further session,' he rejoined.

They kissed and might well have repeated their passionate mating but for the noise of footsteps outside.

'Quick, quick, come out of there,' hissed the unmistakable voice of Katie. 'Mama is ready to leave and I said I would find you and bring you back from your stroll which you took to clear your head.'

'Gosh, thanks Katie,' cried Penny softly. 'I won't be a moment.' She hastily began to dress, saying to Bob: 'Dearest, I won't be able to see you until we are back in London. But in my letter you'll see how I've planned for us to see each other at Hyde Park Gardens.'

'Goodbye, Penny, *au revoir* until we meet again, my beloved,' said Bob – and not for the first time the thought flashed through Katie's mind that young Bob spoke far more graciously than would be expected of a common young gardener from the county of Middlesex.

Penny skipped back to the house in a high good humour and all went well until, later that afternoon, they found themselves at the little railway station waiting for the next London-bound train.

The three ladies scanned the timetables pasted up on the wall but none of them could make much sense of the lists. As Lady Arkley complained: 'The trains always arrive before they are scheduled to go out and I never know whether I should read the page up or down or crossways!'

'It always annoys me,' said Penny crossly. 'For it appears that the stupidest man that breathes can disentangle a railway guide whereas the brightest woman often fails.'

'Oh, look, we will after all have a man to check the times for us,' Katie cried out joyfully. 'Isn't that

Walter Stanton coming down the stairs onto the platform?'

And indeed it was none other but the handsome young student himself who had obtained leave from his Uncle to go up to London (where he could stay at the General's club) on the pretext of spending three days studying hard for his forthcoming examinations.

He walked briskly towards the three ladies and doffed his hat to them. 'This is a most pleasant surprise,' he said disingenuously. 'Are you also travelling to London?'

'We certainly are, Mr Stanton,' said Lady Arkley. 'Would you care to join us?'

'Thank you so much, I would love to. What time is the next train?'

'Could you look it up for us?' said Penny. 'We are finding it somewhat difficult to decipher the information on the timetables.'

Walter scanned the poster and said: 'Well, according to this, we will only have to wait six minutes for the express to Marylebone. However, my experience tells me that there appear to be three classes of trains on this line: those that depart and never arrive, those that arrive but never depart and those that can be caught in transit, going on like the wheel of eternity with neither beginning nor end!'

They laughed heartily at his witticism and the girls chatted animatedly under the benevolent eye of their dear Mama who was blissfully unaware that her golden-haired daughter and young Mr Stanton were on far more intimate terms than she could ever imagine.

When the train finally arrived the party settled comfortably into their first class compartment and it seemed that they would be untroubled by further passengers for there was only one more scheduled stop before they would arrive in the heart of the teeming Metropolis.

But at that penultimate stop a somewhat flustered clergyman scrambled into the carriage just as the train was about to depart.

'Excuse me, everybody,' he asked worriedly, 'but can you confirm that this is the London train?'

'Yes, indeed,' answered Walter. 'We shall arrive in Marylebone in twenty-three minutes time.'

Lady Arkley peered at the newcomer and said: 'Why, it is Reverend Ball unless I am very much mistaken.'

The clergyman looked at her and replied: 'My dear Lady Arkley, how are you? Forgive me in not recognising you at first. I was forced to run down to the platform to catch the train and as you saw I was only just successful.'

Lady Arkley acknowledged his apology and said: 'These are my two daughters Katherine and Penelope and this young gentleman is Walter Stanton, the nephew of old General Stanton who has a house in our village. Girls, Walter, this is the Reverend Ball.'

'Er, Canon, actually,' said the Man of the Cloth.

'Canon Ball?' said Katie delightedly. 'How appropriate a name.'

'Maybe so, but it is impolite to mention the fact,' said Lady Arkley sternly.

'Oh, I do not take offence,' said Canon Ball, shrugging his shoulders. 'But how pleasing to meet you, Lady Arkley. Look, we are next to the refreshment car – do let me have the honour of taking a cup of tea with you. I am sure the young people will forgive me if we leave them until nearer journey's end.'

Walter and the girls could hardly believe their luck! 'I will leave you, too,' said Penny gallantly.

'There is no need, sister.' said Katie. 'Walter and I have no secrets to hide from your eyes.'

Nevertheless, Penny took up a copy of *The Times* Lady Arkley had left on the carriage seat and studiously opened out the paper in front of her, concentrating with might and main on the small, crabbed print. Meanwhile Walter had sidled up to Katie and already had his arms round her. 'Do you think we might –'

'Hush now, you naughty boy!' said Katie but she offered no resistance as his mouth met hers and covered it with a burning kiss. Thrusting his hand into her jacket, he undid the little buttons on her blouse and cupped her rounded, firm breasts, pinching the nipples and firing her with his wanton touches. Her hand strayed down to his lap and he helped her unbutton his trousers and his hard, vibrant cock sprang out to display itself before her, naked and palpitating with unslaked desire.

'Oh, Walter, how it has grown since I last took it in hand,' said Katie mischievously as she grasped his thick shaft.

'Yes, and I have heard my prick groan for a taste of your darling pussey!' said Walter wittily, causing Penny to smile broadly under the cover of her newspaper.

As he spoke he slid his hand up her skirt and placed his hand over her mound. 'Walter, Walter, what shall we do if Mama returns?'

'Don't worry,' said Penny from behind her paper. I am sitting next to the door and I have placed a heavy case in front of me. You will have a couple of minutes warning but you had better get on with it.'

Could the randy couple make love in the time allotted? Swiftly Katie and Walter undressed (for they both preferred to fuck in the nude) and the handsome lad caught his breath when he looked up to see the beautiful naked girl whose arms awaited him.

Katie looked quite the perfect specimen of celestial beauty as she brushed the blonde tresses from her face and her superb young breasts, firm with large exquisitely-formed pink aureoles and high-tipped erect nipples, jounced up and down with the movement. Her flat belly led down to long legs as sweetly shaped as any the finest sculptor might have fashioned, the calves and ankles slender and the thighs fulsome. Between them nestled a mass of light blonde curls that frothed silkily all about her pussey and Walter could see the shell-like lips of her cunney pouting out as his cock swelled up to salute this very goddess of desire.

The lovers kissed and Walter slid his hand into that exquisite muff of golden hair, slipping his index finger into her moistening love channel that opened up to his touch. He dipped his hand in and out, rubbing his thumb knuckle against her clitty in a series of movements that made Katie squirm with delight. They exchanged burning kisses and they locked into a naked embrace as Katie slid onto her back and opened her legs to await the entrance of Walter's proud prick into her yearning cunney.

This lascivious tableau was too much for Penny to bear and almost unconsciously she began to frig herself gently as Walter climbed on top of her sister, ready to insert his dart of love. But Penny could see that whilst the ruby head of his cock was placed between Katie's legs, so huge was his erection that it could not enter further despite the ample flowing of love juices from Katie's pussey.

Walter drew back to wet his knob as Penny moved forward and murmured: 'Let me assist you.' She took the purple-domed monster in her hands and licked and lapped around the crest, washing his knob with her tongue. Then she took the throbbing shaft in one hand and gently opened Katie's cunney lips with the other. She guided the glistening prick till it was fairly lodged just within the portals of that tight yet luscious mouth. Then slowly and gradually Walter pushed his way in and Katie moved excitedly as he continued to swell and move inside her cunney. She felt Walter's lips on hers as he pushed his tongue inside her mouth. His slim, smooth body moved in rhythm, faster and faster until the couple were rocking furiously as he pounded his thick prick into her willing love-box. Katie was twisting in ecstasy, panting with joy as she slipped her hands down his back to grasp his bum cheeks, eagerly lifting her hips to welcome his thrusting penis that slid so beautifully in and out of her sopping cunt.

Walter slowed down his rhythmic thrusting and Katie felt the tingle that accompanies a spend building up inside her. As he then increased the speed of his heaving and bucking Katie took off on her journey to paradise. 'Now, Walter, now! Fuck me hard!' she cried out without restraint and her lover obliged as with short, stabbing strokes he shot stream after stream of creamy jism into her willing womb while Katie herself reached a glorious peak of pleasure.

They lay entwined for a few moments until Penny

broke the magic spell saying: 'Come on, you pair of love birds, hurry up and get dressed! Mama and Canon Ball will be back here any minute!' Katie and Walter scrambled into their clothes as Penny put her ear to the door of the carriage and hissed: 'Damn, I can hear Mama's voice. I'll slip out and try to hold her back for a few more moments.' She moved the case with which she had blocked the door and went out into the corridor where, as she had rightly suspected, her Mama and Canon Ball were making their way towards the compartment.

'Ah, Miss Penelope,' said the Canon as she stepped forward to greet them. 'I was just saying to your Mama how exciting I find even the shortest train journeys. Do you not find the motion exhilarating? Many writers and artists have celebrated this exciting new form of travel. The words of Thomas Gray come to mind:

> *No speed with this, can fleetest Horse compare*
> *No weight like this, canal or Vessel bear.*

Interestingly enough, Mr Gray was a cousin of my father's sister-in-law though I only had the pleasure of meeting him once or twice when I was a small boy.'

'How fascinating,' said Lady Arkley somewhat shortly. 'Penny, would you allow us to pass through to our compartment, please. We will shortly be arriving in London.'

'Certainly, Mama,' said Penny as the train lurched round a sharp bend which enabled the clever girl to pretend to lose her balance. She stumbled forward and reached out with her hand to steady herself on Canon

125

Ball's shoulder. 'Oh, I do beg your pardon,' she smiled at the clergyman as she regained her balance. 'I was just going to mention that my Papa's friend Sir Michael Bailey owns the superb painting of Lordship Lane Station, Dulwich by the French artist Pissarro.'

'Really,' said the Canon, 'I would love to see it. French artists have been foremost in capturing the visual potential of the railways. For example, Monet's magnificent Gare St Lazare must of course be known to you. There's a splendid story attached to that work however which is not so widely known.'

Penny had rightly judged that, like many in his trade, Canon Ball was a garrulous old gentleman and she stood her ground, not letting her Mama pass by as she said: 'Oh really, Canon, I'm sure that Mama and I would love to hear it.'

'Yes? Well, it is just that Monet was desirous of painting the atmospheric effect of fog which the critics had proclaimed could not be captured on canvas. Monet was unknown at that time so he put on his best clothes and called on the Superintendent at the station who assumed that this Monsieur Monet was an artist of importance. Accordingly, he stopped all the trains at Gare St Lazare, cleared the platforms and crammed the engines with coal to produce as much smoke as possible to create the effect demanded by the artist. Can you imagine what short shrift would be given to anyone asking for such co-operation in Britain!'

Canon Ball chuckled and Penny was about to encourage further conversation along these lines but Lady Arkley was now determined to squeeze by her daughter and get back to the compartment. 'One moment, Mama, I will

126

come back with you. I was just going to stretch my legs a little but we will soon be arriving at Marylebone, won't we?'

Happily, the few moments gained by Penny had been well-used by Katie and Walter who were sitting demurely opposite each other when Lady Arkley pulled open the door of the compartment and Walter sprang to his feet to offer Lady Arkley a window seat.

'Walter, where are you staying whilst you are in town?' said Katie in as careless a tone as she could possibly muster.

'At the Rawalpindi Club,' replied her young scamp. 'Usually it is the most comfortable of billets but at the moment it is being redecorated. However, I am only planning to stay there for some ten days or so.'

'You must stay with us,' cried Penny boldly. 'We have at least two spare rooms. Mama, could not Mr Stanton be our guest whilst he is in London?'

'Oh, no,' said Walter, hoping against hope that Lady Arkley would reply in the affirmative. 'I could not possibly impose.'

'It would be no imposition,' added Katie, looking towards her Mama. 'You have been so helpful to us it would be the least we could offer you.'

Lady Arkley pursed her lips as she thought about her decision. It would be no hardship to have Mr Stanton staying at Hyde Park Gardens and if he harboured any intentions towards one of her daughters (for Lady Arkley was not without wisdom in the ways of the world) it might be best to keep the young man in her home where she could keep a beady eye upon him.

'Yes, Mr Stanton, I insist,' said Lady Arkley

graciously. 'I am sure that you will fit most easily into our household.'

'I am sure Walter will fit in very easily and that we will accommodate you with some ease,' said Katie with a little giggle.

'In that case, I accept your kind offer,' said Walter happily and the driver blew the whistle as the train chugged into Marylebone.

Meanwhile at 46 Green Street, George Formbey was busy supervising the arrangements being made to open up the house for his new employer. Count Gewirtz was not expected to arrive for another two days but there was still much to be done to ensure that the house would run smoothly. He glanced at the clock – Mr Edwards of Aspiso's Agency had promised to send him at least seven girls for the remaining domestic duties and the first girl was due at any time now.

'The butler cast a critical eye around the ornately-furnished lounge. He noticed that the Count had purchased one of those new-fangled gramophones and was inspecting the mechanism when Fletcher, the young footman he had already engaged, announced that a young lady had arrived to be interviewed for the post of second chambermaid.

'Show her in here, Tim,' grunted Mr Formbey, sitting himself down on one of the Count's Chippendale carvers. A few moments later the footman returned and announced: 'Miss Elizabeth Stompson, Mr Formbey.' The butler looked up and tried not too successfully to repress a startled stare at the extremely pretty girl who stood before him. Miss Stompson was certainly a most attractive young lady – of about eighteen or nineteen years of age, she was slightly taller than average with a mop of bright auburn curls that set off a cheeky little face, the best features of which were a *retroussé* nose and sparkling blue eyes that glowed with promise. Her slim body was delightfully shown off by a close-fitting costume in the modern style and Mr Formbey's gaze swivelled towards her small but perfectly-formed breasts that jutted out like two firm apples ripe for the month.

'Miss Stompson, yes, I see,' muttered the butler awkwardly, trying to regain his composure. 'Have you a letter from Mr Edwards? I would like to see it. Thank you, I'll just read it and be with you in a moment.'

Surprisingly Mr Edwards' letter was purely one of introduction and merely noted the fact that Miss Stompson had previously worked in Lord Wherry's country home near Chichester and afterwards for a short time for Monsieur Clive L'Abovitch, the French Military Attaché in London.

'Why did you leave your last employer, Miss Stompson?' asked Mr Formbey.

'Oh, do call me Lizzie, sir,' said this delightful girl in a sweet West Country burr that stirred a sensual arousement not only in the butler but in Fletcher the footman whose ear was glued to the keyhole. 'I only left Monsieur L'Abovitch's service as he has been called back to Paris and his successor is not due to arrive in London for another six weeks. So all the staff were given notice.'

'But no references . . .' mused the butler.

'No, sir. No references but no knickers neither,' murmured the young temptress with a saucy grin.

'What did you say?' stammered George Formbey, unable to believe the evidence of his own ears.

'I said "no knickers", she smiled. 'That's why Mr Edwards sent me over for this position. You see, I am very honest and am quite good at making beds but my best asset is that I love a good fuck and so I don't usually bother to wear knickers during the day. It saves time and trouble dispensing with them.

'I would also like to add that His Royal Highness the Prince of Wales has told his friends that I am the best cocksucker this side of the English Channel, a compliment of which I am very proud.

'Mr Edwards said that being able to suck off gentlemen who enjoy that pleasure would be a positive advantage for any candidate wishing to be employed in this house. Mind, I wouldn't expect you simply to take my word about my abilities, Mr Formbey. Perhaps you would allow me to give you a demonstration of my technique.'

The butler cleared his throat and, regaining his composure, unbuttoned his braces saying: 'Well, Lizzie, I suppose it is my duty to examine all would-be employees as scrupulously as possible.'

'Let me unbutton your trousers,' said the lovely lass, tearing at the buttons of her own thin blouse to allow Mr Formbey to pull the garment from her. The sight of her bouncy little breasts with their exquisite saucer-shaped aureoles topped by stalky red nipples caused the butler's cock to stiffen, a process quickened by Lizzie kneeling half-naked in front of him, stroking and squeezing his shaft through his trousers. Deftly she unbuttoned his fly and his hard, hot penis bounded upwards into her hand. She grasped the shaft lightly and said: 'Oh, what a beautifully-proportioned prick! It looks so powerful yet looks good enough to eat. May I be permitted to make a closer inspection of your colossal cock?'

Without waiting for an answer she slipped her other hand round the throbbing staff and her long fingers, working as though they had a will of their own, began to frig the butler's tool slowly, rubbing it up to an even greater height. She leaned forward to take the ruby-coloured dome in her mouth and then she sucked three inches of the shaft into her soft mouth, her wet lips straining to encircle it, finally sliding her head juicily up and down the pulsating prick until she had taken it all deep into her throat. Her pretty auburn curls bobbed up and down while she slid his glistening cock in and out of her mouth, rubbing her nipples against his groin as the butler's body jerked and went rigid as jets of spunk shot out of his twitching truncheon. Lizzie greedily swallowed, milking every drop of love juice from his trembling tool.

To cap this fine performance the delicious girl laid herself face downwards on the sofa and lifted up her skirts to prove that, as she had said, she wore no knickers and Mr Formbey was presented with the sensual sight of her thrilling young bum. Lizzie pushed out her pert little bottom and opened her legs to let the butler have a good view of her pouting pussey. She turned her head and saw Mr Formbey climb up behind her and she reached out to take hold of his still stiff shaft and position it neatly between her bum cheeks.

He went to work with a will and her bottom responded gaily to every shove as the butler drove home, his pendulous balls banging against her smooth rounded bum cheeks. He worked his sturdy cock while she wriggled delightedly, crying out: 'That's it! That's it! Cork me to the limit with your thick prick!' He moved in and out of her juicy cunney with a steady shunting motion and he snaked his right hand across her waist to dive into her silky auburn muff and massage her erect little clitty. Now gripping Lizzie's hips, he pulled her towards him with every inward thrust and pushed her away with each outward movement so she jerked back and forth vigorously which afforded her the greatest of pleasure.

Suddenly she screamed: 'Yes, yes, yes!' and with a great shudder she collapsed onto the cushions and George Formbey too reached his climax, spunking copiously into her sopping cunt before falling on top of her as they swooned away with passion.

They lay exhausted for a while until Lizzie looked up at the butler and said: 'Well now, I hope that my performance shows you that I can do the job.'

Mr Formbey smiled and nodded his agreement. 'Your qualifications may be, ah, unorthodox, but I am sure that you will satisfy Count Gewirtz and myself quite admirably.

'Now tell me, Lizzie, for some reason I think that we have met before. I can't believe that I would have forgotten such a pretty girl as you, yet somehow I have the feeling that our paths have crossed – though for the life of me I can't remember just where.'

'Have you ever been in the West Country, Mr Formbey?'

'Only the once when three years ago I spent a summer on the north coast of Cornwall near Land's End, when the Arkleys rented Lord Rodney Burbeck's mansion at West Penwith.'

'That's where we've met. My cousin Rachel was working as a scullery maid for Lord Rodney and I used to visit her occasionally at the house. She said how different she found it working for Sir Alan Arkley as he never used to fuck her three times a day like Lord Rodney.'

'She must have enjoyed the rest,' commented Mr Formbey.

'For the first week, yes, but then she missed her master's attentions for as they say in those parts, Lord Rodney could fuck like a pirate and Rachel told me that one evening he had the Vicar's wife, Farmer Newman's daughter and herself one after the other.'

'More than I ever had,' complained the butler. 'I spent my free time walking along the cliff land exploring the engine houses of the tin mines. One or two have closed down, I believe, but the Botallack must still be going strong.'

'Oh yes, I should say it is. My brother Tristram is a miner at the Botallack and he told me they've struck a fine new seam about three hundred yards under the sea.'

[*Nearly all the tin mines have now ceased to operate. The Botallack mine mentioned here was the richest of them all but since 1914 has stood as a romantic ruin perched on the edge of the cliffs. – L.L.*]

'I don't miss Cornwall, though,' Lizzie smiled, taking hold of the butler's flaccid penis in her hand. 'I prefer life in the big city. I'm really grateful for the job and I only hope that my friend Estelle is as lucky as I have been.'

'Why, is she also looking for work in domestic service?' enquired Mr Formbey.

'Yes, and her qualifications are just as good as mine,'

said Lizzie, squeezing his shaft gently in her fist. 'I promise you that she will not disappoint you.'

'What else can you tell me about her?'

'Well, her hair is blonde, she has large breasts and she was eighteen years old last Thursday.'

'Good enough, good enough,' said the butler. 'Will you come together tomorrow morning?'

'We'll come together tonight!' said Lizzie roguishly. 'You are kind, Mr Formbey. Estelle and I will show you how grateful we are tomorrow afternoon.'

'I look forward to that happy occasion,' grunted Mr Formbey, pulling on his trousers. 'You know of the generous terms of your employment?'

'Oh, yes, I am really looking forward to meeting this gentleman, Count what's-his-name.'

'Gewirtz, but address him as Your Excellency unless he tells you to do otherwise. Now, Lizzie, I don't want to appear ungrateful for that delicious bout of fucking but I have a great deal to do this afternoon. Be a good girl and get dressed as quickly as you can and I look forward to seeing you and your friend back here tomorrow.'

Lizzie grinned as she slipped on her clothes and gave the butler's balls a fond squeeze before she went to the door. 'We'll be back, don't you worry. I'll let myself out,' she giggled as she opened the door to let in Fletcher the footman who appeared to be somewhat ill at ease in her presence. He looked nervously behind him and after he heard the front door slam shut he informed Mr Formbey that Fortnum and Mason had delivered the twenty-four crates of Maison Deutz and Goldmann champagne and all the other wines ordered Count Gewirtz had ordered via a telegram from Paris.

'Good, that's one less matter about which we have to

worry,' said the butler. 'But are you feeling unwell, Tim – your face is flushed and you look out of sorts.'

'Oh, I'm all right, Mr Formbey,' said the young man, wriggling with embarrassment. 'To tell the truth, I couldn't help overhearing a little of what Lizzie Stompson said to you and it made me feel very frustrated.

'I didn't hear much more after she said she wasn't wearing any knickers,' he added hastily. 'The bell rang after that and I had to supervise the unloading of the crates into the cellar.'

George Formbey laughed and said good-naturedly: 'Don't fret, young Tim! I'm sure that you will get to fuck Lizzie or her friend Estelle.'

'Do you really think so?' said the young footman eagerly.

'Yes, of course I do – here, wait a minute, how old are you?'

'I'm eighteen, sir.'

'Haven't you ever, no I'll bet a thousand pounds that you haven't and that you are still a virgin! Come now, lad, be truthful, there's nothing to be ashamed of here.'

Tim hung his head and muttered: 'Well, it's not something I'm proud of and I'm dying to fuck my first girl. Please don't tell Lizzie or Estelle, Mr Formbey, or I'll die of embarrassment.'

'I won't if you ask me not to, Tim, but I assure you that you'd be foolish to keep your virginity a secret. Why, they'll be fighting over who will pluck your cherry, you mark my words, young man. Mind, I'm a little surprised that a nice-looking lad like you has never managed to find the opportunity to do more than pull his pud!'

'Fate seems against me, Mr Formbey,' said the young man gloomily. 'I thought I was on a winner with the nurse in my last position with Lord and Lady Hartwalsh. They were lovely people to work for but when they decided to live in Gloucestershire I gave in my notice as I'm London born and bred and I don't want to live in the country.

'Anyhow they have a little boy and just before I left they took on a new nurse for the child. She was a pretty girl just a couple of years older than me and her name was Mary Wapping. Well, I almost got to have her, though I suppose I should really say that she very nearly managed to fuck me.'

The footman paused but Mr Formbey said encouragingly: 'No, go on, Tim, tell me all about it. Perhaps you made a mistake and I'll be able to guide you so you'll be better prepared in future. Sit down for a moment and spill the beans.'

'Alright, Mr Formbey, though I think I missed out through sheer bad luck rather than anything else. It all happened one evening about a week after Mary arrived at the house. I had finished supper and I decided to have a bath before I went to bed. To be frank I'd purloined a copy of that rude magazine *The Oyster* that Lord John had hidden in away in the library and I wanted to read it as quickly as possible before returning it to its secret place, and I planned to look through it in the bathroom.

'Anyhow, I enjoyed a luxurious soak and I dried myself off thoroughly before sitting down on the bathroom stool. I opened the magazine and I almost fell off with astonishment when I saw that Lord John himself had written a letter to the Editor!'

Mr Formbey leaned forward and said: 'This sounds good, Tim, let's hear more.'

Tim smiled and fished a piece of paper out of his pocket: 'I've still got the letter as I never got round to putting the magazine back in the library cabinet. I'll read it to you:

'*Sir,*

I must admit to indulging in a fantasy about that lively young filly Jenny Everleigh who writes of her fast and furious love life in the pages of your journal. Perhaps your readers would be interested in my mental meanderings so here we go:

I am sitting at home alone when there is a knock on the front door. I answer it myself as the servants have been given the night off. I open the door and who should be standing there but the beautiful Miss Everleigh herself!

'Hallo, John,' she says. 'I was just passing and I thought I would drop in and see how you were keeping.'

'I escort her in and her perfume drifts up and my tongue appears to freeze. Her well-rounded firm breasts are only partially covered by a turquoise evening gown and I feel a familiar stirring in my groin as my penis begins to swell up.

'How lovely to see you, John,' she coos sensuously, slipping her hand down to rub her palm deliciously over my stiffening cock. We are barely inside the hall when we exchange a most passionate kiss and in a trice her dress is on the floor and she stands naked in front of me.

I tear off my clothes except for my drawers. We stand clasped together as my lips travel down from her pretty face and neck to those gorgeous tits. Jenny then pushes me onto the couch and pulls down my drawers to reveal my throbbing prick as I pull her down to me and suck gently on those lovely nipples, going from one to the other and licking everything inbetween.

'Let's take this whole thing in hand,' she murmurs, wrapping her long, slender fingers round my shaft as she eases down to suck my cock. I bring her pussey to my face in a 'divine sixty-nine' and lick and lap at her blonde muff, working my tongue up and around her clitty, sucking and probing that beautiful cunney as she grinds that silky snatch against my mouth whilst she sucks lustily on my knob, twirling her tongue around the mushroom dome. The sperm is now boiling in my balls and I can feel my shaft tensing itself for the big spurt as I lap furiously at her cunney juices as we both explode in ecstasy.

After we recover we make for the bedroom where my family jewels are polished up to their finest by her talented tongue. We then fuck in every imaginable position until, exhausted by our massive spendings, we drift off into a deep sleep.

As you will gauge from this cock-stirring little letter, Jenny is the girl who I would most like to show round my ancestral seat whilst Lady H*******h is away. Her titties are the perfect size for my mouth and I would bury my face deep in her sweet pussey.

Alas, this remains a fantasy – but who knows what the future may hold?

'Yours sincerely,
John H*******h
Little Prickett
Gloucestershire

'Lord Hartmouth's house is only three-quarters of a mile from Little Prickett,' continued Tim. 'so I knew that he had composed this rude letter. In fact Jenny Everleigh had visited the house a month or so previous when Lady Hartmouth arranged a musical evening with the famous amateur pianist Mr Peter Stockman who had been staying with Mrs Lensen over the weekend.'

'Not the famous gentleman who is reputed to boast of the largest testicles in London?' interrupted Mr Formbey. 'His reputation as a cocksman is supposedly second only to the Prince of Wales.'

'That's the man,' nodded Tim. 'and the talk in the servants' hall was that he fucked four country ladies, the Vicar's daughter and Mrs Lensen's chambermaid within the first three days of his visit. However, to get back to my story, reading Lord Hartsmouth's lewd letter gave me a huge hard-on. I sat on the bathroom stool rubbing my cock and I was so engrossed in this activity that I did not even hear Mary open the door (which I had neglected to lock) and she startled me tremendously as she said: "Well, well, Tim I see that you are very well-endowed for your age. But really, I think this is a job that I can do far better than you." '

'I was too shocked by her entrance to reply but I took my hand away from my fast-shrinking shaft.

' "Let me show you what I mean," she smiled, passing her tongue across her mouth sensuously, licking her lips in anticipation. She came over to where I was sitting which was opposite the long wall mirror – and this meant that I had a perfect view as she knelt down in front of me and proceeded to take my penis in her warm, soft hands. It immediately began to swell up again to its former thickness and with only a little further encouragement, my prick was standing as high and stiff as before.

Mary cupped my balls with one hand and gently squeezed them as she ran her other hand up and down the length of my shaft.

'The feeling I experienced was new to me. My throat was dry and tight and I was as sensuously aware as I had ever been in my entire life. Mary took her hands away from my cock and balls and began to unbutton her blouse. She liberated the last of the buttons and the blouse opened teasingly to reveal the swell of her fully-rounded breasts. Her fingers nimbly worked the hooks and eyes of her skirt and she pulled down the front of her drawers just an inch or two to let me catch sight of her golden curls that glinted in the sunlight streaming through the window.

' "Would you like to see more?" she whispered. All I could do was to nob my head as I was far too excited to reply coherently.

She gave me a wicked grin and knelt down gently in front of me. She grasped my cock again and proceeded to put it in her hot, wet mouth. She sucked and sucked, slowly and skilfully, teasing my balls with her finger-nails, moving her tongue around my knob, gently biting, licking, kissing. I could not control myself as I thrust frenziedly into her throat. I knew I was close to shooting my seed even though she had only been sucking me for a mere minute or so. Mary felt my urgency and she gave my ballsack another squeeze which stimulated a rush of spunk up the channel of my pulsating tool, exploding into a stream of sperm that gushed out wildly into her willing mouth. I felt my balls contract as she happily swallowed all my spunk, milking me beautifully of every last drop of juice. She licked her lips and said: "M'm, I was going to have a cup of cocoa but the juice from your cock is much more satisfying. And my, what a big boy you are, why your cock still hasn't gone down, has it? Well, now, let me think about we can do about that." '

'I stood there dazed as she pulled down her knickers saying: "Goodness, I'm so wet down here, I must take these off and change into a new pair." At the sight of the damp thatch of thick blonde pubic hair, my semi-limp rod leaped up into its former full hardness as Mary looked on in undisguised admiration.'

'Well, for heaven's sake, what did you do then? Take out a pack of cards and play gin rummy?' exclaimed Mr Formbey. 'If you didn't get your end away then –'

'No, I didn't,' snapped the young footman. 'Just as Mary bent over the bath and pushed out her bum cheeks we heard the front door open! It could only be Lord Hartmouth himself as Murdoch the butler was out and only the Master was in town.

'Mary picked up her clothes and ran helter-skelter upstairs into her room at the top of the house. I closed the bathroom door after her and began to get dressed. Lord Hartmouth shouted out for me and I called back that I was in the bathroom. To make matters worse, when I finally reached his Lordship in a state of some dishevelment, who should be with him but the American authoress Miss Patricia Miller, whom all of us downstairs knew was being well fucked by Lord John whenever an opportunity arose.

'So there you are, Mr Formbey,' concluded the unhappy Fletcher. 'My best chance of enjoying my first fuck was stymied by fate. I feel so despondent about it that I sometimes wonder whether I am doomed to be a virgin all my life.'

'Damn bad luck, young Tim,' said Mr Formbey slowly. 'But I'll bet you a pound to a penny that like all of us lucky enough to be in the service of Count Gewirtz, we'll all get fucked on Saturday night, you mark my words.'

Back at Hyde Park Gardens *chez* Arkley there was an air of hustle and bustle as the entire family busied themselves in settling down for their stay in town. One of the first to make himself comfortable was paterfamilias Sir Paul Arkley who, whilst his wife and daughters were enjoying an afternoon concert at the Royal Albert Hall, was enjoying the favours of Charlotte, the somewhat plump yet very good-looking dark-haired servant who Lady Arkley had engaged in place of Connie Chumbley – who as chance would have it was at this very same moment sucking lustily on the naked prick of Inspector Glenton Rogers of P Division, and we will return to them a little later.

Meanwhile Sir Paul and Charlotte were lying totally nude upon the chambermaid's bed and Sir Paul was showing the maid some photographs he had purchased the previous day at Hotton's Bookshop in Piccadilly.

'Look at this one,' leered the baronet. I like this pose of the frisky little French model, Manette. Look at the cheeky cat sitting bollock-naked on a chaise longue, pushing her bum cheeks out towards the camera. Ah, that stirs up my old pego no end, Charlotte. Look at her, the little devil, she seems to be telling me that she wants my stiff cock to push in between those delicious bum cheeks and move in and out with fuck strokes that get louder and harder as I shoot out a thick wad of creamy spunk into her horney pussey. Gad! She's really making me feel randy, look at my prick swelling up!'

'Well that's no compliment to me,' complained Charlotte. 'Here I am just inches away from you in the flesh and it's obvious that a rotten photograph turns you on more than I do. Don't I have just as pretty a face and just as juicy a cunt as that little French tart?'

'Oh, but of course you do, you silly thing,' soothed Sir Paul. 'Let's take a good look at you, Charlotte m'dear. Yes, you have a fine complexion, a pleasing smile and most regular features. Now let's move down to those glorious bubbies, so large, globular and firm with exquisitely saucered red titties. Now, let's move further down to that finely rounded little tummy and, my, my what do I see nestling between your thighs but a beautiful little pussey, all covered up just now and hidden in a most luxuriant growth of jet-black hair.

'Let me brush it aside – ah, that's better, now I have fair view of those pouting luscious-looking cunney lips. Let me salute them in the nicest possible way,' said Sir Paul, pushing Charlotte's legs apart and nuzzling his head between her thighs. 'M'mm, what a heavenly feminine aroma. Oh, what a delightful cunt you have Charlotte. I must suck it and kiss it and pay homage to the mossy shrine of Lady Cunney.'

He kissed her moistening pussey with his tongue running the full length of its parted lips. Charlotte shuddered as his tongue found her hardened clitty that stuck out like a miniature soldier and he sucked and chewed it as the girl gasped with joy, jerking wildly as she moaned:

'Oooh, oooh, OOOH! Sir Paul! More, sir, more, I'm coming, I swear I'm coming!' His hands gripped her hips as she writhed around, making it difficult for him to keep his mouth on her clitty. He moved his head from between her legs and began rubbing and pinching her erect little clitty with his thumb and forefinger.

Now Charlotte was twisting from side to side as her love juices flowed freely and her hands flew to her big breasts and she played with her own nipples, roughly massaging the elongated nipples. 'Rub my clitty harder, sir,' she cried out. 'Go on, rub away!' Her gyrations increased as she twisted and turned, heaved and humped until with a piercing shriek she achieved full satisfaction and she wrapped Sir Paul's hand tightly between her jerking thighs while her spend coursed through her entire body.

'M'mm, that was lovely,' gasped Charlotte. 'Now let me relieve you of all that spunk boiling up in your balls.'

The comely maid ran her nails along the length of Sir Paul's inner thighs and across his stomach. She kissed him lightly on his neck and chin while her fingers danced on the skin of his cheeks. She moved close enough for her hardened nipples to graze his chest then slowly moved down and, as his cock sprang up to greet her, she flicked at it with her tongue before taking the shaft into her wide mouth and swallowing it whole. She sucked on the baronet's shaft as if she had not tasted cock for a year and very soon Sir Paul was ready to spend. She gave his knob a final kiss and she moved quickly to lie back with her legs wide apart, her hands rubbing her cunney to moisten her pussey for Sir Paul's prick which would be soon inside her.

She lay on the bed with her legs wide open and her knees pulled up as Sir Paul came over to lay on top of her and Charlotte took hold of his cock and coaxed the knob between her pussey lips. He gently pushed forward and the girl began to breathe heavily while he began to thrust his shaft in and out of her moistening cunt. She raised herself to meet his strokes as he shafted her faster and faster. He pumped in and out of her pussey and he rubbed her red stalky nipples with one hand whilst the other snaked round to squeeze her luscious bum cheeks.

'Fuck me now!' Charlotte yelled uninhibitedly. 'Fill my cunney with your hot spunk!' Sir Paul spent almost immediately, crashing great globs of frothy love juice into her pulsating pussey, working his shaft in and out until the last drops of cream trickled out and his shaft began to deflate.

'That was absolutely marvellous,' panted Charlotte. 'Oh, you do know how to please a girl, Sir Paul. I spend every time we fuck and I bet Lady Arkley does too, the lucky woman, having you in her bed every night.'

'Thank you m'dear,' said Sir Paul politely. 'They say the way to a man's heart is through his stomach but you and I know that his cock is a far more responsive organ. Praise a man's penis and he will be mere putty in your hand.'

'Oh, I wouldn't want you to think that I let you fuck me just for those lovely presents,' said Charlotte with a note of reproach in her voice.

'Maybe so, but I've spent enough on you to buy a boat,' said Sir Paul.

'And you've spent enough in me to launch it!' replied

Charlotte wittily. 'But don't let's argue, darling. Have I time to suck your cock just before we get dressed?'

'I'm afraid not, my love,' sighed the baronet. 'But look, I do have a little something for you.' He sat up and padded across to his jacket which he had thrown across over a chair. He took out a small packet and tossed it over to Charlotte who caught it cleanly.

'Call it an advance birthday present for next week,' he suggested.

'Oh, thank you, darling. I don't know if I can wait all that time before I open it!' said Charlotte excitedly.

'You don't have to wait – open it now,' he said with a smile.

She tore open the paper and opened the little box. 'Oh, Sir Paul, it's lovely!' she murmured as she took out a small enamelled brooch which showed four naval flags. 'It will look so nice on the blue dress you bought me last month. These flags are very pretty. Do they spell out a message of some kind?'

'Yes, as a matter of fact they do – that is, only to someone who understands naval signals,' he replied with a smile.

'How exciting! It's like a secret code. Do tell me what they say!'

'Well, the message of the flags is: "Position open ahead, I am about to fire a torpedo." '

'Ha, ha, ha! You really are a clever old stick.'

'Now so much of the old, you cheeky girl. But I cannot claim credit for the idea. To be honest, His Royal Highness the Prince of Wales asked the famous Mr Smolask of Hatton Garden to make up this brooch for Mrs Keppel and this is a copy of it. I don't mind admitting that HRH had Mrs Keppel's brooch flags set in diamonds but I couldn't afford that and even if I could, you would hardly be able to wear it!'

'I don't mind about that. It's a lovely brooch and I'm going to give your cocky a special seeing-to next time I see him,' promised Charlotte as she kissed Sir Paul on the lips.

They dressed quickly for Lady Arkley and the girls would soon be back from their concert.

And indeed they had only a few minutes grace after they had finished dressing before Lady Arkley, Katie and Penny returned from the Albert Hall.

Their *paterfamilias* greeted them warmly in the drawing room and said that he hoped that they had enjoyed the concert which had been performed in aid of one of Lady Arkley's favourite charities.

'It was most enjoyable, Paul, you really should have come with us rather than study those stupid Government reports,' said Lady Arkley who may have been a martinet in many ways but whose manner could always be softened by music, of which she was extremely fond.

'Duty calls, I'm afraid,' muttered Sir Paul. 'I spent a great deal of time on an important affair. Er, Charlotte, ask Cook to prepare tea for us as soon as possible, please.'

Fortunately neither Lady Arkley not the girls noticed the smirk on Charlotte's face as she left the room.

'One of your favourite works, Beethoven's Fifth Symphony was performed, Papa,' said Katie.

'And it was well played, too,' Penny chimed in. 'The Paris Conservatoire Orchestra performed magnificently. It's such stirring stuff too, isn't it? As our music teacher

Herr Tockhess has always told us, the Fifth Symphony is a deeply personal outpouring of music, the outward manifestation of a great and turbulent spirit.'

'Ah, but for me the highlight of the afternoon was the Schubert Fantasia in F Minor *fur Klavier zu vier Handen**. The pianists were Frederick Cohen and one Martina Motkaloswki, a fine-looking young Polish lady who certainly impressed me with her performance,' said Lady Arkley.

'Really?' said Sir Paul, pricking up his ears. 'I am sure that she is on the guest list for Count Gewirtz's party tomorrow night. Yes, I recall now she was mentioned in a letter the Count sent me last week. I look forward to meeting her.'

'So do we, Papa,' said Katie. 'We will congratulate her on her performance.'

So shall I, thought Sir Paul to himself, but on her performances away from the piano – for in his letter Count Gewirtz had described a beautiful Polish girl who played the piano like a dream and who turned out to be the most enjoyable fuck since the fiery English Lady Jenny Everleigh and her cousin Molly Farquhar entertained the Count *à deux* at Lord Titchfield's Spring Ball three months before.

The family enjoyed a quiet tea with Sir Paul pondering how he would be able to arrange an assignment with Martina the pianist and Katie concerned as to how Walter would be able to slip into her bedroom that night without being seen by either members of the family or the servants. Penny meanwhile was working out when

* For piano and four hands

she and her beloved Bob might next enjoy a good bout of fucking. But what of Lady Arkley? Truth to tell, she was only engaged in deciding just what dress from her huge wardrobe would be suitable for Count Gewirtz's grand party. Not knowing the eccentric Galician, Lady Arkley was somewhat at a loss to know whether a glittering outfit or a more restrained appearance would be appropriate and finally she decided to ask her husband's opinion on this important matter.

'Paul, what should I wear for Count Gewirtz's party tomorrow night?'

'Absolutely nothing, my dear,' replied her spouse absent-mindedly, his thoughts now centred on the silky-muffed pussey of Charlotte who was busying herself clearing the table. 'Absolutely nothing at all.'

'I beg your pardon,' said Lady Arkley sternly as the girls began to giggle.

'I asked your opinion as to what I should wear for tomorrow's function and you have suggested I meet Count Gewirtz in a state of nudity,' she said, drawing herself up to her full height.

'No, no, no, my love,' said Sir Paul hastily. 'I thought you asked if we should present our host with a gift and so I said that he would not wish us to bring anything, absolutely nothing at all.'

Lady Arkley was still not fully convinced but before she could reply the front door chimes rang out. 'Saved by the bell!' muttered Penny to her sister. 'I'll say,' Katie giggled. 'What on earth can Papa have been thinking of?'

In fact to Katie great joy, Sir Paul's saviour was none other than Walter Stanton who had been spending the afternoon in study and who had come back on the off-chance that he and Katie might be able to find themselves alone and uninterrupted for an hour or even less.

'Ah, Walter, my boy,' said Sir Paul trying to disguise the relief he felt at not being pressed further by his wife. 'Good to see you. Will you want some tea? Charlotte has cleared away but it's no bother to have a kettle put on for you.'

'No thank you, sir. I took tea at the library. I came back early to see if the girls would like to take a stroll round Hyde Park for an hour as the weather is so pleasant.'

'I'd love to go with you,' said Katie hopefully.

'Well, I'd rather finish an excellent novel I started last week.' said Penny.

'Would you have any objections if Katie and I went out unchaperoned?' asked Walter.

'Not at all, my boy. It will do you both good to have a constitutional. We dine at eight so you have plenty of time for a walk before changing for dinner,' said Sir Paul. 'I'm off to the library to look over some government papers.'

Lady Arkley had no objection so the young pair slipped out and enjoyed the warm rays of the late afternoon sun as they strolled beneath the trees away from the hurly burly of Rotten Row and Knightsbridge. Walter took her sweet little hand in his as they walked into a little cluster of leafy trees near the centre of the park.

'Inside this copse I discovered there is a small hillock upon which we can sit, unobserved from public view,' murmured Walter.

'All we have to do is make our way unseen through that thicket on your right and hey presto! We will disappear like magic from public view,' he added.

Walter led the willing girl along a half-hidden track and they were almost at their goal when they heard sounds of what seemed to be a feminine moaning in front of them.

'What's that noise, Walter?' whispered Katie with a frightened look in her eyes.

'I don't know, darling, but I'm sure it's nothing to be worried about,' he said soothingly. 'Stay here a moment and I'll look through that bush on the left and see what's going on.'

They heard the moaning again and Katie said: 'No, we'll go together. Someone might be in need of assistance.' So they crept forward and Walter was first to peer through the bush. He looked for a full twenty seconds or so before he turned to Katie and grinned:

'Don't worry, darling. No-one needs any assistance. I doubt if the girl we heard would welcome an interruption.'

'Why, what do you mean?'

'See for yourself,' he laughed quietly.

Katie pressed forward and brushed aside the branches to look upon the grassy knoll which faced her only some twenty yards away. A handsome young couple, believing themselves well hidden, were engaged in a most voluptuous fuck. The girl's white globular breasts were bare for they had spilled out of her unloosed bodice. The boy was unclothed below the waist and Katie caught her breath as she looked on his tight, muscular bottom cheeks pumping in and out while he nuzzled and sucked on the long engorged nipples that crowned the girl's splendidly fleshy orbs. Katie breathed deeply as the young scamp grasped the girl's bum and lifted her upwards and she pulled up her skirt. He removed her knickers in one swift movement and Katie caught her breath as he moved slightly sideways and his veiny cock stood up as stiff as a flagpole while the girl reached out to give this extraordinarily big shaft a friendly rub.

Slowly he eased his monster prick into the girl's willing cunney and she opened her thighs to their fullest extent to accommodate him. She held her own legs wide apart with her hands as his reached out under hers to grip her bum. Her hips arched towards him as if trying to entice every inch of cock as far as possible inside her. Now the boy thrust effortlessly in and out of her pussey and she began to moan again in delight, faster and deeper, until both prick and pussey exploded in a gigantic simultaneous climax.

Walter squinted as he peered forward earnestly and then turned round to Katie with a large grin on his face.

'This is quite a coincidence,' he said. 'I do believe that I know that chap over there. Yes, I'm sure that prick belongs to young Godfrey Hendon or I'm a Dutchman.'

'Who is Godfrey Hendon?' Katie queried.

'Oh, he is an old college chum from Cambridge. Yes, I'm sure that's him. We rowed together for Trinity Hall and many is the time I've seen him in the showers. He wasn't a marvellous rower but as you can see he possessed the biggest prick in the crew! I haven't seen him for at least a year. Perhaps I should go and say hallo.'

'Well, perhaps not just now,' said Katie with a little giggle for Godfrey was now lying back on the grass with his girlfriend coaxing his cock back to life with a series of butterfly kisses on the uncovered dome. Her hands ran around the cluster of thick dark hair around his prick and Katie craned her head forward to see the girl let her mouth travel along the length of his shaft which began to throb and swell as she grasped it and began rubbing it up to a fine erection. She then stroked the rampant cock as Godfrey (for it was he) said, 'Sally, I want to fuck you again. You have an adorable bottom. May I have the pleasure of inserting my cock *au derrière*?'

'Yes, if you must. But be careful how you poke me as we don't have any cold cream.'

'Alas, there was none at the chemist's, Sally.'

'Why didn't you try Boots?'

'Because I wanted to slide in, not march across, you silly girl!' laughed Godfrey and the two voyeurs were hard-pressed not to join in the peal of laughter from Sally as she undressed and stood naked before rolling herself over onto her tummy. Godfrey pulled her bum up into the air by gently manoeuvering her hips and then he knelt behind the delicious creature, clasping his arms around her waist and positioning his knob between her firm bum cheeks.

He drew back his cock, wet his knob with spittle and squarely aimed the head of his charger towards the wrinkled little rosette that beckoned his now iron-hard rod.

'Ouch!' cried Sally. 'That's painful!'

He tried again but could not penetrate the winking brown orifice. 'I can't bear this,' said Walter. 'I must show him how to bottom-fuck or that poor girl will not be able to sit down tonight.'

'Hello there, Godfrey,' he called out as he scrambled out from behind the bush. 'How nice to see you again.'

'God Almighty! If it isn't Walter Stanton! How are you, Walter? Permit me to introduce Miss Sally Sunshine, a dancer from that marvellous show at the Holborn Empire. Sally, this is Walter, an old friend from my college days. Don't be embarrassed, the talk in Cambridge was that Walter might not obtain a good degree in law but that he would gain a first class degree in fucking.'

'That's very kind of you,' said Walter modestly. 'Look, old boy, I don't want to interfere, but I don't think you are going about this the right way.'

'Well, I am somewhat inexperienced in bottom-fucking,' admitted Godfrey.

'Ease into her slowly but firmly, my dear chap. Here, permit me to assist you.' And Walter took hold of the young man's pulsating prick and eased the glowing dome of his noble weapon between Sally's superb bottom cheeks that were fairly aching to be split. He pushed forward again but withdrew when again he found difficulty in penetrating – so this time Walter moistened the gleaming, rubicund dome with more spittle and placed the knob fairly to the mark.

'Try now,' he advised and his work achieved the desired effect as Godfrey's shaft this time enveloped itself between the in-rolling cheeks of the girl's beautifully-proportioned arse. A little fearful in case he injured his beloved, Godfrey pushed slowly at first but soon realised that he was now absorbed well enough in her tight little bum-hole. So he began to work himself with vigour, pushing his entire body forwards and backwards, making Sally's bum cheeks slap loudly against his belly as she cried out, this time with unalloyed pleasure.

Godfrey's penis was now fully ensconced in her warm, tight bum and he screwed up his eyes in sheer bliss.

'Christ, what a great bum-fuck!' he panted as he leaned over Sally to fondle her luscious breasts and play with her erect titties. As she waggled her bottom provocatively she lifted her head from the pillow and Walter and Katie could both see that there was no doubt of her complete enjoyment of Godfrey's thick prick pounding in and out of her gorgeous bum.

'Now, Godfrey, now!' she gasped and the slim lad needed no urging, for almost immediately he flooded her arsehole with such vibrant shoots that Walter swore afterwards that he could actually see the ripples of orgasm running down Sally's spine as she shuddered to a delicious climax. As she artfully wriggled her bottom, spout after spout of creamy spunk filled her juicy hole and with a succulent 'pop' Godfrey withdrew his still-stiff shaft and sank back on his haunches. Sally turned round and with an exclamation of rapture, dropped to her knees and sucked his glistening cock, eagerly swallowing the last drains of sperm, gobbling greedily as her hands jerked up and down on his shaft. Then, when she had milked his shrinking cock of the final drops, she sat sedately on his lap, her hands round his neck.

'Thanks for your help, Walter,' said Godfrey. 'I told you he was an expert at fucking, didn't I, Sally?'

'Yes, we owe you our thanks, kind sir,' giggled the girl. 'If you like I will suck you off, too. I can see from the bulge in your trousers that you have a fine weapon concealed between your legs.'

'Very kind of you, I'm sure,' said Walter, a hint of a blush colouring his face. 'But actually I am with a young lady and –'

'You don't want to make her jealous!' finished Godfrey. 'Where is she, Walter – behind the bush?'

Katie decided to break her cover and Walter stepped forward to take her hand as she made her way to the others.

'Permit me to introduce Miss Katherine Arkley,' said Walter.

'Charmed, I'm sure, Miss Arkley but you catch me in a state of some embarrassment,' said Godfrey with a little smile.

'And how about me?' enquired Sally. 'I'm hardly in the right state to greet any visitors.'

'Except my cock!' Godfrey corrected her. 'You look just right to receive a visitor such as he.'

'Boasting again! I bet you can't get it up, Godfrey. I've been fucked by Sir Ronnie Dunn, the greatest cocksman in London and even he wouldn't be able to perform again after what we've just did.'

'Don't be so sure,' said Walter. 'At Cambridge Godfrey took part in a contest with Dr Terence Slacker of Magdalene – known to all as Terry the Tool – and two ladies from The Titchfield Arms much experienced in the arts of fucking. After three hours Terence was forced to concede defeat and, as I recall, Godfrey won a purse of ten guineas.'

'Twenty guineas, actually,' said Godfrey. 'I would like nothing better than to fuck you again, Sally, though as a gentleman I feel I should offer Miss Arkley first refusal.'

'No, no, that's quite all right. I prefer to watch,' said Katie hastily.

Sally decided to make matters in hand and ran her long fingers along Godfrey's broad chest. Then, moving quickly, she slid herself on top of him, hungrily searching for his lips as they kissed passionately once more. They moved their thighs together until their pubic muffs were entangled and Godfrey's stiff prick probed the entrance to her exquisite little crack, throbbing with a powerful intensity until Sally eased her hips with a yelp of delight while the swollen knob forced its way between her cunney lips, massaging her clitty, as Godfrey arched his own frame upwards, plunging his trusty tool inside her wetness. She clambered up to sit upright, her knees either side of Godfrey's slim frame, to ride a superb St George and she gurgled with joy as Godfrey shot great gusts of sperm deep into her womb just at the point that, she, too, reached the pinnacle of pleasure.

'This exhibition makes me fearfully randy,' muttered Walter, nibbling Katie's ear.

'Wait till we get home,' she replied, giving his swollen cock a friendly squeeze which caused an even greater bulge in his trousers.

'We must be going now. So nice to have met you both,' said Walter.

'I'll look you up when I'm back in London,' said Godfrey. 'I'll leave a message at the Rawalpindi Club. I'm off tomorrow down to the West Country for some birdwatching.'

'Are you now, Mr Hendon? A good friend of mine, Henrietta Boston-Coxe, is a keen ornithologist and spends a great deal of time in the Scilly Isles.'

'Really – well, I will pass on your regards if I see her for I am also going to the Scillies. It's just about the only place where one can observe several species including the Manx shearwaters which breed nowhere else in Britain.'

'I didn't know you were interested in birds, Godfrey,'

said Sally. 'I've never been to the Scilly Isles. Are they nice to visit?'

'Oh, yes, I always enjoy a trip out there. Not many people know that there are actually forty-eight isles but only five are inhabited. I do like the mild sub-tropical climate and the peace and quiet far from the London crowds.'

'Perhaps you will take me there? The show finishes on Saturday week and I've nothing else booked for a while. You'll have to buy me a ticket for the train but we could have such fun,' said Sally.

'We'll see. Meanwhile, these good folk must take their leave,' said Godfrey.

'Yes, indeed. Though really it should be us who stay and you to go,' said Walter.

'Why is that?' asked Godfrey.

'Because then I could say "thank you for coming"!' said the witty Walter and the four young people burst out laughing as a sudden evening breeze sent the still naked Sally and Godfrey running for their discarded clothes.

As Katie and Walter strolled back to Hyde Park Gardens, not far away, at 46 Green Street, George Formbey was opening a telegram from Count Gewirtz which informed him that the Count would be arriving one day earlier than expected and that a suite of rooms should be opened up for his travelling companion Madame Vazelina Volpe.

Thank goodness Connie and Mrs Beaconsfield arrived on time, thought the butler. But what of Lizzie and Estelle, the two maids he had engaged – would they be up to scratch?

In fact the two girls had presented themselves punctually for service and were upstairs in Estelle's bedroom giggling about Estelle's escapades in her last position at the country home of Captain Gerald Edward Stanton-Harcourt near Newmarket.

'The Captain was a keen horseman and though well into his forties was still a fine figure of a man, muscular and well-proportioned,' said Estelle to Lizzie as they lay together on the luxuriously appointed bed – and like the other servants, the girls had noted with appreciation the high standard of accommodation Count Gewirtz provided for members of his household. Mrs Beaconsfield, for example, was amazed and delighted to find that she was provided with her own private bathroom.

'Captain Eddie was married but he and his wife led almost separate lives,' Estelle continued. 'She cared little for country pursuits and spent as much time as possible in London with well-known rakes such as Sir Ronnie Dunn, Lord Gerald Horne and Captain Goldstone of the South Oxfordshire Rifles.

'However, I always wanted to try riding so when after serving him breakfast Captain Eddie asked me whether I would like to join him for a trot round the estate, I jumped at the chance. I told him that I had never climbed up on a horse before. He said that didn't matter and that he would offer to teach me – and as his wife and myself were similar in build, I could borrow some riding gear from her wardrobe if I wished to do so.'

'This does sound like a good story. I hope it will all end with a poke,' laughed Lizzie.

'Wait and see, you rude thing!' Estelle scolded her with a merry smile. 'Anyhow, I changed into a pair of her jodhpurs. Now, despite being slim, I have often been complimented on my particularly plump cunt and I was delighted to see that though the jodhpurs were cut loosely around the hips, they were extremely tight-fitting from the thighs to the ankles which accentuated the shape of my pussey. To obtain an even better effect I managed to pull the seam right up into my cunney so that the shape of my generous outer lips would be revealed and even the swollen rosebud of my clitty could be discerned especially – as I didn't put any knickers on and was totally nude underneath.

'I didn't have any underclothes underneath my white blouse either and I undid the top two buttons so that the Captain would get a good view of the swell of my breasts. As I walked out to the stables I noticed the two stable lads staring with excited eyes at my bottom cheeks which wobbled gracefully encased in their tight covering. Captain Eddie, as he was known to all, was hard at work composing a poem about the end of the hunting season for Baily's Magazine. He was sitting down at a small table Mrs Donaldson the housekeeper had prepared for us.

' "Pour yourself some coffee, m'dear," said Captain Eddie, his brow furrowed as he put a line through some of the verses he had written. "I'm damned if I know why I agreed to take on this job. The only poems I know are the kind you can't write in magazines."

' "You mean limericks, sir?" I said. "I know some of those naughty ones like:

> *There was a young lady of Glasgow,*
> *And fondly her lover did ask 'Oh,*
> *Pray allow me a fuck'*

160

> *But she said, 'No, my duck,*
> *Though you may, if you please, up my bum go!'*

or:

> *There was a young girl of Pitlochry*
> *Who was had by a boy in a rockery.*
> *She said, 'Oh, you've come*
> *All over my bum;*
> *This isn't a fuck – it's a mockery.'*

'Is that the sort of poem you are writing, sir?'' '

' "Ha, ha, ha! No, it's not though I'm sure that the readers of Baily's would prefer your verses to mine! I'll read what I've managed so far. I call this poem: *The End of the Season* and it begins: –

> *My hunter may rest in his stable,*
> *No more sitting down on his back,*
> *Shall I push him as fast as I'm able*
> *In the wake of the musical pack.*
> *No more shall I canter to covert,*
> *No more across country be borne,*
> *Goodbye to the season, it's over –*

Now I just can't thick of a final line." '

'I thought for a moment and suddenly I was fired by inspiration. "How about: "Goodbye to the Hound and the Horn." I suggested.

' "Capital, capital!" boomed Captain Eddie. "You are a natural rhymer, Estelle." He looked up at me for the first time and added: "What's more you are a fine look-

161

ing filly at that. Bugger all this poetry. Let's saddle up and
then we can enjoy ourselves back in the house.''

' "With indoor sports?" I said, for I have always preferred older men, as you know. 'I sincerely hope so,' said
the Captain as the stable lads, Fred and Louis brought our
horses up to the table.

'I won't bore you with details of the ride but Captain
Eddie said I rode excellently well for a complete novice. I
must say I did enjoy bouncing up and down on the horse's
back in my tight jodhpurs. It made me feel quite randy
and I was more than happy when after an hour we can-
tered slowly back to the house where Fred was waiting to
assist me to dismount. The Captain and I went indoors
and the Captain gallantly allowed me to be the first to
mount the stairs. Well, perhaps he wasn't gallant but just
randy as he pinched my bum just as we reached the first
floor. "Captain Eddie!" I said with mock severity.
"What are you doing?" "Sorry m'dear," he replied.
"But your rounded bottom cheeks look just too delicious. Why don't you take your togs off and join me in a
nice warm bath?"

'I was more than happy to agree to his suggestion. I
peeled off all my clothes and took a look in the mirror at
my naked body. I know you have always admired my
large breasts and the blonde little muff of fluffy hair
covering my crack. Would Captain Eddie also approve? I
slipped on a bathrobe and opened the bathroom door.
The Captain was standing under a hot shower, soaping
himself in the warm steamy water pumping out over his
head. He had strewn his clothes on the floor but my eyes
quickly focused back on his muscular body and his beautifully formed tight buttocks. As he turned round slowly

he saw me standing there. I slipped off my robe and instantly his thick cock stiffened up into one of the hardest rods I have ever seen. He took hold of his prick and stroked his shaft up to its full height until it stood stiffly against his belly with the tip reaching his navel. My nipples were trembling with excitement at the idea of that juicy cock crashing into my love channel. I knew I was getting wet as I slipped my hands down between my legs and stirred the moistness around. My clitty was already swollen with desire, popping out of its hood for more attention.

'I stepped into the big bath and found out that cleverly, Captain Eddie had kept the plug in so that there was a bedding of warm soapy water in which we could lie down. I let myself be pulled down and I enjoyed his tongue and fingers running over my body. Now his mouth came down on me with practised expertise and I shivered with delight as I bucked and humped into his face, trying to let his tongue slip deeper into my crack. He was eagerly lapping at my juices, his teeth nipping at my clitty, his lips sucking as he licked and lapped until I cried: "Yes, yes, yes. Don't stop, suck it out, suck my clitty!" That's what I wanted and that's what he did. I felt an enormous spend building inside me as he pushed his fingers into my throbbing slit. I arched up to meet his mouth, and then, ahhhh! The tension snapped, the energy came in waves and so did I from the top of my head to the tips of my toes as my body went limp.

'Of course we finished with a grand fuck. I stayed on my back, cossetted by the warm water as his thick cock wriggled its way between my pulsating breasts and into my mouth. I pursed my lips tightly around it and let the feel of his ribbed stick run in and out as he soaped my titties with his fingers. He then eased back, taking his cock from my mouth and down towards my blonde thatch until his knob was poised between my cunney lips. He tenderly pushed it in, sinking down slowly until our hairs crunched together. We bounced, we shook and I ground my hips as we fucked beautifully in a glorious rhythm of long slow movements in perfect unison. As my own body felt the force of the sexual tide begin to build he increased the speed of his thrusts.

'His cock throbbed violently in my sopping cunney until he exploded into me in a rush of liquid fire. I spent again instantly as my saturated clitty sent ripples of bliss throughout my body. Oh, we fucked away for what seemed like hours as the glorious warm water coaxed our bodies to new heights of delight and the heady, steamy atmosphere added to the sheer fun of it all. It was certainly the highlight of my stay at Harcourt Manor and Captain Eddie gave me a crisp new ten pound note as a birthday present when I left his service last week to come back to London.'

There was a pause as Lizzie digested the details of her friend's erotic encounter and then she said slowly: 'Dear Estelle, I envy you what sounds like a jolly fine fucking. I've had Mr Formbey the butler and he knows how to use his cock but your Captain Eddie sounds like a first class cocksman, and as we both know, a hard man is good to find!'

'M'mm, Captain Eddie was a first class fuck,' agreed her jolly companion. 'I do feel like a fuck right now. See, my little pussey has already juiced up whilst I was recounting my lewd tale.'

'Well, at least we have each other,' said Lizzie, her hands moulding Estelle's large breasts, her fingers lazily encircling the nipples, making them stand out hard. Estelle leaned back on the bed, breathing heavily as Lizzie kept her hands on her breasts, massaging them firmly. Then she took one hand away to slip it under Estelle's bum. She pressed against her and their nipples touched as they trembled with unslaked lust. They kissed, quite softly at first and then harder, slipping their tongues in each other's mouths as their pussies ground hard together and they fondled each other cracks through the thin material of their knickers.

Lizzie pulled down her friend's drawers and inserted a finger through the blonde bush into Estelle's moist cunney. She wriggled on the intruding finger as her pussey walls contracted around it.

'Oh, that's gorgeous, Lizzie,' she breathed. 'Make me come!'

They drew apart for a moment to pull off their clothes and then resumed their love-making, kissing and cuddling as Lizzie jerked her fingers in and out of Estelle's sopping muff. She clamped her cunney walls round them, contracting the muscles as she moved them back and forth.

'Oooh! Oooh! Oooh!' panted Estelle as the sensation of Lizzie's mouth and tongue all over her titties and her hand in her pussey sent the pretty girl into tremors of ecstasy. Her legs threshed around as Lizzie moved her head between her thighs and sucked at her hard little clitty, whilst slipping a hand between her own legs to bring herself off at the same time. Estelle repaid the compliment by nibbling at Lizzie's uptilted titties until they both spent copiously.

They were woken from their blissful reverie by a knock on the door.

'Who is it?' Estelle called out.

'It's Tim here,' replied a youthful voice. 'Mr Formbey wants all the staff downstairs in ten minutes time for an important meeting.'

'Right, we'll be there,' Lizzie chimed in. 'Don't start without us.'

'But we've already started without him,' she added quietly so that Tim would not hear. 'I must fuck that good-looking boy, Estelle, and I'm sure you want him, too. How shall we go about it?'

'I don't think it will prove too difficult a problem,' commented her friend as she pulled on her dress. 'Let's find out what Mr Formbey has to say and we'll think about Tim Fletcher afterwards.'

Mr Formbey sat at the head of the table and looked benignly at his assembled staff. Estelle and Lizzie were the last to scamper through the door and Mr Formbey motioned them to sit on the floor whilst he delivered his address: 'Now everybody, I've called you all together because the master of this house, His Excellency Count Gewirtz –'

'The gobbling Galician!' interrupted a voice from the corner where Nicholas the coachman and Christopher the page were standing. The boy let out a snigger and Mr Formbey glared at the pair. 'I want no more of that kind of talk – ever. You all know on what generous terms we have been engaged on by Count Gewirtz and we owe him our total loyalty, obedience and respect.

'And I'll remind one and all that besides the wages, we'll be given a fat bonus if the Count likes the way we run things here. We'll all have to work very hard, though it'll be well worth it if all goes well. But it won't be free and easy, I'll tell you that for nothing. So if there's anyone who doesn't want to stay, now's the time to say so. I'll contact Mr Edwards of the Aspiso Agency and he'll pay out a week's wages to anyone who hands in their notice today.'

There was a deep silence until the errant cockney coachman gave an embarrassed cough and said: 'Sorry, Mr Formbey, I was aht of order by passing that remark. You're quite right, of course. This 'ere Count Gewirtz is a rum cove though, that's for sure. I mean, did you know that 'e 'as police protection during his stay? Someone I know in the force is on dury every evening from tomorrow until Count Gewirtz leaves London. It was him that told me that the Count was known as wot I called him just now.'

'It wasn't Inspector Glenton Rogers, was it, Nick?' asked Connie Chumbley, remembering her tryst with the randy police officer Mrs Beaconsfield, the equally sinsual cook.

'No, I don't know any Inspectors. This chap's a plain P.C. Frankie Fulham's his name and he's often on traffic duty at Marble Arch.'

'All right, all right,' said Mr Formbey with a touch of irritation. 'At least we now all know where we stand. Now, I have to tell you that the Count will be bringing a lady friend with him tomorrow from Paris. Her name is Mademe Vazelina Volpe and she is a famous artist, a little temperamental, I expect, so Estelle and Lizzie, I want you two to be on your best behaviour. Nick, you don't need to meet him as the Prince of Wales is sending a carriage to Victoria Station to meet them and I dare say His Royal Highness will accompany the Count and Madame Volpe back here.

'Mrs Beaconsfield, I rely on you to provide a tasty tea. They'll probably be too exhausted to want a substantial dinner so I suggest something like a simple soup, white-bait, veal with just three vegetables, a sorbet and fresh fruit. I'll check that all the wines have been delivered satisfactorily.'

The butler mopped his brow and concluded: 'Good luck, everybody; I'm sure everything will turn out for the best and we'll have the opportunity of enjoying ourselves along the way. So long as the first dinner party goes off with a bang, then I'm sure all will be well.'

CHAPTER FIVE

By coincidence, the next morning as Mr Formbey and his team scuttled around putting the final touches to their efforts in making his Green Street abode ship-shape and Bristol fashion, Count Gewirtz paced the first floor deck of the cross-Channel ferry wondering whether he had been hasty in offering hospitality in London to Madame Volpe. She was certainly a fine fuck, thought the Count as he grasped the handrail to look back at the busy port of Calais from which they had set sail just five minutes before.

'But bringing a woman to London is, how does that English saying have it, like bringing coals to Newcastle,' muttered the Count softly to himself. 'A man who cannot find a woman in London must be soft in the head – or more likely soft in the cock!'

'What did you day, Your Excellency?' boomed a hearty voice behind him and Count Gewirtz turned round to see a portly gentleman in full morning dress complete with top hat, standing just a couple of feet away.

He squinted into the sunlight and then broke into a grin as he recognised his companion. 'For heaven's sake, it's Tommy Arbarthnot unless I'm very much mistaken,' said the handsome Continental aristocrat. 'We haven't met since Major-General Newman's Summer Ball in Sussex two years ago when His Royal Highness the Prince of Wales and . . .'

The Count's voice trailed off into silence as he suddenly remembered that the final image of HRH was that of the Prince enjoying the royal cock being sucked by none other than the pretty young wife of Tommy Arbarthnot who was at the same time receiving from between her bum cheeks the substantial shaft of the Duke of Cambridge in her cunney whilst she manipulated in each hand the throbbing cocks of Lord Hampstead and the Bishop of Brighton.

'Christ, what a wonderful memory you have, Count. Still it was a splendidly enjoyable evening,' said Lord Arbarthnot who appeared quite unruffled by Johnny Gewirtz's recall of that orgiastic affair. 'I'm working for HRH these days, y'know, as a special equerry and I've been commanded to welcome you to our sceptred isle and all that business in style. A private carriage awaits us on the London train when we get to Dover and the Prince wants you to come straight to see him before you go to Green Street. Don't worry, I'll have three men on hand to look after all your luggage.'

'That's very kind of you, Tommy. But I should tell you that I am not travelling alone.'

'Yes, I know that you are taking Vazelina Volpe to London. HRH is particularly pleased as he wants to meet the lady himself. When I told him that Madame was accompanying you he was absolutely delighted – and so was I. I cannot think of anything better to do than pleasing Prince Tum Tum.'

[*Tum Tum was the affectionate nickname for the Prince of Wales, later Edward VII, whose ample appetites led his developing a portly figure by the time he was thirty five – L.L.*]

Count Gewirtz stared hard at the courtier and said: 'You must forgive me, Tommy, but between ourselves, I cannot for the life of me see what the Prince has done to deserve such loyalty. After all, not to beat about the bush as I think your British saying goes, you know that I know that the Prince of Wales fucked your wife at Major General Newman's Ball. No, forgive me, I should never have brought up this delicate matter. Please accept my sincere apology.'

'No, no, no, I don't mind at all,' exclaimed Tommy Arbarthnot. 'I regard it as a very great honour to my household and the whole business helped me out of a personal spot of bother as well.'

'Really,' said the Count, genuinely interested in hearing more of this strange tale. 'How long has the affair been going on?'

'Since last January,' replied his companion as they slowly walked across the empty first class deck. 'It started during a country house weekend party at Sir Ronnie Dunn's place in Hertfordshire. On Saturday afternoon I decided to take a walk through the woods alone to ponder over a serious problem. For some reason my old pego hadn't been working as well as I or my wife would have liked. You know that Sylvia is much younger than me and I was upset that I couldn't fuck her as often or as well as she would have liked. Mind, she is a dear girl and never complained when, even *after* she had sucked my cock, I couldn't keep it up.

'I wandered around for a while but then the snow began to fall quite heavily so I turned back after just half an hour or so. When I returned to the house I heard a buzz of chatter in the living room and found some of the guests enjoying a joke from Sir Ronnie who, as you know, is perhaps the best raconteur in London Society. I messed the end of the story he had just told but as I came in he called out: "Ah, Tommy, just the man. Will you answer a question for me – why can't a Jew ever become a Morris Dancer?" I replied that I had not the faintest idea. "Because, old boy," he said triumphantly, "because to be a Morris dancer you have to be a complete prick!"

'We all laughed heartily at this witticism and I looked around for Sylvia, my wife but she, the Prince of Wales and several other gentlemen were missing from the gay company. I took my leave and looked into the games room where I found two of the absent guests engaged in a game of billiards. I decided to go to our suite and lie down for an hour as the evening was bound to be a hectic affair. In case Sylvia had also had the same idea, I opened the door as quietly as possible and shut it behind me also with the minimum of noise.

'At first I thought my ears were deceiving me for I could have sworn I heard the sound of giggling from the bedroom. I stepped quietly to the half open door and straightaway I saw that I had not been hearing things. There, spreadeagled on the bed, lay my wife, totally nude, her large breasts swinging free and her legs wide open to reveal her long crack that protruded from the black thatch of hair between her legs. Kneeling besides her was none other than HRH smoking a large cigar and clad only in a pair of drawers. Sylvia was brazenly fondling the crotch of his shorts. He put the cigar in an ash tray and lay down besides her, his naked cock now thrusting upwards out of the hole in his pants. He turned to suck at her rosy nipples and slid his hand into her moist muff as he arched his back to aid my wife pull off his drawers.

'She then grasped his thick shaft and worked it up and down with long, slow strokes, the way she had rubbed mine many times, stopping to squeeze it occasionally to test the hard strength. I felt my own cock rising and, as if in a dream, I took out my own tool and began stroking it in time with the rhythm with which my wife was stroking the royal prick.

'Right in front of my eyes they began to fuck with complete abandon. At first my wife was on all fours over him, her head bobbing up and down as she slid his thick prick in and out of her mouth, rubbing her nipples against his groin whilst he was under her, his hands round her hips and parting the cheeks of her bum as his tongue darted in and licked and lapped at the entire length of her long, juicy slit.

'The Prince then threw himself over her and knelt between her thighs as she spread her legs apart and then wrapped them round his back. "Now as my cock enters your cunt I shall tickle your little bum-hole," said the Prince in a hoarse voice. My wife let out a gasp of pleasure as his prick slid into her and entered her in one long, deep thrust. She let out a little cry and then they set about humping and bumping as I rubbed my own shaft excitedly, shooting out a stream of sperm just as the Prince pulled his prick out of my wife's cunney and spunked copiously over her titties.

'He dressed almost immediately afterwards as he said

that he had better go downstairs or people might guess that he had been upstairs with her. I slipped into the bathroom and he did not see me as he closed the door behind him.

'I waited a couple of minutes and this time opened and closed the door normally. Sylvia was still lying naked, dozing on the bed and the memory of what I had just witnessed made my blood boil and my prick was rock hard as I threw off my clothes and to her great delight fucked her most beautifully. Her pussey was still juicy from the Prince's jism and soon we were grunting and groaning so loudly that the guests downstairs must surely have heard us. She begged me to pump into her again and again and I responded by thrusting so hard that her bottom cheeks banged against my thighs and I thought that my balls would be sucked into her wildly jerking pussey. We screamed with delight as I shot a huge fountain of white frothy love-juice into her adorable cunney.

'Since then I have deliberately absented myself when I know that the Prince and my wife could find time to be together. If possible I try to sneak in for a look but since that fateful day I have never had any trouble in making my prick swell up. Just thinking about how another man had enjoyed my wife's beautiful body gives me a terrific cockstand in seconds.

'So you see, Johnny, that I shall always be eternally grateful to the Prince of Wales for fucking my wife!' ended the grateful courtier.

Live long enough and you hear everything, thought Count Gewirtz to himself. 'Well, I'm delighted that your story has a happy ending. Let's go down and pay our compliments to Madame Volpe. But I must warn you,

Tommy, that if I find anyone, from the Prince of Wales to the cabin boy in bed with her I shan't be as tolerant as you!'

'Oh dear, I hope I have not offended you.'

Count Gewirtz grinned and said: 'In no way, Tommy. My opinion is exactly the same as Mrs Patrick Campbell's – consorting adults must be free to fuck as they like, so long as they don't do it in the street and frighten the horses!'

The two men strode downstairs to the Count's cabin where Madame Volpe was lying on the bed reading a copy of a Continental newspaper.

'*Ach, Johann, wo warst du*?' she exclaimed.

'Speak English, my love,' replied her mentor. 'Not only are we now in British territorial waters but we have an English guest.

'Vazelina, may I introduce Lord Thomas Arbarthnot, special equerry to His Royal Highness, the Prince of Wales. Lord Arthbarthnot, Madame Volpe.'

After the formal introductions had been made, Madame Volpe said: 'Lord Artbarthnot –'

'Oh, call me Tommy, please Madame.'

'Thank you – well, Tommy it does seem to me to be rather unfair that we Europeans must always speak English whilst you Britishers appear unable by and large to learn any foreign languages at all except a little French and Latin.'

'Are we, as insular as all that? Johnny, I appeal to you to judge the matter.'

'I'm afraid that I must side with Vazelina,' said Count Gewirtz carefully. 'Mind, a dear friend of mine is old Sir Henry Layard, the archeologist who discovered Nineveh. Unfortunately he is rather ill and I must visit him on this trip. Anyhow, Henry speaks Arabic and Farsi perfectly as well as other European tongues.'

'And he is an Englishman?' enquired Madame Volpe.

'Ah, well, he sat in the House of Commons but I must admit that he was not exactly of pure British stock. If I recall correctly his mother was Spanish, his early upbringing French and his education was completed in Italy.'

[*Sir Henry Layard was a famous archaeologist and politician who after retirement was sent briefly to Turkey to be the British Ambassador in Constantinople by Disraeli. Sir Henry died in July, 1894, a year almost to the day after Count Gewirtz visited him at his London home – L.L.*]

'He cannot be counted as British then,' said Vazelina Volpe triumphantly. 'After all, you cannot call him British.'

'Oh, I don't know,' ruminated Count Gewirtz. 'After all, if a man was born in a stable that does not make him a horse! But I will admit that Sir Henry is an exception to the rule and that far too many Englishmen cannot converse in any language but their own.'

Madame Volpe took a large sip of brandy from the glass by her bed and from her slightly slurred speech it was obvious to both the gentlemen that, to use the appropriate nautical term, she was three sheets to the wind.

'Speaking French and German is something the British don't do well,' she announced. 'And Tommy, I hope you will forgive my saying so, but I'm afraid that when it comes to eating pussey, you Englishmen don't do very well either.'

'Is that so?' said Tommy Arbarthnot politely. 'Do you speak from practical experience, Madame?'

'I most certainly do. I have enjoyed men from all over Europe and the United States and though I grant that Scotsmen especially are well endowed when it comes to size, even they don't use their equipment to the best advantage.'

'So what do you suggest they do about this lack of expertise?' said Count Gewirtz lightly.

'Well, for a start, I think that your French friend Doctor David Lezaine's little book *Fucking for Beginners* ought to be distributed free to all Englishmen over the age of eighteen. Mind the best way to learn is to actually see a master fucker like Johnny Gewirtz in action rather than pore over the pages of a book, even one as well written by Doctor Lezaine.'

Tommy Arbarthnot's eyes gleamed in anticipation as he said: 'You make a very point there, Vazelina. Why, I was saying to Johnny only a few minutes ago how much I learned from seeing the Prince of Wales's prick on bedroom duty. Nothing would give me greater pleasure than to see a true expert at work.'

Count Gewirtz sighed and said: 'Are you asking me to show you how I won my reputation as a lover?'

Madame Volpe licked her lips and said: 'I don't see why we should disappoint Lord Arbarthnot – as the Chinese say: "It is better to travel hopefully than to arrive" and we have at least another hour to kill aboard this little ship.'

'My goodness, you are both so kind. It certainly shows the worth of daring to ask,' murmured the noble Lord as he made himself comfortable in an armchair.

'Oh, very well,'said the Count good-naturedly as he unbuttoned his shirt. 'Vazelina, take off your clothes.'

'I only fuck in the nude,' he added to Lord Arbarthnot who was already leaning forward in his chair, his eyes gleaming with anticipation.

Vazelina Volpe slipped down from the bed and quickly undressed, bending to one side and the other and lastly, forward. When she straightened up her superb naked body glowed in the subdued light, shadowed in mystery and toned to excite. Both Lord Arbarthnot and the Count gasped with admiration at the lissom suppleness of her curves. The thought flashed through the mind of the handsome Galician that she had grown even prettier since he had first fucked her four months ago in the spacious apartment situated in a pretty square off the Champs Elysée, which he had purchased on extremely favourable terms in 1889 from the Duc de Teguise.

Her chestnut locks fell thickly to her shoulders which appeared to the two men to be of a dazzling whiteness. Her nose was neither too long nor too short, being enhanced by large liquid blue eyes that seemed to hold a smouldering took of sensuality. The Count feasted his eyes upon the proud thrust of her full, uptilted breasts that were crowned by the lush red nipples that were already pouting out their firmness, the snowy white belly and the fluffy crisp thatching of brown hair that nestled between her ivory-columned thighs.

This vision of feminine allure turned and bent down to sweep up her clothes that had fallen to the floor. Her bottom was a perfect peach, its firm dimpled cheeks sent the Count's cock swelling up to the hardness of steel. He shrugged off his trousers and drawers with difficulty and his prick stood as high as a flagpole, the head rubicund and gleaming as Vazelina turned and jumped back on the bed, her legs splayed out, waiting for her lover to perform his devotions at the Temple of Venus.

'Go to it, Johnny, fuck the arse off her,' Tommy Arbarthnot whispered hotly though unnecessarily, for in truth Count Gewirtz needed no extra encouragement. He vaulted athletically upon the bed and knelt between Vazelina's long legs. He placed his hand first upon her thickly-curled bush and then he leaned over her and their mouths joined in the sweetest of kisses. Now his hands roamed as he fondled her plump breasts and ran his palms across the upturned nipples. His eyes shone with passion as he glided a hand between her thighs and she writhed in response as a questing finger slid into her already-moist cunney.

The Count broke off the embrace to caress with attentive lips first her throat and then, moving from side to side, to suck in turn each quivering nipple that jutted out. Gradually he eased his mouth down to the mossy bush of brown hair that covered her cunney lips. He buried his face between her thighs and she clasped his head between her legs as he nuzzled her pussey with his lips and tongue, causing the delightful girl to moan sensuously with delight and her pussey moistened at the touch of the Count's questing tongue.

Lord Arbarthnot's right hand flew to his fly buttons which he ripped open to clutch hold of his throbbing cock as he heard Count Gewirtz's tongue licking and lapping around the labia of this gorgeous girl who ran her hands along the Count's head while she urged him to lick harder. He placed his lips over her jerking little clitty and sucked it into his mouth where the tip of his tongue began to explore it from all directions. This triggered an uncontrollable little scream from Vazelina as a tremendous spend shuddered through her body and her pussey drenched the Count's face in a spray of love juice and huge waves of orgasm swept through her entire body.

She unclasped her legs from around his neck and the Count rolled back and let the delicious girl take hold of his hot, rigid rod at the base of his shaft. She kissed the smooth, velvety dome of his knob where a small bead of liquor already stood in tribute to the passion to come and then sucked in at least six inches of his throbbing tool, letting the knob slide against her cheek as she slurped noisily on her succulent sweetmeat.

'Ah! Aah, Aaah, Aaaah! I'm coming, I'm coming, Vazelina! Here I go!' choked the Count, his dark eyes full of fire as his shaft trembled and shot great jets of frothy spunk into Vazelina's mouth while she sucked and smacked her lips with great gusto and the creamy love juice flowed down her throat.

This was too much for Lord Arbarthnot to bear. He was now standing not more than a foot away from the bed and his hand moved up and down his shaft at an increasing speed until he, too, spent and his fountain of sperm arced upwards before raining down upon the lovers. Unfortunately, some drops landed in Count Gewirtz's eye but the resourceful Galician nobleman wiped away the offending liquid on Lord Arbarthnot's shirt.

'You have seen the *hors d'oeuvres,*' panted Madame Volpe. 'Now sit back and enjoy the *entrée*.'

Lord Arbarthnot resumed his place in the armchair as

the loving couple resumed their exquisite love-making. Vazelina soon sucked up the Count's prick to its former startling thickness while he played with her juicy pussey, dipping his fingers in and out of the delicious dampness.

Then the Count mounted her and guided home his ramrod cock between her aching cunney lips. Directing every centimetre of his sizeable shaft snugly inside her pussey, she closed her thighs, making Johnny Gewirtz open his own legs and lie astride her with his prick well and truly trapped inside her cunt. 'Note well this position,' panted Vazelina Volpe across the cabin to Teddy Arbarthnot. 'I love to do it this way as the sensation is so pleasing to both of us.'

The Count could hardly pump in and out of her pussey because her cunney muscles were gripping him so tightly but then, as she began to grind her hips round, his cock was massaged exquisitely. It throbbed powerfully inside her juicy pussey which was dribbling their spendings down her thighs. He sank his fingers into the cheeks of her soft bum, inserting the tip of his finger into her bottom-hole which made her squeal and wriggle in a new ecstasy of passion. She shifted her thighs and, as the pressure around his prick eased, the Count began to drive wildly in and out, fucking at such an intense speed that Teddy Arbarthnot marvelled at the style and how he managed to refrain from spunking into that delicious crack.

Meanwhile Vazelina Volpe was being brought off time and time again, working herself up to a magnificent climax as the fierce momentum sent her pussey into new heights of delight. She brought her legs up against the small of the Count's broad back, humping the lower half of her body upwards to meet the violent strokes of his raging prick. He bore down on her yet again, his body now gleaming with perspiration, fucking harder and harder, the rippling movement of his cock playing lustily against the velvety walls of her cunt. Then suddenly the end approached, he tensed his frame and with a cry he crashed down upon the girl, his shaft jetting spasms of spunk streaming inside her slit as she quickly squeezed her thighs together and milked every last drop from his spurting length, not releasing him until his staff began to shrink and he pulled it out of her sopping cunney.

They lay exhausted on the bed as Lord Arbarthnot, who unlike the Count, could not even keep his shaft stiff after spunking let alone being able to spend twice in a short time, broke into a round of applause. 'My cabin is only a moment's walk away. Turn right and it is the fourth door on the left, number forty-seven. If you would care to join me there after you have dressed I will have champagne and caviare waiting for you.'

The trio sat sipping champagne and picking daintily at the caviare thoughtfully provided by Lord Arbarthnot for the remainder of the journey. Madame Volpe regaled the gentlemen with a fascinating account of her last love affair with the gifted violinist and music teacher Doctor Harold Hodfrey, who as you probably know was a great friend of the composer Robert Schumann.

'I thought he was happily married to the famous mezzo-soprano Mavis Balloney,' said Count Gewirtz mildly.

'So he is and of course she must never be told of our little affair,' said Vazelina, draining her glass of champagne. 'It was quite fascinating really for several reasons.

For a start, I was only eighteen at the time, studying in Germany under the great Professor Webowski. Doctor Hodfrey was in Germany to receive an honorory degree in music from the University of Frankfurt and afterwards he agreed to give a short series of lectures at the conservatorium. He was already well into his fiftieth decade but after the second lecture when a group of us met him at a reception given by Professor Webowski, I thought he looked down my admittedly low-cut dress with more than a glimmer of interest.

'Soon we were on first name terms and Harold invited me to come back to his rooms later that evening when, as a special treat, he would show me his Stradivarius. In my innocence I accepted his invitation and indeed later that evening he did show me his instrument – though he never took his violin out of its case!' she added with a hoarse little laugh.

'This sounds a most interesting anecdote,' observed Lord Arbarthnot. 'I saw him perform with his quartet at the Albert hall only three years ago at one of Bailey's gigantic benefit concerts.'

'Well, his performance with me was strictly solo, or rather a duo,' drily remarked Madame Volpe. 'In his room he plied me with champagne and the finest delicacies and in no time at all I found myself sitting next to the great man on a couch, his arm wrapped round me and answering all kinds of intimate questions that he was firing at me.'

'Really, how odd. What sort of question do you mean?' asked Count Gewirtz.

'Oh, you would both be surprised. I don't pretend to recall them all but I am sure that one of the first was:

"Tell me, my dear, do you have a preference for huge cocks?" Well, *in vino veritas*, (*in wine there is truth - L.L.*), and I told him bluntly that with present company excepted - for your cock is one of the biggest I have ever taken inside me, Johnny - I preferred smaller pricks. In my experience they get so much harder and they appear to be more manoeuvrable when thrusting into a juicy, slippery pussey.

'How pleased I am to hear you say so,' said a delighted Tommy Arbarthnot. 'I have always suffered from a feeling of inferiority as my cock only measures five and a quarter inches.'

'Don't worry, Tommy, it's not the size of the waves, it's the motion of the ocean,' responded Vazelina Volpe brightly. 'Anyhow, I do remember that he then asked me which were my favourite positions for fucking. I told him that I enjoyed the good old standard missionary position with my legs wrapped around my man's waist or neck as I love to kiss and be able to see my partner when we make love. Mind, I do enjoy fucking doggie-style occasionally as variety is the spice of life.'

'The dirty old devil!' exclaimed Count Gewirtz. 'I expect he then asked if he could fuck you and made some extravagant promise of reward.'

Vazelina laughed and said: 'How did you guess? He said that he would pay for a trip round Europe for myself and a friend if I sucked his cock and let him fuck me.'

'Did you?' enquired Lord Arbarthnot.

'Yes, but because I wanted to and not for any financial or other inducement,' she replied.

'Oh, do tell us all about it,' said Lord Arbarthnot. 'I do so enjoy listening to a randy tale. It's almost as good as watching the Prince of Wales fuck my dear lady wife.'

'Very well, let's sit down here and I will recount the experience in detail. It was so agreeable that it gives me great pleasure to think about Harold Hodfrey who was a most charming and attentive lover,' said Madame Volpe brightly. 'Are you sitting comfortably? Then I'll begin . . .

'I did not waste too much time in preliminaries once I had decided to accede to Harold's request. I went across and sat on his lap and I gently caressed the bulge between his legs. He gasped and I saw such a sensual look on his face that I knew he was genuinely excited. This made me feel very excited, too, and I felt wet between my legs. So I jumped off his lap and told him to close his eyes whilst I disappeared behind the Chinese screen that stood in a corner of the room.

'When I came out I was stark naked and I called out: "Harold, you can open your eyes now." He did so and *Mein Gott*! His eyes nearly popped from his head as I ran my hands up and down my body, squeezing my breasts and tweaking my nipples so that that stood up like little red bullets. "Now you too must undress completely," I murmured. Harold obeyed my command with commendable alacrity as I sprawled out in front of him on the cushions I had draped on the carpet whilst he tore off his clothes.

'Harold stood there, his long prick bobbing with excitement whilst I continued to caress my body. I opened my legs wide and drew up my knees, showing him a glimpse of my glistening pussey. I stroked my cunney lips slowly and Harold licked his lips as I slid one, two and three fingers into my aching cunt. My juices were already running down my open, spreadeagled thighs as I said: "Come here, Harold and kneel besides me with your nice thick cock next to my face, for although my pussey is dying to meet your shaft I think you want something else first, don't you?"

'I grasped hold of his hot, hard staff and opening my mouth I slipped in the luscious knob, enclosing my lips around it as firmly as I could, working on the ultra-sensitive tip with my tongue. I eased my lips wide to swallow another inch or two as my hands circled the base of this gigantic shaft, working the loose skin up and down while I began to bob my head up and down in a slow rhythm. Now I cupped his balls in one hand and kept his shaft from twitching too much with the other. I sucked away lustily as I savoured his juices, my soft tongue rolling over the dome.

'Somehow I managed to coax practically all his shaft into my mouth and I sucked noisily until I felt the sperm boil up inside that bursting prick and then I knew he was about to spend. Harold could contain himself no longer and he thrust his hips forward and spurted a stream of white frothy juice into my mouth. I tried as hard as I could to swallow all of his tangy spunk but some of his precious fluids dripped from my lips onto the cushions. "Never mind," cried Harold for he correctly judged that I was concerned about staining the material. "I will dab some of Professor Kidderminster's Famous Elixir on the cushions. I have used it for years as a laxative for my servants, a cough remedy for my horses and as a most effective spot-remover."

'I swallowed as much of his creamy emission as I could and continued to suck his delicious cock until it went limp in my mouth. "I do love sucking a good thick cock,' I told Harold. "It is almost as good as getting fucked but most men squirt off too quickly. I do like a man like you who shoots off great spurts of spunk and yours tastes absolutely delicious."

' "Does it really?" exclaimed Harold. "I am so pleased that you enjoyed it. But now I can feel my shaft rising again and I would very very much like to fuck you." "It will be my pleasure," I said, clambering over to sit astride him, gripping his head and body between my feet and lifting my dripping crack directly over his mouth for a good licking. Harold's face was buried in my bushy mound as he rapturously lapped the juices of my sopping pussey and then his tongue found my clitty and I writhed in uninhibited ecstasy as he sucked furiously on my erect little clitty which throbbed under the ministrations of his wicked tongue. We knew that the time had arrived for the *coup de grâce* and he wriggled free as I turned over on my back and opened my legs to await his huge battering ram. He took hold of his cock and nudged the knob against my pussey lips. I was so juicy that he entered me easily, sliding his cock deep, deep inside my cunt. Gently at first his shaft moved in and out in slow thrusts and ah, what delights I savoured as I felt his massive tool push in and withdraw, push in and withdraw and how exciting was the sound of the slurp as our juices eased the passage of his prick.

'Then Harold began to work up a faster pace, burying himself inside me with deep, strong thrusts that mashed my clitty against his pubic bone, making me spend yet again. He held us together very still, smiling as my spasms stopped as I lay there gasping for breath. Now he began to stroke his prick in and out, penetrating with lightning force and speed. He managed to keep this up for maybe thirty seconds or so and then with one almighty heave he groaned and I felt his body stiffen. A second later, my pussey was flooded with a boiling river of his spunk and I screamed out my ecstasy as a truly superb spend coursed through me and his gushes of juice creamed my cunney in a glorious mutual orgasm.

'I can tell you that Harold Hodfrey was one of my ten best fucks,' concluded Madame Volpe. 'He proved to me that – how does the English proverb put it – there are plenty of good tunes to be played on an older instrument.'

Count Gewirtz thought briefly about offering his pretty lady a further spearing upon his aristocratic member but decided instead that the three of them should prepare for disembarkation. 'I have no servants travelling with us,' he told Tommy Arbarthnot, 'although I must say Captain Allendale has been most attentive and has assured me that a guard has been kept over our luggage which will be the first pieces to be taken off the ship.'

'Jolly good. I assure you that your journey to London will be even smoother than this sea-crossing,' promised Lord Arbarthnot.

And the Prince of Wales' equerry was as good as his word. All travel formalities were waved aside for the threesome and in no time at all they were approaching Charing Cross Station. There the stationmaster himself was on hand to escort the party to the carriage that awaited to whisk them off to see the Prince whilst their luggage was taken by a large van directly to Green Street.

'We're going to Bedford Square where HRH is taking tea with Miss Lily Belsey, the music hall actress, at Sir Ronnie Dunn's house in Bedford Square,' explained Lord Arbarthnot as the carriage turned into Great Russell Street from Tottenham Court Road. 'He has to meet her away from the Palace, of course, as she is too common to mix with Society.'

'Balls! Why do you have to fashion up such a nonsense, Tommy,' snapped Count Gewirtz. 'He's meeting Lily here as he wants to take her to bed and he can hardly do so in the royal apartments! Really, I do so tire of your English snobbery. Why, in Europe, I assure you, things are far better arranged.'

Lord Arbarthnot smiled weakly as the carriage drew up outside the entrance to one of the fine Georgian town houses in Bedford Square. A uniformed policeman stood outside the door of number sixty-nine ('A most suitable number for both Sir Ronnie and the Prince,' commented Count Gewirtz whose uncharacteristic little bout of irritability had been brought on by indigestion and the fact that he too had coveted the pretty Miss Belsey but had no intention of vying for her favours with the Prince of Wales.) A flunkey ushered them into the lounge where Prince Edward was standing with his back to the fireplace, a cigar in one hand and a glass of whisky in the other.

'Ah, ha, Johnny Gewirtz, how good to see you again,' he boomed out in his deep gutteral tone. 'When did we last meet now? Why it must have been last summer at my sister Beatrice's birthday party in Windsor Park! You remember, Johnny, that the damned rain suddenly descended upon us and you kindly sheltered my mother from the storm with your jacket. My God, how time flies! Are you keeping well, my old friend? No doubt you are still basking in the compliment paid to you by Princess Yokle of Moravia at the Kaiser's party in Berlin last year. What was it again? Oh, yes, in her opinion and in the opinion of twenty-eight princesses and other ladies of quality from the courts of Central Europe, no other man can match the talent of Count Gewirtz in *l 'arte de faire l 'amour*.'

'It is always pleasant to visit London and always an honour and pleasure to see you, Your Royal Highness,' smiled the Count, now restored to his usual good humour by the huge compliment paid to him.

'So this must be the beautiful Madame Volpe, the most distinguished singer in all Europe and currently the toast of Paris.' Prince Edward continued. 'Please introduce us immediately.'

'But of course. Madame Vazelina Volpe, I have the honour to present you to His Royal Highness, Prince Edward,' said Count Gewirtz.

The Prince took hold of Madame Volpe's outstretched arm and kissed her hand. '*Enchanté, Madame. Bitte, mochst du deutsch sprechen? Ou vous préférez français peut-être*?'

'Oh, English is very acceptable and most appropriate since we are in your presence,' simpered Madame Volpe, fluttering her long eye-lashes at the Prince.

'Are you sure? I speak German very well. After all, it is a language I have heard spoken all around me since my childhood. In their domestic life my parents spoke probably more German than English. My French is not quite so fluent though I am able to improvise effective little speeches when necessary.'

'His Royal Highness belies your comment earlier today that we Englishmen do not speak other people's languages,' chimed in Lord Arbarthnot.

The Prince turned and glared at him and growled: 'Tommy, go and busy yourself with something or other until my guests leave. Then I will find some other menial tasks for you to perform.'

The crestfallen equerry slunk out of the room as the Prince turned back to Count Gewirtz and continued: 'I know you have not even yet set foot in your house in Green Street, Johnny, but I did want to see you before tomorrow night's party. Princess Alexandra will be with Mama at a dreary concert in aid of some good cause but I said that I would be with the Arbarthnots. Now Gertrude Arbarthnot and I have an understanding and Tommy won't breathe a word to a living soul about where I will actually be which, of course, is with you in Green Street,' he continued.

'You can rely on our total discretion,' said Count Gewirtz. 'Will you be joining us alone or with a companion?'

'A good question, indeed, and the answer, my dear Count, is that I shall be accompanied by the pretty little filly who is standing behind you.'

Both Count Gewirtz and Madame Volpe turned round to stare at the extraordinarily attractive blonde girl who had quietly entered the room during the conversation. The Prince continued: 'Count Johann Gewirtz of Galicia, Madame Vazelina Volpe of Paris and Berlin, I have the pleasure of presenting to you Miss Lily Belsey of London, known to us in England as the prettiest little showgirl ever to grace our theatres.'

Madame Volpe smiled at the girl whilst Count Gewirtz took her hand and murmured: '*Enchanté*, Miss Belsey. I have admired you from my box at the Alhambra many a time. The last time I was in London I saw you in ''Kisses By Moonlight'' and I enjoyed your performance so much that I rebooked my box for the next night.'

'Did you really?' said the delighted Miss Belsey. 'I am so pleased you enjoyed the show so much. I don't suppose you were the gentleman who sent round a dozen red roses with an anonymous note to ask me whether –'

'Yes, well, never mind all that,' interrupted the Prince with hint of asperity. 'You can ask him all about that tomorrow night. You see, my dear, the Count is giving a most select dinner party at his home in Mayfair and I would be delighted if you would come with me. I warn you, though, that you may have to sing for your supper.'

'Oh, how marvellous, sir, I would love to go,' said Miss Belsey happily, curtsying slightly to the Prince. 'Is it all very formal? What sort of dress should I wear?'

'Some frock that is easy to take off,' grunted the Prince. 'Madame Volpe, Johnny, I know you will want to unpack so I won't detain you any longer. I look forward very much to seeing you tomorrow night.'

They took their leave of the Prince and the showgirl and were soon at Green Street where Mr Formbey was waiting in the hall to welcome them and to present the staff who were lined up in the hallway to greet their employer. After making the introductions Mr Formbey asked the Count if he wished to say a few words.

'I only want to say this – I don't believe any of you have worked for me before. Now, I expect total devotion to duty and I expect that you will all be working very hard for, as I will be in London only a short time, Mr Formbey has been instructed to employ only a skeleton staff.

'However, whilst I demand the highest standards of efficiency, I will not stint in showing my appreciation to you when I return to Paris in about three week's time. One final piece of advice: if anyone finds the work too onerous or the terms of employment not to their liking, tell Mr Formbey immediately. He has my ear at all times. Now, Mr Formbey, Mrs Beaconsfield, please spare me ten minutes to run through the menu for tomorrow night. We will have to be on our toes, for the Prince of Wales is honouring us with his presence and we must pull out all the stops.'

At the breakfast table the next day Sir Paul Arkley was browsing through the sports pages of *The Times* when his younger daughter, Penny, asked him about any arrangements he and Mama had planned for that evening.

'Why do you wish to know, Penelope? Have you or Katherine any plans for tonight about which I am unaware?' broke in the gimlet-eyed Lady Arkley.

'Certainly not, Mama, I just enquired out of idle curiosity,' said Penny in as innocent a voice as she could muster.

Lady Arkley's eyes narrowed but she refrained from further comment as Sir Paul answered: 'As it happens, I shall be dining with Count Johann Gewirtz in Mayfair.

'Rather a nuisance, really,' he added shamelessly. 'But some important people will be there and no doubt I will spend a boring evening discussing some wretched international political business. However, your Mama has been invited to a reception given by the League of Ladies Committee of the Royal Free Hospital to raise money for whatever is needed these days. Princess Alexandra is the guest of honour but your Mama can no doubt provide you with fuller details. Of course I shall miss her company at Count Gewirtz's but she rightly believes that she must support her Committee.'

'Yes, your Papa and I will both be dining out tonight and I am grateful to you for raising the matter, Penelope. Perhaps you and Katherine will now inform us of any arrangements you may have made,' said Lady Arkley grimly.

'Mine are very simple, Mama. Walter Stanton has been asked to bring a partner and dine at Sir Heddon and Lady Court's home this evening. It is their daughter Louise's twentieth birthday tomorrow and a group of young people have been asked to come round for a little surprise party. I have accepted Walter's invitation to accompany him,' said Katie.

'Yet I do not recall you asking my permission for such an outing,' said Lady Arkley.

'I was going to tell you about it later this morning. It is all perfectly respectable and Papa plays bridge with Sir Heddon at the Cockfosters Club so I am hardly venturing into the unknown. I waited until the last minute to tell you and Papa because Louise's parents are trying to ensure that the gathering will come as a complete surprise to Louise who at present is under the illusion that she is to be taken to the self-same reception where you are bound, Mama.'

'That's understandable,' said Sir Paul hastily for

neither his wife nor daughters were cognisant of his dalliance with Marie, a pert French waitress at the Cockfosters Club, and he was more than happy to change the flow of conversation as quickly as possible. 'But how about you, Penny? It seems sad that you will be here all alone whilst your sister, Mama and I are out enjoying ourselves.'

'You need not fret, Papa, I shall not be alone. Alicia Marchmont-Clarke is coming round for supper and afterwards we will, practise our piano duets for Mrs Durie's charity concert next week.

Her reply, which was truthful as far as it went, satisfied her parents and the rest of the day passed off uneventfully in Hyde Park Gardens, though elsewhere certain events are worthy of record.

Walter Stanton spent the latter part of the morning in study but at half past twelve decided to take a break from his labours and partake of a light luncheon at the Rawalpindi Club. He was sitting alone in the bar, sipping a whisky and soda, when in walked Alexandra Boxe-Meredith and 'Madcap' Molly Farquhar, by far the most outrageous girls in all London. Indeed, Walter had not realised just how liberated these ladies were until two months previously when he discovered through the Club's newsletter that in one afternoon the naughty pair had deflowered every boy in the Fifth Form at Nottsgrove Academy, that select private school near Barnet in Hertfordshire much favoured by the cream of English Society.

'May I offer you ladies some liquid refreshment?' enquired Walter politely, rising to his feet.

'How about a double spunk on the rocks?' suggested Molly with a loud laugh.

'I don't think Walter Stanton goes in for fucking,' retorted Alexandra gaily. 'I wouldn't be at all surprised if he were still *virgo intacto*.'

'Is that so, Walter?' giggled Molly. 'I do love fucking virgin boys. Is it true you have never poked a girl?'

The young man flushed with embarrassment and said: 'If you believe that, you will believe that Man will someday plant a flag on the Moon. However, I will nevertheless repeat my question. Would either of you ladies like a drink?'

'And I will repeat my answer – a double spunk on the rocks!' cried Molly who in all fairness had just finished a bottle of champagne in the company of Oscar Wilde in the plush setting of the Club lounge. But though champagne acted as a powerful aphrodisiac upon Molly, the plump man of letters had not responded when she placed her hand upon his flaccid penis. 'Walter, I mean it, let all three of us now retire to a *salle privée* and enjoy each others bodies for an hour or so. I was only teasing you – please don't hold it against me.'

'No, stick it in her pussey instead! But it sounds like a good idea to me, Molly. What do you think, Walter?' said Alexandra, slipping her hand between Walter's legs to feel his substantial cock and balls. 'Come on, now, do be a good chap and please the ladies.

'Barman, send round a magnum of the house champagne and three glasses to the Chelsea Suite immediately,' she added without even waiting for his reply.

'Oh my account, Oliver,' Molly called out as Molly took hold of the young man's arm. 'No, no, Walter, I insist. My Papa allows me £500 a year for entertainment and there's plenty left in the kitty. You can buy me champagne once you have passed your examinations for the Institute.'

This warm-hearted gesture could not be ignored and Walter allowed himself to be marched off to one of the Rawalpindi's well-appointed private rooms. Moments later the champagne arrived in an ice bucket and after the servant had closed the door. Molly felt the bottle and said: 'H'm, not cold enough yet – it won't be drinkable for half an hour at least. So, dearest Alex, would you like to fuck Walter straightaway or may I have the first suck of his prick?'

'Oh, please, Molly, I don't mind either way,' replied the gorgeous girl with due politeness.

'Wouldn't you prefer to have his knob between your luscious cunney lips before I suck out his love juices?'

'No, no, no, I insist on waiting upon your pleasure, Molly. After all it was your idea in the first place and you even bought the champagne.'

Walter was stung to interject: 'Well, if you can't make up your minds, why don't you take your luncheon together. After all, it is almost one o'clock.'

'What a splendid idea! That's just what we mean to do,' said Molly, unbuttoning her blouse. 'Quite right,' chimed in Alexandra, climbing out of her skirt to reveal that underneath she was wearing only a pair of crisp white cotton panties.

'You look good enough to eat, Molly,' she continued with undisguised admiration as she feasted her eyes on her friend who now stood naked in front of her. 'Let's go over to the bed,' said Alexandra huskily as the two girls embraced. Walter licked his lips as the two girls kissed and cuddled lasciviously. Molly was totally nude but Alexandra was still wearing her white panties and, ever the gentleman, Walter went across to the bed and pulled them down, exposing her beautifully-rounded bum cheeks which wriggled delightfully when he squeezed them, before taking his place again in the armchair by the side of the bed.

'Oooh, I love to feel your nipples swell up in my palm,' panted Molly. 'Don't you just adore having your breasts caressed, darling? Aaah, that's simply divine.'

They covered each other's mouths with the most passionate of kisses as they fingered each other's pussies. Molly then threw herself backwards on the bed and opened her legs wide as Alexandra moved her head down and nuzzled her lips around her playmate's curly brown pubic bush. 'Ah, what a truly lovely little cunney you have, Molly. My, how warm and inviting it is inside! How it sucks and envelops my fingers! If only I had a prick I would fuck you so beautifully.'

'Darling, ohhhh, darling . . . Alex . . . that feels so good . . . please, angel, finish me off,' Molly gasped, clutching Alexandra's blonde-haired head in her hands whilst the delicious girl frigged her passionately, burying her mouth in the moist, succulent padding of silky curls until the lovely Molly screamed: Yes! Yes! I'm spending my darling!' and her cunney juices flooded out all over Alexandra's mouth and chin.

'There's no substitute for a woman's touch,' said Alexandra smugly after Molly had completed her spend. 'Men just cannot match our light handling and feminine finesse!'

Molly frowned and said: 'I'm not so sure about whether that is completely true. Girls are usually more skilled at licking and lapping but even though your tongue makes my titties stand up like little bullets, I must admit that I do love having a big, hard cock smothered between my breasts. Oh, how I just adore rubbing a fat knob up and down my nipples just until I think he is ready to shoot his spunk – I don't let him, though, as I like him to straddle me so that his balls are dangling over my breasts and his cock is in my mouth. Then as I suck his shaft I want him to lean back and massage my pussey whilst his ballsack brushes against my nipples. Oh, I must admit that just talking like this makes me so randy.'

'Nothing like making a clean breast of it,' came Walter's voice from the armchair. 'Just let me get undressed and let me relieve your feelings.'

In a trice the handsome young man was on the bed as naked as the two girls who squealed with delight as he kissed each of them in turn, wiggling his tongue inside their mouths as their hands met together, clasped around his rigid cockshaft. 'Fuck Alex whilst I kiss your balls,' whispered Molly as Alexandra scrambled up on her knees and turned round, presenting her exquisite bottom for Walter's delectation.

Molly bent forward and planted a wet kiss on Walter's rubicund knob. She then took hold of the throbbing shaft and teasingly planted the red-plumed helmet between Alexandra's bum cheeks. 'Here we go!' said Molly as she inserted the tip of his knob against Alexandra's pussey lips which gratefully enclosed the top of his dome. 'Brace yourself, darling!' added Molly as she pushed three inches of Walter's thick stiffness into

Alexandra's willing wet cunney which made her friend squeal with delight. Molly then moved her head down to suck Walter's heavy balls as he built up a rhythm, slowly pushing and pulling his glistening prick in and out of her juicy cunt. Her bum cheeks wriggled joyously as Walter drove deeper and deeper, pumping and thrusting as she reached back and spread her cheeks. 'Empty your balls, Walter!' screamed the lovely lass as her own climax exploded whilst Walter pumped spurt after spurt of hot, creamy cream into her cunney.

Now the only question was whether Walter could raise his standard for a second joust with the gorgeous Molly who decided that she could not live another hour without Walter's prick lodged in her pussey. So, without giving the student more than five minutes in which to recover his senses, the lewd girl commenced to "play" with his prick, pressing it to her generous breasts, squeezing it between them, pressing it against her cheeks, gently rubbing it with her hands and taking the uncapped knob between her lips, softly biting it and tickling it with the end of her tongue. Then she suddenly thrust the whole shaft into her mouth and by her erotic palating and sucking, proudly erected the shaft till her lips could hardly enclasp the ivory column.

She pushed Walter onto his back, his cock now stiffly waving as Molly eased herself upon it and began to ride a St George on his shaft, her teeth flashing in a lustful smile as she slid up and down, pumping her tight little bottom up and down furiously, digging her nails into his ribs as she held onto his body. Each voluptuous shove was accompanied by a wail of ecstasy. Walter grabbed her large breasts and brought them down to his raised head to suck on her rosy nipples and Molly moved even faster under this added stimulation.

Walter could feel the first stirrings of frothy love juice swirling in his aching balls as Molly's pussey squeezed even more tightly round his soaking shaft. He gave a quick scream as the first jet of spunk shot up into Molly's cunney, drenching her pussey as she gyrated wildly upon his jerking shaft. Molly, too, was now besides herself with the joy of sexual abandon and she let out a cry of unmuffled delight while she orgasmed, her pussey juices running over Walter's shaft, mingling with his own spend which spilled out of her sopping cunney and trickled down her thighs.

Alexandra had watched the lustful pair with interest. Now she padded over to the champagne and filled three glasses to the brim. 'I'll order some smoked salmon sandwiches to go with this wine,' she called out. 'Venus and Priapus deserve the finest refreshments especially if Walter is to perform again after our luncheon.'

At Green Street Mr Formbey was busy supervising last-minute arrangements for the party whilst Lizzie was in her bedroom writing a letter to Sergeant Stanley Watforde of the Royal Marines who had won her heart at a Whitsun funfair on Hampstead Heath the year before but who was posted to faraway Calcutta on a two year mission. Lizzie gave her old friend all the news about her new job and then added:

Oh, Stanley, it is only two o'clock in the afternoon and I have just forty-five minutes break before I start work again. If only I were in your arms, I want you so badly! I murmur your name as I fondle my breasts and roll onto my right hand. My fingers find the wetness in my pussey and spread it all over my clitty. Slowly I move my fingers, sliding them into my hot, wet cunney and as I part the soft folds of skin I think of how you like to touch me with your fingers and your lips.

Do you remember how we made love in your little flat in Museum Street? How quickly your expert fingering of my pussey had me writhing with pleasure. Your finger and thumb found my hardening clitty and you tweaked it so perfectly, knocking it from side to side as you said: 'What a delicious pussey, Lizzie, and what a heavenly womanly scent!' You brought your head to my blonde bush and let your tongue run the full length of my parted cunney lips, sucking the juices out of me and cooling me with your breath, making my pussey feel like the most loved place on earth.

If only you were here now, Stanley Watforde! My body is aching for you! I do so wish you were here to fuck me. Instead I must play with my own titties, massaging the elongated red berries and then as I slide my thumb into my cunney I think of your thick, veiny cockshaft slowly dipping into me, then moving stronger and harder just like I am moving my fingers now. I keep rubbing until I squirm into a juicy spend, holding my titties now and pressing them tightly together – by bending my head I can lick my nipples and run my tongue back and forth between them.

You would love to be on top of me now, wouldn't you? Thrusting that hard eight-inch tool into my crack, watching me lie back with a blissful smile as you fondle my soft breasts and tweak up my titties to their full

*height. I would wrap my long legs around your waist and
beg you to fuck me as hard and as deep as you can. Your
cock would now begin to twitch and then I would thrill to
the warmth of the cascading fountain of spunk that
shoots out of your beautiful cock . . .*

I must go now. Write to me soon.

Love,

Lizzie

She neatly folded the notepaper into an envelope which
she inserted in the book on her bedside table. 'Ah well,'
muttered Lizzie aloud, 'there is not a word of lie as such in
that letter to Stanley but I suppose I could well be accused
of being selective with the truth.'

I would love to have Count Gewirtz fuck me, she
thought to herself as she tidied her hair. He is such a handsome man and though a little plump he is still physically
very attractive – and how rich he must be! There can't be
many houses that have policemen guarding the entrance
night and day. Who on earth can be arriving to warrant
such concern? 'This business is probably all to do with the
Prince of Wales,' said Lizzie to Tim Fletcher as they put
the final touches to the arrangements for the evening
under the direction of the eagle-eyed Mr Formbey.

Lizzie was gratified when Count Gewirtz smiled at her
in the hallway as he was preparing to go out for a short
afternoon walk. 'You are sure you do not require a cab,
sir?' asked Mr Formbey.

'No thank you, I feel like taking a brisk walk in the
Park. Madame Volpe is resting upstairs but I need a little
exercise,' said the Count, adjusting his hat. 'I should be
back within the hour.'

He walked up Green Street but near the junction with Park Lane a man was sitting on the pavement, his back pressed against the gate of Lord Plattslane's town house. The Count's first instinct was simply to step over the semi-prostrate form as experience had warned him against the advisability of helping inebriates to their feet. Inevitably, when dragged upright they would flail like drowning swimmers and clutch wildly at anything within reach. Supine however, they were harmless as they enjoyed the blissful security of the floor where balance is effortless. Yet this man seemed too well-dressed to be lying drunk at half past three in the afternoon so the kindly Count sighed as he approached the man and bent down to apprise the situation from close quarters.

'Good God,' said Count Gewirtz with no little surprise. 'Unless I am very much mistaken it's Arthur McCann, the explorer. Arthur, my old friend, what on earth have you been up to? Here, let me get you up on your feet.'

He helped the man to his feet but Arthur McCann – for the Count was not mistaken – could keep upright only by holding onto the Count's shoulder. 'Johnny, it's good to see you,' he gasped. 'I didn't know you were in London. By George, old boy you've arrived in the nick of time.'

At this point the constable who had been standing outside 46 Green Street ambled up to see whether he could be of any assistance. Coincidentally, he happened to be none other than P C Fulham who, as readers may remember, had for the last three years been fucking Grace, Mrs Beaconfield's sister, and via these ladies news of what had happened to poor Mr McCann was soon known to all members of Count Gewirtz's staff.

'I'm not drunk, Johnny, though I dare say it looks that way,' gasped the explorer.

'Don't worry about it,' said Count Gewirtz soothingly. 'The constable and I will help you to my house just a few yards away. We'll get you comfortable and then you can tell us all about it.'

Twenty minutes later Arthur McCann was sitting in the Count's drawing-room, dressed in his shirt and trousers as Lizzie brought in a pot of steaming hot coffee.

'Drink this, Arthur, it will revive you and then afterwards tell me how on earth you came to be lying on the pavement. I know you haven't been drinking as there is no smell of alcohol on your breath. Take your time, my old friend,' said the Count encouragingly.

'Has the policeman gone?' asked Mr McCann somewhat fearfully.

'Yes, he is outside the front door but I can ask him in if you want to speak to him.'

'No, no, no, that's the last thing I want. After all, one doesn't want the whole world to know how bloody stupid one has been.'

He leaned forward in his chair and said: 'Johnny, my head is clearing now and so first let me thank you from the bottom of my heart for your kindness. I owe you an explanation and you shall have one. No, please, I want to tell you of my experience this afternoon.

'As you may know, I have been out in West Africa for the last eight months helping our soldiers in Nigeria. We have delivered some sharp blows which have broken the power of the slave-owning Fulani chiefs and the people there have welcomed us and made possible the permanent and willing submission of a numerous population to the protection of England.

'I returned home last Friday and you can well imagine that my wedding tackle has been getting more than a little rusty. There just weren't and chances of enjoying the delights of the pretty native girls as I was working alongside Reverend Lionel's Evangelical Crusade and my own dear lady wife has been taking the cure in Carlsbad and won't return to London for another week.

'So when a pretty girl handed me an advertisement leaflet whilst I was walking down Piccadilly this morning, instead of throwing it away I actually read it. The leaflet gave the address 129 Albemarle Street and across the top in capital letters was printed 'Poses Plastique'. [*Poses Plastique was the Victorian equivalent of strip-tease. Actresses would pose in so-called classical backdrops which gave the necessary excuse for girls to appear scantily clad or even semi-nude – L.L.*]

'I thought that if the girl who gave me the advertisement was anything like the girls who would display their charms in the poses plastique, it would be worth while turning into Albemarle Street and having a look at what was going on. It took only five minutes to reach the place and I rang the bell. The door was opened by a swarthy-looking fellow, rather stout, dark moustache, going thin on top. He took me into a room and demanded a sovereign which I gave to him. I asked when the poses plastique would begin and he told me to wait where I was for a moment.

'Two or three minutes later the door was thrown open and there stood an attractive well-endowed girl of about twenty-five. She was wearing a thin cotton tennis shirt and a sports skirt that reached down only to her calves. "Hello there, what's your name?" she said brightly. "My name is Barbara and I am your own personal pose plastique."

' "My name is Arthur," I stammered. "But what does my own personal pose plastique actually mean?"

' "Why it can mean just about anything you want," she cooed, thrusting her melon-sized breasts, which were covered solely by a wispy gauze, into my face. Instinctively I took hold of one of these great breasts and pressed it to my face.

' "Not so fast, Arthur," giggled this dark-haired minx. "What show you see depends upon what you pay. Would you like the three guinea show or the full five guinea performance? If you can afford it I would go for the dearer one as you'll get more out of it, I promise you." And as if to prove her point she moved even closer to me, her hand rubbing my thighs, tracing the outline of my stirring cock and reaching down to cup my balls. "Wouldn't you love me to suck off your big fat prick, Arthur?" she said, moving her mouth to my ear and gently biting on the lobe before slipping her wet tongue inside.

'Of course I immediately gave her five guineas for the de luxe performance and she smiled sweetly and said that she would be back in a few minutes. You can well imagine, Johnny, that my cock was stiffening as my mouth was watering at the same time.

'Barbara came back, only this time she was quite naked. Her beautiful big breasts were crowned by nut brown nipples and she had a neatly-trimmed inverted pyramid of pussey hair. At her command I knelt on the ground in front of her and began to lick her thighs while my hands were pulling her plump buttocks closer to me. Her hands were on the back to my head, forcing my face further into her moist depths. I worked my tongue in deeper and deeper, searching for and finally finding her erect little clitty which sent her into a delirious spasm of delight as I was kissed and sucked upon the delicious morsel. "Aaah!" she screamed as I worked my tongue until my jaw ached. Heaving violently the lovely girl spent copiously, drenching my face with her juices as she came with a shuddering orgasm which rammed through her body.

'She then unbuttoned my trousers, sending them sliding down to my ankles and slipped her hand into the opening of my drawers to bring out my naked swollen shaft to view. Her tousled dark hair was now between my legs as she kissed my purple bulb and her tongue flicked out to tease my cock before she opened her mouth and popped in the luscious knob, working on the ultra-sensitive tip with her tongue. Her mouth was like a cave of fire that warmed but did not burn as her wicked little tongue circled my knob, savouring the juices that were already dribbling from the 'eye'. Her teeth scraped my dome as she drew me in between those luscious lips, sucking hard as her smooth soft hands rubbed my shaft up and down.

'I told her that I would spend if she continued to suck my cock so she straightened up and we covered each other's mouths with burning kisses. I took all the liberties I desired with her, kissing and sucking her pretty lips, the nipples of her globular breasts, handling her soft bum cheeks, frigging her erect little clitty and drawing up my bursting tool between her thighs and rubbing her pussey lips till I felt myself succeed in making an entrance to her moist grotto. She the while moaned with delight, hugging me in her arms, giving me kiss for kiss, grappling with the ruby knob of my cock to push it firmly inside her.

'We sank to the carpet and she made me lie on my back whilst she bounced up and down on my thick prick which was firmly inserted into her tender cunney and as she moved her hips faster and faster the feel of her throbbing cunt soon brought me to the peak of pleasure and I could no longer hold back. With an exclamation of delight I spurted a stream of warm spunk up into her very entrails. Her cunt gripped and throbbed on my shaft so deliciously that my staff stayed as hard as iron while she rolled over onto her back, my cock still inside her, and we were soon running another delightful course.

'She grabbed my arse cheeks and pulled me forward so that each millimetre of my shaft was inside her. Our pubic bones mashed together as she began moving her hips up and down. With her hands gripping my bum I matched her movements and soon my glistening prick was thrusting in and out of her cunney at a considerable pace. Our movements speeded up even more until I felt myself exploding into her as I reached my climax, shooting further rivulets of love juice into her willing pussey. Afterwards she told me to rest and I lay my head down on her delightfully large titties while she gently played with my now limp cock.'

'Well she sounds like a perfectly charming girl,' said Count Gewirtz with an air of puzzlement in his voice.

'You certainly can't complain too much, even though five guineas is a great deal of money to pay for a fuck.'

'Ah, if only it had ended there and then I would have been well content,' continued Arthur McCann. 'We were, as I say, resting from our endeavours when another girl came in – the very same girl from whom I had taken the leaflet in Piccadilly.'

'She asked us if we would like a drink and my new amorata said immediately: "I would adore a glass of champagne, wouldn't you?" The idea did not displease me so I gave me assent. We dressed ourselves and the girl came back with a bottle of champagne and three glasses. "You won't mind my joining you?" she said pertly, sitting on my lap and fondling my thighs. "No, not at all." I replied politely. "You had better give Polly a sovereign for the champagne," said Barbara so I reached inside my jacket for my wallet and I thought I detected a gleam in the girls' eyes when I fished out a Treasury note from a pile of its fellows. Anyway, we drank just a little champagne and the conversation deteriorated into lewdness. One of the girls insisted that I could not tell the difference between their titties with my eyes closed and wagered the cost of a second bottle on the matter.

'I accepted the challenge and my cock began to stir again as both girls stripped to the waist. Polly's breasts were almost as large as Barbara's, her white globes delightfully topped by dark brown nipples that looked impudently away from one another. I was instructed to close my eyes and Polly said that they would take it in turns to place their titties in my mouth as I sat on a chair. "Just wash your mouth out with another drink. The champagne will make the exercise even more pleasant for

Polly and myself,'' said Barbara, handing me a brimming glass. I toasted the pair and drank about half the contents which I thought at the time tasted somewhat differently to the previous glass I had consumed.'

'Oh, no, don't tell me that they had slipped a sleeping drought in your drink!' exclaimed the Count.

'Absolutely correct, Johnny,' said Mr McCann. 'I felt myself falling off the chair and the next thing I remember is waking up sitting on the pavement looking like a foolish drunkard.'

'Oh dear,' said Count Gewirtz. 'How much was in your wallet which I presume has been purloined?'

'About seventy pounds – and my watch has gone, too. I could inform the police but it will be my word against theirs and I would hardly like my name splashed all over the front page of the *Evening News* or the *Illustrated Police Gazette*.'

The Count grimaced as he realised his old friend's predicament. 'Arthur, I'm afraid you're right and I think it best to enter the whole incident in your ledger of experience. But look here, I'm having a little dinner party and you are most welcome to join us.'

'No, no, really I could not impose.'

'You would not be imposing, my dear friend, in fact you would be doing me a great favour. Dr Frederick Nolan was to have joined us but he has been called at short notice to Windsor as Her Majesty is suffering from a severe bout of influenza and her personal physician Sir James Reid has asked Dr Nolan to give a second opinion.'

'Well, if you are really sure . . .' said Mr McCann with some hesitation.

'I won't take no for an answer,' insisted the Count.

'I'll order a Prestoncrest cab to take you home and to pick you up again at eight o'clock. Fine, that settled, I look forward to seeing you.'

'It's very kind of you, Johnny. Have you invited anyone that I know?'

'One or two Cremornites, Arthur, including your old friend Sir Ronnie Dunn. Oh yes, and HRH will be bringing his latest *amour*, a very pretty lady indeed. I know I can rely on your total discretion, my friend.'

Arthur McCann's eyes brightened as he asked: 'May I assume that the chance of a good fuck is not out of the question?' And although Count Gewirtz did not directly reply, the broad grin on the Galician nobleman's face sent Mr McCann home in a far happier state than he could possibly have dreamed of only an hour or so before.

CHAPTER SIX

What huge good fortune that my dear lady wife was unable to be with me tonight, thought Sir Paul Arkley as he surveyed Count Gewirtz's exquisitely-furnished drawing-room, clutching a pre-dinner whisky and soda. He had already been introduced to Vazelina Volpe and to Martina Motkalowski the Polish pianist whose praises, reader, you may recall were sung by his wife and daughters who heard her performance at the Royal Albert Hall the previous day. She was accompanied tonight by the Italian violinist Bernado Rubeno, a slim young sallow-skinned man with long black hair and dark, fiery eyes.

Sir Paul decided to make polite conversation with the three artistes who appeared to be engaged in an animated conversation. Sir Paul walked up to the little group and listened to their discussion.

'Yes, yes, there have been many works written for the piano,' said the beautiful Martina Motkalowski in her attractively-accented English. 'But Beethoven's Emperor Concerto is not merely an arrangement of sounds to be judged favourably or adversely. It is the standard composition, the bench-mark by which all other pieces are to be gauged. Beethoven mustered an unprecedented energy of expression to create a master-piece that will never be bettered.'

Sir Paul coughed discreetly and said: 'I would stand with that opinion, Mademoiselle Motkalowski. But could you explain to a simple concertgoer like myself why Beethoven dedicated the concerto to the tyrant Napoleon?'

'I don't think he did,' said the pretty pianist. 'I doubt whether he ever heard the term as I believe it was only after his death that his English publisher, Mr Cramer, gave this story some currency.'

'Not many people know that,' commented Sir Paul. 'However, may I take this opportunity to introduce myself? I am Sir Paul Arkley, an old friend of Johnny Gewirtz whom I first had the pleasure of meeting in Biarritz eight years ago.

'I know who you are, Mademoiselle, as I heard you play at the Albert Hall yesterday afternoon. It was truly a memorable experience,' he added, hoping that she would not question him too stringently for readers will recall that instead of accompanying his family to the concert, Sir Paul spent the afternoon fucking a plump chambermaid.

Martina smiled graciously and accepted his praise with a slight incline of her head as she introduced her companions. By now the room had filled up and Count Gewirtz came hurrying over with the news that the guest of honour had arrived. No sooner had he informed them of this fact than Mr Formbey the butler opened the doors and announced; 'His Royal Highness, the Prince of Wales and Miss Lily Belsey.' The men bowed and the ladies curtsied as the Prince entered the room arm in arm with

Miss Belsey. There was a momentary silence broken by the Prince who said cheerfully: 'Now Ladies and Gentlemen, this is an informal occasion. Let us eat, drink and be merry without any undue standing on ceremony. Am I right, Johnny?'

'Well said, Your Royal Highness. Let me present my guests to you.' said Count Gewirtz. Besides Sir Paul and the musicians there appeared to be a preponderance of unattached men, for as well as Sir Paul, the Jewish financier Sir Ronnie Dunn and the last-minute guest Arthur McCann appeared to be without female company. 'Are we not waiting for three more ladies?' asked the Prince when soon after the introductions Mr Formbey announced to the company that dinner was ready to be served.

His host grinned and said: 'I have made special arrangements for the gentlemen and I don't think they will be lonely for very long.'

'Ah-ha, if you have made the same arrangements as you kindly made for me in Cannes four years ago they will certainly not be displeased!'

'You remember that party, sir? Forgive my repetition of the ploy but Madame Volpe has asked me to further her education in *l'arte de faire l'amour* and I judged this method to introduce our sport in the best possible taste.'

The Prince nodded his head in approval. 'Johnny, I am sure I will enjoy this party but I now make one firm stipulation – no one must fuck Miss Belsey before me.'

'Of course not, Teddy, I wouldn't dream of it. After all, isn't there something known as your royal prerogative?' piped up the cheeky Miss Belsey, taking hold of the Prince's arm.

Count Gewirtz chuckled as he moved away to escort Vazelina Volpe into the dining-room. The guests took their seats but there remained three vacant chairs at the table. Count Gewirtz clapped his hands and called for silence, saying: 'Your Royal Highness, fellow guests, as you see we need three ladies to make up our party. Now Formbey and Fletcher will fill our glasses and then retire and then our three missing guests will make a musical entrance, highly appropriate with so many artistes present.'

He waited for the servants to leave the room and then placed a cylinder in his gramophone, adjusted the horn and the sounds of a popular music hall tune filled the room. [*The early acoustic gramophones first used cylindrical wax records and flat discs did not come into general use until the first years of the twentieth century – L.L.*] The Count flung open the door and said: 'Let me introduce our three missing guests, directly from the Empire, Leicester Square! Sir Paul Arkley, your partner for tonight is Miss Bella Burman!'

At the sound of her name in danced a nubile young girl of not more than nineteen years, totally nude and of such ravishing beauty that even the Count himself, who had fucked at least four hundred women by the time he was thirty, licked his lips in anticipation. Bella was extraordinarily well-proportioned, her hair being dark brown and worn long so that it tumbled down in silky strands over her shoulders. Her cheeks were rosy red and her full lips were as ripe cherries and her teeth were even and firm. Her small but superbly-formed uptilted breasts each crowned with a tiny button of a pink nipple bounced merrily as she danced and between her long legs

216

nestled a silky brown bush in which Sir Paul Arkley immediately noticed, a delicious-looking slit. This acme of sensuality pirouetted gracefully in front of him as the music stopped and then sat herself down on his lap, her arms around his neck.

Count Gewirtz changed the cylinder and announced: 'To partner my old friend Ronnie Dunn, I have the pleasure of introducing Miss Patti Pottesman!' and a second striking girl, also stark naked, came tripping into the room. She was tall, almost five feet ten inches in height with a willowy figure and a pert, pretty face that was encircled by a mop of curly hair. Her breasts were fuller than those of the previous girl and each and every man in the room felt his penis stiffen as the curvacous temptress took her soft globes in her hands and flicked up her tawny nipples to erection.

'And to complete our party,' intoned the Count. 'It is my pleasure to present the lovely Susannah Sullivan who has promised to make this an evening to remember for the lucky Arthur McCann!'

The nude girl who skipped through into the dining-room earned a round of spontaneous applause from the assembled company. She was deliciously beautiful with cornflower blue eyes, a tiny nose but with generously wide, red lips, a face that was somehow disembodied as she smiled to show pearly white rows of teeth that sparkled as her mass of blonde hair, set in simple loose tresses, scantily covered her full, firm breasts. She, too, sat on the lap of her designated partner and there was not a man at the table who did not envy Arthur McCann as the girl's taut, tawny nipples acted as magnets to his roving hands.

Fletcher the footman and the two maids, Lizzie and Estelle, brought in the *hors d'oeuvres* which consisted of simple raw vegetables – *crudités à la français* – with a selection of sauces in which the vegetables could be dipped whilst Mr Formbey kept himself busy refilling the glasses with ice-cold champagne.

And as the servants arranged the food, a quartet of musicians, two girls and two men, entered the large room. Sir Ronnie Dunn chuckled when the man sat down at the piano for he recognised none other than David Jackson, one of London's most talented amateur musicians and the proud possessor of one of the biggest pricks in London. He vaguely recalled seeing the men but at this time he could not quite place where he had seen the attractive girls before. The gorgeously pouting Patti, who was stroking the banker's thighs with one hand and caressing his face as he popped tid-bits into her mouth, also recognised the male musicians.

'Johnny Gewirtz must certainly have some influence in musical circles,' she whispered in his ear, 'for is that not the great Mr Webb himself performing on the piccolo? How extraordinary it is that a man with so huge a physique should be able to coax such marvellous sounds out of so tiny an instrument.'

'M'mm, quite extraordinary,' replied Sir Ronnie somewhat indistinctly, burying his lead between Patti's generous, full breasts.

'When you told me this party would broaden my horizons I had no idea that you had this in mind,' murmured Vazelina Volpe to Count Gewirtz who was looking round the table with satisfaction as all the guests were obviously enjoying the entertainment he had provided.

'You have seen, shall we say, only the tip of the ice-berg, Vazelina,' said the Count. 'I hope this sophisticated evening is to your liking?'

'Of course it is, Johnny, only I am just wondering what happens now, that the overture has been played and the curtain is about to rise.'

'You will not be disappointed,' promised the Count. 'Now I think we will let our three nude lovelies open the proceedings.' He rose to his feet and announced 'Ladies and Gentleman, do partake of these light *hors d'oeuvres*. Meanwhile, the delightful dancers who have just joined our party will perform *Le Ballet des Tribades* devised by Monsieur Yugerputz of Petrograd, which will be the first time, I believe, that the uncensored work has ever been seen in its entirety in this country.

The little orchestra struck up a gay melody as Bella, Patti and Susannah gave the company a graceful exhibi-tion of their dancing skills, although the members of the audience were puzzled when Patti left the floor to leave Bella and Susannah entwined in passionate embrace while the music slowed in tempo to a soft romantic theme. The two naked girls writhed their bodies around as they stroked each other's breasts, bellies and thighs. The other guests were so engaged in watching this lustful exhibition that no one noticed Patti re-enter the room with Mr Formbey and Tim Fletcher the footman in tow, carrying in a large divan bed covered in creamy satin sheets. They set the divan in the centre of the floor and retired to the door and, to his great delight, the young footman was allowed to stay whilst Mr Formbey slipped back to the servants' hall where the nubile Lizzie was waiting for his return.

Bella and Susannah leaped upon the divan and Bella tweaked up Susannah's nipples to a fine erection as the blonde girl grasped Bella's delicious bum cheeks and fondled them lasciviously. Susannah pushed her titties up in front of Bella's face and she sucked and licked on the red cherries as she opened her legs to receive Bella's hand on her neatly-trimmed golden-haired pussey. Bella put her hands on the trembling girl's inner thighs and pulled them apart, displaying to perfection the pink outer lips of her cunney peaking through the blonde moss. Susannah was now whimpering with pleasure and Bella slid two fingers into her moistening crack as she athletically leaped on top of her partner and straddled her so that her bottom was directly over the blonde girl's mouth. She gently lowered her bum so that Susannah could take hold of her arse cheeks in her hands and insert her tongue into the fleshy, quivering folds of her pussey. Bella leaned forward and dived into Susannah's silky muff to complete a perfect 'sixty-nine' to the polite applause of Count Gewirtz and Sir Ronnie Dunn who were both aficionados of tribadistic displays. The girls licked and lapped each other's cunneys, probing, sucking, and rubbing, frigging their clitties and making each other shriek with pleasure as they shuddered to a glorious mutual climax.

The girls continued to play with each other, grinding their pussies together and then Susannah climbed on top of Bella who lay on her belly and rubbed herself off on Bella's back, raising her bum cheeks delightfully to the assembled company and opening her legs so that her prominent pussey could be well seen by all.

Patti stole across to Sir Ronnie Dunn and unbuttoned

his trousers, letting his circumcised cock leap into the air. She crouched down besides him and taking his boldly upright shaft in her hands she said: 'Ronnie, I have this fancy that you want to fuck Susannah's bottom – but I have been promised first refusal on your fine-looking prick.' And so saying she took his not inconsiderable length into her soft mouth, sucking thirstily on his shaft while reaching down to delicately finger the baronet's swollen ballsack. She nibbled daintily at his purple-coloured knob as Lily Belsey called out: 'Now, my dear, do remember that every mouthful must be well chewed before it is swallowed!'

Sir Ronnie trembled under the provoking vibrations of Patti's giggles as her mouth closed firmly once again over his prick, and this time she pursued an insistent passage down the shaft. He pressed her head down as she sucked in his cock to the very root, cupping his hairy balls in her hands. He felt the hot waves of spunk flood along his tool as with a gasp he flooded her greedily receiving mouth with a copious emission of love juice. Swallowing and sucking, she soon drained him of his resources and, squeezing the last few drops of milky sperm from the head of his prick, she carefully took his happy but now wilting cock in the palm of her hand before deftly tucking it away inside his trousers. 'We don't want Mr Pego catching cold. Go to bed for a little while and I am sure that later in the evening he will be able to get up again!'

Susannah and Bella now disentangled themselves from their own love-making and pulled all the men out of their seats – Bernado Rubeno, Arthur McCann, Sir Ronnie Dunn, Count Gewirtz and (after a moment's hesitation) the Prince of Wales himself – and sat them on the divan. Patti then asked Mademoiselle Motkalowski for the use of her napkin which she used to bind round Susannah's pretty face so that her eyes were covered.

'Ah, we are about to play Blind Man's Buff,' said Sir Ronnie.

'Not quite – rather this is a variant of the game that we call Blind Girl's Cock,' trilled Bella, her hands busy opening up Bernado Rubeno's fly buttons and bringing out a red-domed prick of a not unsubstantial size. Patti performed the same service for Arthur McCann, Count Gewirtz and Sir Ronnie whilst Bella had the honour of holding the royal prick in her hands when she pulled down the Prince's trousers and brought his majestic bone-hard cock out into the open.

'Now gentlemen, stay as you are for a moment,' said Patti, nodding to the band who struck up *What The Wild Waves Are Saying* as Bella led Susannah forward until she was standing in front of the five naked cocks. She then dropped to her knees and gave each of the men a thorough going-over with her tongue, licking each cock from the tip all away along to the balls and back again. Then she put her lips to each one and pushed down on it to take part of the shaft in her mouth for a few moments before pausing and moving on to the next shaft.

'Right, now that Susannah has tasted all your cocks, she will put her hands over her eyes to ensure that she cannot see even a shadow,' said Bella. 'Gentlemen, you can now change places and when you have settled down again, Susannah will suck you off. She wins a guinea for every prick she identifies correctly and we girls will pay any of you twenty guineas if you manage not to spunk during the three minutes Susannah will have to suck your cock.

'Perhaps you would act as timekeeper,' she added, looking across to Martina Motkalowski. 'Mr Webb the flautist will be pleased to loan you his pocket watch.'

'Oh yes, I would love to do so. This is just as exciting as playing the Emperor Concerto,' said the concert pianist, her eyes sparkling with anticipation.

'Very well, are you ready, steady, go!' called out Patti.

Susannah dropped down her knees again and felt for the first prick which happened to be the throbbing Napolitan shaft of Bernado Rubeno. She began to pertly sticking out her tongue to tease his knob, running the tip of pink tongue all round the edges of the springy cap whilst at the same time gently manipulating his balls through the soft wrinkled skin of the bags. Then suddenly she opened her mouth and enveloped the red dome which the company could almost see swell in her mouth as she lustily sucked on her throbbing lollipop, moving her head up and down until with a shout of '*Mamamia*!' Bernado spurted his jets of love fluid which Susannah swallowed with great enjoyment. She rubbed his cock with her hands until every last drop of spunk had been milked from his prick and his shaft began to droop in a rather pitiful manner.

'Susannah, can you identify the tool you have just sucked off?' asked Patti.

'I am almost certain it belonged to the Italian gentleman, Mr Rubeno,' giggled the blindfolded girl to a round of applause, sipping a glass of champagne thoughtfully given her by Vazelina Volpe so her palate would be clear for the next erotic encounter.

'How long did he last?' enquired Bella.

'Bernado spunked after one minute and seven seconds,' intoned Martina who took her position as timekeeper most conscientiously.

She took hold of another penis at random and this time found herself stroking the stiff, thick prick of her host, Count Gewirtz. Her soft hands caressed his hairy balls as she slowly licked up and down the length of his shaft, taking her good time to reach the uncapped crown until she suddenly lashed her tongue around his huge pole and noisily sucked and slurped while her hands encircled the base of his shaft and started a sliding action up and down. This was too much for the Count to bear and he shot a torrent of spunk over Susannah's face. She licked her lips and managed to swallow enough to recognise the salty tang and she cried out: 'I just know that this prick must belong to Johnny Gewirtz. His love juice has such a distinctive flavour I would recognise it anywhere.'

'Absolutely correct, you clever girl. How long did our host manage to last, Martina?' said Patti to the audience who again applauded this unusual entertainment.

Perhaps the erotic entertainment had taken its toll on the Count's stamina but Martina informed the assembly that he had only managed to last fifty-eight seconds before drenching Susannah's face with his copious emission.

The beautiful fellatrix now turned her attention to a third throbbing pole and this time she grasped the majestic prick of HRH the Prince of Wales. Count Gewirtz grinned as Susannah said: 'This is a mighty weapon indeed. It is so big that I don't know whether it will all fit into my mouth. Still, let's see what we can do.'

'There's a clever girl,' murmured the Count to Vazelina Volpe. 'I will wager ten thousand pounds she knows full well that she is holding the crown jewels in her hands – and she also knows how to flatter the Prince for as we say in Galicia, *ven der putz shtayt, ligt di seichel aroys de fenster.*'

Vazelina giggled her agreement as he translated: 'When the cock stands up, common sense flies out of the window.'

Meanwhile the sly Susannah was taking her time in bringing the Prince's prick to the boil. She let his shaft fall from her mouth and instead nibbled and sucked at his hairy ballsack which caused the heir to the throne to breathe heavily as the girl's soft tongue worked its way slowly from his balls and slowly up his shaft, teasing his red-mushroomed knob, encircling it and licking lazily at the large bead of pre-cum which had oozed out from the 'eye'. Then, licking her lips, she lapped quickly and gently across the royal knob and, filling her mouth with saliva, plunged six inches of his thick staff into her willing mouth, sucked hard for a short time, withdrew, then plunged her pretty blonde curls down again. She did this four times, quelling the pressure and then building it up again whilst the Prince squirmed, unable to resist. On the fourth plunge he let out a great bellow and heaved upwards, filling her sweet mouth with steaming cock and boiling spunk and she drank him dry to the cheers of the onlookers.

When she had recovered the cheeky girl called out: 'That right royal cock can only belong to His Royal

Highness.' And Martina added: 'And he managed to last for two minutes, twenty-eight seconds before spunking!'

'Goodness me! That is the longest anyone has ever held out. No one will ever beat that record so Bella and I will finish off Arthur and Ronnie,' yelled Patti, jumping up onto the divan and ordering Arthur McCann to suck her titties. He immediately took one into his mouth and began licking and lapping at the engorged nipple, playfully pulling it with his teeth as he caressed the other erect little tawny soldier, rubbing the teat against the palm of his hand while she wiggled her way across him so that she could brush her wet pussey lips along the length of his straining shaft.

'Now I am going to sit on your cock,' announced Patti as she slid on top of his prick, ramming herself up and down, squeezing her cunney and buttock muscles which sent Arthur into the very seventh heaven of delight. His excitement soon overflowed as she moved her hips faster and faster, her cunney gripping and releasing in such exquisite a fashion that with an exclamation of joy he spurted a fountain of warm sperm, shooting into her very entrails. But her cunney gripped and throbbed so deliciously that he was delighted to find that his cock stayed as hard as iron and they were soon running another fine course.

Sir Ronnie's shaft was now standing stiffly up against his flat belly so Bella caught hold of his circumcized cock and guided it between her lips, slurping uninhibitedly as she sucked the swollen member up to bursting point. Then suddenly she opened her lips to release the twitching tool and taking it in her hand brought it behind Patti who, without missing one beat of the rhythm as she slid up and down on Arthur McCann's cock, leaned forward so that the charming wrinkled orifice of her pink bum-hole caught the baronet's attention. The girl reached for Sir Ronnie's cock and placed his knob between her plump rounded bottom cheeks. He grasped them and opened wide the crack. Fortunately the fact that his tool was of a length rather than a thickness enabled him to push hard from the start. With only a short cry of initial discomfort from Patti, the two men jointly rammed in and out. At one stage they pushed in together and they could feel their pricks rubbing together with only the thin divisional membrane running between them. It was simply too exciting for them both and all too soon they pumped jets of frothy white juice into her bum and cunney simultaneously as Patti, too, reached the summit of the mountain of love, causing them to fall back onto the divan quite sated from this novel experience.

Count Gewirtz clapped his hands and suggested that the party avail themselves of a short interlude from the erotic proceedings and the three naked girls slipped on the silk robes that the Count had thoughtfully provided for them.

The young footman Tim had stood transfixed by what he had seen but was brought out of his trance by Mr Formbey, Lizzie and Estelle who had brought in the next course on silver salvers which they wheeled in on the Count's Louis XIV serving tables. 'It's Welsh lamb,' announced the Count, ' which seemed to me to be most appropriate considering we are honoured tonight with the presence of the head of that Principality. I have omitted to serve a fish course as I do have some further indoor sports planned and I believe it is healthier to eat more sparingly than would be usual on a more formal occasion.'

The main course was consumed with relish – for the previous activity had increased the appetites of those concerned – and the conversation consisted mostly of Sir Ronnie Dunn's light-hearted jokes as it was not without cause that he was regarded as one of the wittiest men in London.

'Johnny, did you hear the story of the sailor who returned home after two years at sea to find that his wife had been delivered of a bouncing baby just three weeks before?' he said to Count Gewirtz. 'Well, he was astonished by this news so he went to see the local priest. "Oh dear, my son," said the priest. "I'm afraid that you are the proud father of a grudge baby." "A grudge baby – what's that?" asked the sailor. "Well, put simply, it just means that someone had it in for you!" replied the cleric.'

'Ha, ha, ha!' responded his audience. 'Tell us another story, Ronnie.'

The genial baronet smiled and turning to the Prince of Wales said: 'Sire, do you know the difference between a railway carriage with the Prime Minister, the Home Secretary and the Foreign Secretary inside – and a hedgehog?'

'No, but I'm sure you'll tell me,' laughed the merry Prince.

'With a hedgehog the pricks are outside!' quipped Sir Ronnie.

After a few more stories, Lily Belsey, who had been uncharacteristically subdued during the high jinks, asked whether members of the company found certain foods or drink acted as sexual stimulants for them. 'I find that eating peaches in brandy to be a great stimulant. It takes just about twenty minutes but then I feel myself get damp between my legs, my nipples swell up, my clitty throbs and I'm ready for action,' she commented. 'How about you, Bernado, we've all heard of Spanish Fly, does it really make you randy?'

Bernado looked across the table mischievously at Lily and said: 'I am sure that neither you nor any of your sex need special stimulants. In my country we say that the only chaste women are those who have not been asked! But whether or not this is true, I would never recommend Spanish Fly. This preparation made from the dried bodies of blister beetles is used medically as a diuretic – to help people pass water. It certainly does not arouse sexual desire.

'As for food, I have always found that eating olives makes me think of love-making. If I take an olive in my mouth and roll it around I begin to imagine that I am sucking on the nipple of a beautiful young girl such as yourself.'

'Imagination is all,' chipped in Vazelina Volpe. 'When I eat a plum I enjoy the flavour, the hollow you can stick your tongue in once the stone has been removed . . . sucking a plum gives me a real thrill! Teasing the juicy flesh with my tongue makes me think of sucking a big, fat cockshaft – which reminds me that Lily and I have not taken part in any fucking so far tonight.'

'Have no fear, you will have your share after the dessert,' promised Count Gewirtz as he turned to the butler standing behind him. 'Formbey, you may clear away and then please bring in the *bombe surprise* immediately.'

The staff cleared the table quickly and retired for a few minutes. Then Mr Formbey and Tim Fletcher wheeled in a large table set on castors covered completely by a dazzling white cloth which reached down to the floor. Whatever it was under the table cloth seemed to move as Mr Formbey solemnly announced that the *bombe surprise* was ready to be served.

'Thank you, Formbey, I think it best if we serve ourselves,' said Count Gewirtz, dismissing them with an airy wave of the hand.

'Perhaps His Royal Highness would do us the honour of unveiling our dessert,' added the Count, turning to the guest of honour. 'I'm sure he is not afraid of this kind of bomb.'

'I don't think you would harbour any anarchists, Johnny,' laughed the Prince, heaving himself up to his feet. 'Ladies and Gentlemen, I give you Johnny Gewirtz's special dessert. And after all this build-up, I certainly hope that we won't be disappointed by whatever is underneath this cloth.'

With a fine flourish, the Prince swept off the cloth – to reveal round the edges of the table beautifully arranged mounds of the most colourful fruits – oranges, pineapples, mangoes, bananas, strawberries and more – whilst in the middle, posed as still as for a photograph were the nude bodies of Estelle the blonde parlourmaid and a handsome Negro youth. This lucky lad was lying on his back, his skin shining from the fruit juices Estelle had rubbed onto his skin. Estelle herself was kneeling across him, her golden muff just inches away from his mouth as her own lips touched the tip of his semi-stiff cock which was rising perceptively from the mass of dark curls at its root and where Estelle's hands were placed strategically on either thigh.

The guests applauded the spectacle and Lily Belsey remarked on how pleasing was the contrast between the blonde girl and black boy, whose name Count Gewirtz announced was Ben Botley, a dancer who performed with Bella, Patti and Susannah at the Empire, Leicester Square. Ben's enormous black cock was now fully extended and without further ado Estelle jammed down his foreskin and began to lick and lap around the monster uncovered dome. At the same time she lowered her cunney onto his lips and he noisily nuzzled into her glorious golden thicket, enveloping his nose in her juicy honey pot, flicking his tongue upon the parted lips, to find and lick into erect life her enticing clitty before plunging his tongue into her soft, juice-eased cunt as she sucked vigorously upon his huge tool, taking as much as possible into her mouth, cupping his ballsack with one hand and holding his throbbing shaft with the other.

Count Gewirtz clapped his hands twice and the pair reluctantly drew back from their classic sixty-nine position. 'Don't spend now,' advised the host. 'You'll have to wait to pleasure each other after my guests have been served. Your Royal Highness, could Estelle offer you some fruit salad?'

'Indeed she may,' smiled the Prince, catching the spirit of the offer by unbuttoning his trousers. Ben jumped down from the table to sit between Lily Belsey and Martina Motkalowski who took it in turns to grasp his huge penis and admire the thickness and length of the dark shaft. Meanwhile, Estelle reached for a banana and placed it lasciviously between her cunney lips. As the Prince of Wales, now also nude, climbed on top of the trolley beside her she applied a generous helping of thick cream to the royal prick and they lay on their sides, the Prince eating the banana down to her pussey lips whilst she gobbled the cream off his princely pole. The Prince ran his warm tongue over her engorged clitty as his hands squeezed her firm young breasts. Showing a surprising agility for a heavily-built man, the Prince was now astride the quivering girl and the company delighted in her passionate sighs as the Prince pushed his knob between the yielding cunney lips. Estelle lifted up her bottom in answer to his urgent thrustings, her legs curled around his back. There was little doubt that she was enjoying this right royal fucking and she screamed: 'I'm going to spend! Give it to me! Come into me deep! Do it! Do it!' The Prince thrust forward again a few times but this time on the last stroke he held his cock inside her for a while before pulling out his shaft and then with one almighty push spunked great gushes of love juice into her welcoming cunney.

Meanwhile Martina and Lily were vying for possession of Ben's big cock. Lily's velvet lips were spread round his knob whilst Martina grasped his thick cock with both hands and jerked the shaft up and down. This double stimulation proved too exciting for the poor boy and he soon ejaculated his spunk in short, sharp bursts which Lily swallowed, continuing to suck on his great organ until it finally began to go limp.

'M'm, a fine tangy bouquet, I really enjoyed the taste of that libation,' said Lily, smacking her lips. 'Oh, I do love sucking a grand, stiffstanding cock! And I do so love the taste of the salty spunk – but if only boys wouldn't squirt so soon.'

'Yes, well I don't mind kissing and licking cocks,' said Martina doubtfully. 'But unlike you, I prefer to have a man shoot his spunk in my cunney. So if a lover wants me to suck his cock I will nibble his knob for a little and wash round the ridge with my wet tongue. Then I like to have his hard rod between my pussey lips and begin fucking!'

'Well, it would be very boring if we all enjoyed the same things,' said Lily cheerfully. 'But I am sure you will agree that so few men know how to suck pussies properly.'

'Here, here!' chimed in Bella and Patti who had heard Lily's comment. 'The British are poor pussy eaters compared to the French or Italians.'

'Oh, I don't know,' said Martina thoughtfully. 'Sir Paul Arkley is giving a fine demonstration of the noble art right now on the dessert table.'

The girls craned forward to watch as the baronet, asked by Count Gewirtz if he would partake of some fruit salad, was gulping down the little arrangement of strawberries Estelle had set out on her blonde bush. Sir Paul slipped one hand under her small but perfectly-formed bum, and lifted her cunney up to his mouth. He buried his face between her pouting cunney lips and pushed his tongue into her juicy crack, shoving it as deeply as he could until he found her clitty, rolling the erect flesh as she gasped with delight. His clever tongue jabbed again and again at her erect clitty as he sucked it into his mouth, trying to obtain a hold on its slippery surface with his teeth.

This erotic sight was too much for Vazelina Volpe who stripped off her clothes and, somehow finding room on

the fortunately strongly-built table, joined the couple.
She managed to place her head under Sir Paul's waist
and she took his hairy ballsack into her mouth, sucking
slowly first on one ball and then the other. The sight of
Vazelina's delightful bottom caused all the other pricks
in the room to rise but it was Bernado Rubeno who was
first, leaping up behind her, his prick at the ready as he
pulled apart her delicious bum cheeks to give fair view of
the wrinkled little bum hole that winked up at him. He
edged his knob towards the mark but Vazelina took her
mouth away from Sir Paul's balls for a moment to cry
out: 'I'd rather you fucked my pussey than my arse,
Bernado. I hope you have no objection?'

'It saves me having to choose between the brown and
the pink, as the snooker player said,' laughed Bernado,
guiding his cock towards the pouting lips of her juicy
cunt. She reached behind her and guided him into her
chosen port. Effecting a safe lodgement for his knob,
with one vigorous shove he buried his not inconsiderable
cock to the hilt and his balls flopped against her heaving
buttocks. He thrust again and again and, as he clasped
her to him with a compulsive thrill, he poured out a
torrent of creamy spunk in an ecstasy of enjoyment.

The little orchestra struck up '*Why Don't We All Join
In*?' and the quartet clambered down from the table onto
the divan and resumed their lovemaking. Only this time,
whilst Estelle was on her back having her pussey sucked
by Sir Paul Arkley, whose balls were being similarly
attended to by Vazelina Volpe who was in turn being
fucked from behind by Bernado Rubeno, Sir Ronnie
Dunn and Arthur McCann knelt on either side of Estelle
who handled their cocks expertly whilst gobbling the

majestic shaft of Count Gewirtz.

This fired the company to new heights and they formed a superb fucking chain with Sir Ronnie fucking Patti while she tickled Bella's cunney. Bella was being fucked from behind by Bernado Rubeno as Susannah sucked his cock whilst Ben drove his black monster in and out of her pussey as Count Gewirtz worked his prick into her tight little bum hole. The remainder of the company changed positions as the participants tired but both the men and women gave satisfaction to each and every one of their partners until even Count Gewirtz and Susannah Sullivan, who were the last two remaining players, were finally *hors de combat*, and they collapsed into a sweaty, naked heap of bodies around the room.

Outside in the hall Mr Formbey put his ear to the door. 'I think they must have all screwed themselves silly by now,' he muttered. 'Tim, you go in and begin to clear the table while I go downstairs to the kitchen for a chat with Mrs Beaconsfield.'

The young footman opened the door quietly and popped his head round to see what was going on. His jaw dropped as he stared at the slumbering form of the Prince of Wales, lying naked on the carpet with two equally nude chorus girls, Patti and Bella, resting their heads on his thighs and both with their hands clutching the royal cock. On the other side of the room the blonde Susannah was gently frigging the upright prick of Count Gewirtz who, though half asleep, was tickling the large titties of Vazelina Volpe. Bernado Rubeno and Arthur McCann were deep in the arms of Morpheus whilst Martina and Lily were locked together dozing, their hands placed over each other's cunnies.

Lily Belsey stirred and met Tim's gaze boldly. 'Well, what are you staring at, young man? Haven't you ever seen naked women before?' she asked with a giggle.

'Not as often as I would have liked,' stammered the handsome youth.

'Indeed? I suppose you will tell me now that you are a virgin,' laughed the pretty soubrette. 'No, surely you cannot still be waiting to lose your cherry!'

Tim blushed his admission and Lily's blue eyes sparkled with glee. 'Are you really telling me the truth? Look at me now, are you saying that you have never been to bed with a woman?'

'I wish I could deny it but, alas, somehow I have always been denied the opportunity,' said Tim sadly.

'We can't have such a good-looking boy as you looking so melancholy,' she said, scrambling to her feet and stepping towards him. 'What's your name, then, you poor deprived lad?'

'Tim Fletcher, ma'am.'

'Very well, Tim Fletcher, I think this may well be the night that you lose your unwanted encumbrance. Wouldn't that be nice?'

Tim caught his breath as he drank in the proud thrust of her full, uptilted breasts crowned by the tawny nipples that were already pointing out their firmness, the sweep of her thighs that moulded into Lily's long legs and the fluffy, crisp thatching over her pouting crack that nestled between the tops of those lovely limbs.

She took hold of him and pressed her lips against his, darting her tongue between his lips as she slipped her hand down to feel his swelling shaft. Tim shivered uncontrollably as she unbuttoned his trousers, sending them sliding round his ankles as she slid her hand inside his drawers to bring out his hard smooth-skinned prick. 'This is a fine instrument,' she murmured. 'If this were a piano, I would say that it ranked along a Bechstein or a Zanerowski.

'Wouldn't you agree, Martina?' she added as the other girl yawned and stretched her limbs.

'Yes, that's a very well-shaped cock – now take off the rest of your clothes, young man, and let's see what else you can offer,' said Martina lazily.

Tim trembled as he tore off his shirt and trousers and pulled off his shoes and socks. Lily looked on with amusement and whispered to Martina: 'Tim has told me that he is a virgin but he won't be one for very much longer!'

The boy was now naked and his slim yet muscular frame heaved as he took Lily into his arms, mashing her soft breasts into his chest as they kissed wildly, their tongues deep in each other's mouths. His hands slid down her body to her smooth thighs and ran up behind to grip the firm globes of her bum before running his fingers along the crack of her arse until he found her dampening cunney. Lily sighed and moved her hips, rubbing her pussey along the length of his palm, her juices coating his hand and Tim felt her hard, hot clitty as she rubbed herself faster against him. His eyes smouldered with passion as they sank to the floor with Tim pressing his mouth to that wonderfully soft body, kissing, licking and lapping until his lips found the fluffy bush of honey-coloured down that covered her pubic mound.

Tim buried his head between her thighs as she clasped his head between her legs. His tongue slurped around the labia and Lily slid her hands into his hair, urging him to lick her harder as he tasted her sweetness, exploring her very essence with his lips and tongue. Her hips were now moving in synchronised rhythm with his mouth and she cried out with joy as she reached the summit of pleasure.

He straightened up and knelt in front of her but nervousness had overtaken him and his prick dangled down limply. He looked down in horror at his flaccid shaft but Martina, wisely guessing that the youth was suffering solely from nervous excitement, reached out and rubbed his shaft up and down until it began to harden in her hand. She drew back the foreskin until his red knob swelled bounded in her hand. She pushed him down so that he was lying on his back and Lily hauled herself up until she was in a sitting position on top of his thighs. Martina still held Tim's staff in her hand and she rubbed the end of his smooth-domed knob lightly over Lily's silky pubic bush. 'A-h-r-e, that's divine, just divine,' groaned Lily. 'Oooh! What a lovely feeling!' Martina kept the moist end of his penis hovering between her friend's cunney lips until Lily pulled herself over Tim's twitching tool and sat down suddenly so that all of his thick shaft was embedded inside her.

'Yes! Yes! Yes!' she squealed as she leaned forward and brushed her nipples against his chest as they kissed with renewed passion. 'Now, Tim, I want as much of your darling cock as possible for as long as you can keep that gorgeous stiffness inside my juicy wet cunt!' And she bounced up and down upon him with a gleeful expression on her pretty face, then she sat still for a moment, pausing to savour the delicious sensation of having her cunney filled with Tim's throbbing tool. Her cheeks were flushed, her nipples standing out like little red rocks as her breasts bounced gaily in time with the pumping of her bottom cheeks as they smacked rhythmically against the top of his legs. What Tim lacked in experience he made up for in enthusiasm, meeting her downward plunges with his own upward thrusts, feeling for the first time the delicious caress of a cunney sheath around his shaft.

She whimpered with excitement as she held her hips hard down upon him, rubbing from side to side, clenching her cunney muscles as a series of exquisite spasms rocked her lithe body. Then she threw back her head and spent just seconds before Tim's juices came boiling up from his balls through his shaft to soak her love channel with a full libation of thick, creamy sperm. Lily rolled off him, gasping for breath but Martina, who had amused herself by frigging her own pussey during the bout, took hold of Tim's tool which was still hard and licked the last of the spunk off his twitching mushroomed knob.

'You have no objection to letting me be the first to suck this lovely prick now that it has entered its first pussey?' she asked. 'Not at all,' Lily replied gaily. 'and I am sure that Tim won't exactly mind either!'

'I should say not!' gasped the happy youth, hardly believing that he had now travelled that long-awaited journey from imagination to actuality. Martina smiled as she bent her head down to rest on his thighs. She began by jamming down his foreskin and teased the uncovered cock head by running the tip of her tongue all around the ridges of the springy cap whilst at the same time manipulating his heavy balls through the hairy, wrinkled skin of his bags.

Lily watched her friend's technique in earnest as Martina gave Tim's cock a few hard sucks with which to open the proceedings and make the young man's prick swell almost menacingly in her mouth. She pulled it from her lips and lapped up the pre-cum juices that were already oozing out of the tip. She flicked her tongue delicately along the shaft and Lily joined her to lick slowly along the bottom of his tightening ballsack. Tim groaned and his prick began to twitch uncontrollably and Martina jammed her mouth over the bulbous dome and slurped greedily as the frothy white jets of spunk spurted out into her throat. She gulped and sucked to milk his prick dry, draining the last drops of juice, rolling her lips around the shaft, nibbling round the funny 'eye' until his movements ceased and his shaft softened into flaccidity.

Sir Ronnie Dunn now stirred himself and came ambling over to join the girls. 'Is this a private party or can anyone join in?' he enquired with a smile.

Martina giggled and reached up to grab hold of the baronet's swelling shaft as he sat down between the girls. He kissed Martina boldly on the lips but at the same time inserted his wicked fingers into Lily's juicy cleft, thrilling her with his gentle yet firm touch. His pulsating prick stood high as Martina continued to rub the purple shaft up and down from the base to the dome and back again. This spectacle quite fired Tim who stroked his stiffening prick up into a further fine erection – what a splendid introduction to *l'arte de faire l'amour*, as he later commented to Mr Formbey – and Martina wriggled her hand to invite the footman in for a further session of fucking.

Sir Ronnie took Lily's erect little nipple into his mouth

as he continued to slide his fingers in and out of her sopping cunney. Martina opened her legs to accomodate Tim's bulging prick and she gave Sir Ronnie's thick prick a final loving rub before letting him roll on top of Lily and slip his meaty weapon into her welcoming pussey. The baronet pounded away merrily in and out of Lily's succulent crack as with one hand he toyed with her nipples and with the other tweaked Martina's titties to add further fuel to the fire raging inside her. Meanwhile Tim thrust home, withdrew and then re-entered, initially at a slow pace and then, on Martina's command, at a faster rhythm.

With one hand Lily reached down between Sir Ronnie's legs and squeezed his balls whilst Martina performed the same ministration for Tim. This additional stimulation soon had the desired effect and the two men spunked copiously into their respective pussies as the girls, too, reached delicious orgasms.

Tim's tool was now in need of recuperation but Sir Ronnie's blood was still up and he scrambled to his feet, his long staff dangling between the two girls. 'Suck me off, please, ladies,' he said huskily and the two girls were pleased to accede to his request, their pretty heads closeted together as they tongue-flicked his shaft and balls until they glistened with saliva. Lily continued to suck lustily on the fast swelling sugar-stick while Martina suddenly moved her mouth away and buried her head between Lily's long legs, driving her tongue between the pussey lips right into the ring of her cunney, tossing it round the quivering walls, withdrawing and then plunging in again rapidly, in and out, in and out. Lily continued to suck Sir Ronnie's prick and Martina continued to attack the trembling girl's engorged clitty, passing her tongue over the most sensitive parts before taking Lily's glorious clitty in her mouth, rolling her tongue around it and playfully biting it with her teeth. With each stroke of her tongue Lily arched her body in ecstasy and, without changing her rhythm, Martina let her hands wander along the carpet as if searching for something much needed. Tim guessed that she wanted her handbag and passed it to her. Still sucking the tangy juices that were now flowing from Lily's velvety grooves, Martina fished inside her bag and brought out a beautifully-fashioned, India rubber dildoe complete with a strap which she immediately fitted round her waist. She lowered herself back into position and began to suck Lily's erect nipple with one hand whilst guiding the dildoe straight into Lily's willing slit.

Count Gewirtz had now regained his appetite and moved across, his hand stroking his formidable prick up to its full majestic height. He looked down on Martina's rump moving to and fro and exclaimed: 'What an adorable bottom. May I have the pleasure of inserting my cock *au derrière*?'

'Help yourself!' Martina panted and pushed her delightful bottom out to ease the passage of the Count's pulsating shaft. He slipped the glowing dome of his noble tool between Martina's superb cheeks that were waiting to be split. He pushed forward and his prick quickly enveloped itself between the globes of that mouth-watering bum. The Count absorbed himself in her tight little orifice and began to fuck with vigour, pushing his body forwards and backwards, making her bottom cheeks slap loudly against his belly as she moaned with delight. He bent over to fondle and weigh her lush breasts and she wriggled her arse provocatively which made the Count's cock pound even more quickly in and out of her gorgeous bum.

Other guests now sauntered over to enjoy the show. Sir Ronnie stood with his head thrown back, breathing heavily as he pushed his shaft further into Lily's sweet mouth as the ecstatic girl sucked lustfully around his knob as at the same time Martina raised herself up and down sending the dildoe crashing in and out of Lily's pussey whilst Count Gewirtz caught the rhythm as he fucked Martina's bottom with long, powerful strokes of his thick prick.

'Help me to complete the chain,' cried Vazelina Volpe, running up to plant a burning kiss on Count Gewirtz's lips. Patti whispered to Bella that this reminded her of a stage tableau and they had the splendid idea of lifting Vazelina up so that she continued to kiss the Count with her legs resting on Sir Ronnie's shoulders. 'Pull her legs back so that Ronnie can gamahuche her pussey!' called out Bernado Rubeno, the first to see how this could be best achieved.

'A splendid idea!' called out Sir Ronnie and Patti and Bella carefully moved Vazelina's legs until her bushy mound was directly above his mouth and the lecherous financier was able to bury his face in her silky brown bush. His tongue raked her clitty as it slid wickedly between her lips and now all engaged were replete.

Sir Ronnie was not unexpectedly the first to spend, squirting jets of spunk into Lily's mouth which she gulped down with joy. Her pussey now tingled with delight as a great shattering orgasm sped through her body. Martina, too, now reached the highest peaks as she climaxed from the joint stimulation of Count Gewirtz's hands running in and out of her cunt and his thick prick spurting globs of hot love juice into her bum-hole.

His Royal Highness led a round of applause for the performers and sitting down on the couch, patted his thighs to give an open invitation to any lady present to sit there and caress the princely prick which was standing bolt upright from the mass of shaggy brown hair at the base of his belly. Patti and Bella asked if they might be fucked by the royal rod and the Prince graciously nodded his assent.

'Let's get you in the mood first,' said Bella gaily and the two naked girls stood in front of him, stroking each other, kissing, rubbing each other's breasts and bums and the kissing soon turned into licking and lapping. Then fingers were rubbing at cunney lips and gradually the girls were pushing their fingers deep inside each other's pussies as they moved to a soixante neuf position on the floor, licking each other's cunnies, little pink tongues probing into juicy, warm vaginas. Bella's hand was pumping away merrily at Patti's sopping cunt and glistening juices ran down the crack of her arse and dripped down onto the carpet. 'More, more. Push harder. Push everything in!' gasped pretty Patti. 'Which man has a nice, thick prick ready to slide into my aching pussey?'

The gentlemen all looked towards the Prince as none wished to be guilty of the sin of *lèse-majesté*. 'I am at your service, ma'am,' he grunted as he heaved himself to his feet and joined the two tribades. He chose to fuck

Patti, rolling her onto her back and, after juicing her pussey up even further by inserting two of the royal fingers, pushed his shaft deep inside her. She pushed her groin up against him, wiggling her hips to ensure that every last centimetre of that rigid rod was embedded in her love channel.

Besides them Sir Paul Arkley had moved on top of Bella, pushing his prick in and out of her sopping cunney, his hips bucking to and fro as his purple knob, coated with love juice, squelched in and out of her haven.

As the Prince and Sir Paul fucked the beautiful dancers, the girls, who were lying side by side, turned to each other and started kissing each other again, kissing, licking and stroking nipples while the men were plunging their pricks into their pussies.

'Ah, *quando viene il desiderio, none' è mai troppo*,' exclaimed Bernado Rubeno, his arms around Susannah who was gently frigging his massive cock.

'When desire comes it is never excessive,' translated Arthur McCann, idly letting his hand slip down to forage around Susannah's blonde cushion of hair which lightly covered her puffy cunney lips.

Sir Ronnie Dunn then had a brilliant idea – with the aid of Count Gewirtz he lifted Patti and Bella onto the dining-room table. Patti was on her back and Bella lay on top of her, continuing their kissing and fondling as the Count spread their legs wide and positioned their luscious cunts level with the edge of the dining-room table.

Naturally the Prince of Wales was offered first choice of the two ripe cunnies and first he plunged into Bella's love tunnel from behind and then withdrew to thrust into Patti's pussey for a while before settling into Bella's sopping sex hole. Sir Paul Arkley went round to the other side of the table and inserted his uncovered purple knob between the lips and flicking tongues of the two girls who appeared to be more than happy to accommodate the intruder. They set about licking his prick in style, their tongues working their way along his rock-hard cock with expert precision. What a delightful duo they made, opening their mouths till their lips met round his swollen shaft. Then, as if kissing each other, they moved their heads from side to side, giving Sir Paul a wonderful sucking off which he obviously enjoyed immensely.

The Prince was still happily pushing his prick in and out of Bella's cunt from behind and her lithe body quivered as he rammed home with gusto, sheathing his mighty cock so fully that his balls banged against her bum cheeks.

'Oh, what joy! What bliss! What a grand fuck!' he cried out as he leaned forward to slip his hand between the girls' writhing bodies to diddle Bella's erect little titties. She wriggled her bottom artfully and this manoeuvre so stimulated the Prince that with a strangled roar he sent spout after spout of spunk into her juicy wetness and the spectators could see the ripples of orgasmic joy running down Bella's spine as they shuddered to a magnificent mutual climax.

The Prince reeled back into a chair, quite exhausted from his huge spend but Bernado Rubeno gallantly took his place to try out the pleasures of the double-decker pussies. Both gaped open invitingly as Bella and Patti continued to rub their pussies together in a frenzy, lascivious lubricity. He paused for a moment and then decided to edge his sturdy staff into Patti's wide pussey that was already wet with her own juices and the Prince's spunk which had dripped down from Bella's cunney. Bernado made a slow, sensual entry as Patti raised her legs to wrap round his waist, making Bella 'the meat in the sandwich' as Arthur McCann commented, and Bernado's ivory-smooth hardness was soon fully buried in her delicious crack, his long tool working backwards and forwards as Patti tightened her cunney lips as best she could to feel the ridging of his knob.

At the other side of the table Sir Paul had somehow managed to prolong his period of continuous ecstasy but now he could wait no longer and a great wash of white sperm came flooding out of his prick into the open mouths of Patti and Bella who sucked up as much of his cream as they could before kissing wildly, exchanging mouthfuls of spunk as they climaxed together.

Bernado was now pounding like a piston, bringing Patti to a second orgasm with every peak of his cock's jutting strokes, which quickly ended with his drenching her womb with a perfect shower of spunk.

This little scene set Susannah's blood on fire and she dropped to her knees, rolled back Arthur McCann's foreskin and took his stiffening shaft in her hands to lap at the uncovered dome. Rapidly his cock began to swell and he moved forward instinctively to push his hardening prick into her mouth. The blonde beauty was an excellent cocksucker who obviously enjoyed this exquisite form of sexual gratification. Her mouth worked up and down, licking the length of his rod, playfully flicking at the knob with her impudent tongue.

Her magic mouth circled his knob, savouring the juices and her teeth scraped the tender flesh of the underside as she drew him in between those luscious lips, sucking slowly to bring Arthur to hitherto new peaks of sensual delight.

When she felt Arthur approach his climax her hand gripped the base of his penis and, with the other, she pumped the shaft up and down, taking his balls into her mouth and sucking on them as she rubbed him up to orgasm. A rush of excitement surged through his body and he filled her mouth with huge globs of frothy jism. She eagerly swallowed his copious emission and gurgled to see that his cock remained semi-erect even after discharging its load of love juice.

'You really are a game old chap, Arthur,' she exclaimed, laying herself down on the carpet. 'Now I'll just give your prick a nice little rub to bring it back up to the mark and then I want you to pop it in my pussey.'

Arthur needed no second invitation and he viewed the luxuriant blonde bush as Susannah parted her legs and stroked her delicate little notch. He lay down beside her and felt for the soft, warm lips of her pouting pussey which moistened at his first touch.

'Still feeling randy?' teased Susannah, one hand still holding on to his hardening staff.

'I feel as if I could satisfy you, Patti, Bella and all the other ladies present.'

'Don't brag, Arthur, just show me what you're made of,' she replied, as she lay back, stroking her nipples and spreading her legs apart.

Arthur positioned himself on top of her and lifted her legs until the back of her knees were just above his waist. Her cunney was so juiced up that his shaft slipped in immediately up to the hilt. As he jammed his erect, rampant cock inside her she put her arms around his neck and clamped her legs around his torso. He thrust deeper and deeper and between the thrusts he withdrew his shaft up to the ruby mushroomed knob and then pushed right in again as far as he could go. When he was fully inside he gyrated his hips so that his prick moved in all directions within her love channel and then he withdrew and paused once more before plunging again into her welcoming wetness.

'That's really marvellous, Arthur,' panted the sensuous Susannah. 'Now push as hard as you can. Oooh! Ooooh! Ooooh! I love to feel your hard, strong cock roving inside me.' So as he pushed he shifted his position slightly – first to one side and then to the other – to make sure that his prick went in at a different angle to give the quivering girl a little extra enjoyment.

Each time his thick prick slid into her she let out a cry and dug her fingernails lightly into his shoulders, her large breasts crushed against his hairy chest as he clutched the cheeks of her bum in his hands and continued to fuck her with regular but forceful movements. He quickened the tempo and Susannah shouted that she was about to spend. Arthur felt the muscles of her cunt clasping and rippling along the length of his shaft sending waves of exquisite pleasure down his spine. He could feel the pressure building up in his balls as he gripped her bum cheeks tightly, his fingers digging into the soft flesh, straining hard against her until he felt his hot jets of spunk speed along his tool to spurt out in fiery bursts into her sopping pussey.

'Aaah! Aaah! What a fine fucker you are Arthur! Empty your balls! Yes, that's it! That's it! What a lovely spend!' yelled Susannah uninhibitedly as she reached a crescendo of pleasure and great shudders of delight fairly shuddered through her.

This superb coupling ended just as Mr Formbey wheeled in a trolley of *entremets* and ice creams. Although all were still naked, the combination of their strenuous exertions and the effect of the modern central heating installed at no expense spared by Count Gewirtz, meant that the company were more than ready for the cooling desserts, and even for a break from all the fucking.

Vazelina Volpe sat on the Prince's lap, spooning ice-cream into his mouth whilst Lily perched herself on the Count's thighs, offering him little bites of the chocolate eclair which she had first rubbed gently between her legs. The two men took their partners by their waists to make them comfortable but their discussion centred around the new-fangled motor car which was already making its appearance on London's crowded roads.

'Mark my words, Your Majesty,' said Count Gewirtz earnestly. 'At present motoring is only for the few but it will not be long before they become our chief means of conveyance and cars will soon be built to such a standard that the occupants will be able to arrive at their destination in the same state of cleanliness as if they had been for an old-fashioned carriage drive.'

'You really believe that these horrid machines are here to stay?' sighed the Prince.

'Without a doubt, sir, and our coachmen will have to show the greatest skill in controlling their horses because so far my experience is that the animals are severely frightened by any vehicle travelling at more than ten miles an hour. This is what I have discovered in Paris, at any rate, and I am sure that you will find this to be so in London very soon.

'I would hazard a guess that within the next few years most motor cars will be easily able to reach four or even five times that speed so the Government had better begin planning for this explosion of fast traffic on the roads as soon as possible,' said Count Gewirtz.

'I'll mention it to the Prime Minister,' said the Prince, nodding his head in agreement. 'Have you one of these infernal motor cars, Johnny? I would like to experience a ride in one of them.'

'Not in London, I regret to say, but I'll bring one over from Berlin on my next trip,' said the Count. 'And I think that a ride in my Daimler automobile may well convert you to the joys of the horseless carriage.'

'Good, I'll hold you to that promise. I wish you would come to London more often, Johnny, as we always have a good time together. You'd be surprised how little time I do actually manage to have for private amusement. God, next week I have to waste a whole evening dining with a boring bunch of lawyers in the Middle Temple, an occasion I could well do without.'

'Well you surely don't have to go very often, although funnily enough I seem to recall that you missed one of my parties a few years ago because of some legal dinner – or is my memory playing tricks?'

'No, no you are not mistaken,' said the Prince

gloomily. 'It was in 1887 when as Prince-Bencher I held the office of Treasurer and presided at the Grand Day banquet in Trinity Term.'

'Was not this the special dinner being held in celebration of the Queen's Jubilee?'

'You are again correct – and I was really annoyed about missing a party given by Count Gewirtz! Actually, it did not turn out as badly as I feared. As you may well imagine, a more than usually distinguished and numerous company assembled in the Hall and the activities were on a more extended scale and of a more unrestrained character.'

'This sounds interesting, Your Majesty,' chirped Vazelina, offering the Prince another spoonful of ice-cream which he gratefully accepted.

'It turned out quite well,' grinned the Prince with a wicked smile playing about his lips. 'By the time it came to the brandy and port, many of the legal gentlemen were, not to put too fine a point on it, absolutely blotto. I had drunk more sparingly as I had to make some damned speech and it would not be right to stand up and spout in an intoxicated condition. Still, I felt very merry, especially when this attractive young waitress leaned over me to fill up an empty decanter. She wore a really pretty blouse and as the top buttons were open I was given a delightful view of the swell of her deliciously rounded breasts. My arm reached out as if it had a mind of its own and gently caressed her sweet backside . . .

'Now you know, Johnny, that I have never taken advantage of my high position to make girls do anything they would not wish to do, so if this dark-haired little minx had blushed with embarrassment or moved away smartly, I would have thought nothing more of it. But she wriggled her arse seductively against my hand and whispered: 'My name is Sally, sir, and I'll be in the ladies cloakroom in about ten minutes if you've the time and fancy for a quick fuck.'

'That was all I needed to hear for I hold that there is nothing to beat the unexpected chance of love-making to make the adrenalin course through the veins.

'Anyway, I was dining in an all-male company so the ladies cloakrooms would obviously be unused. I made my excuses and slipped away to find Sally waiting for me, already partially undressed, sitting on top of the long table where hats and coats were deposited. She had thoughtfully brought two cushions and was clad only in her blouse and underskirt. I climbed up besides her and undid her blouse to reveal her extremely large breasts which were topped by equally large aureoles and stiff, strawberry-coloured nipples. I unwrapped her skirt and drank in the beauty of her delightful mound which was covered by a profusion of rich brown hair. The swelling lips pouted so invitingly – the glowing red chink between looking most luxurious and welcoming!

'After a preliminary embrace Sally laid down with a cushion under her bum and with her legs wide open to present me with a fair mark as I pulled down my trousers. I prefer to fuck in the nude but there was so little time that I could not waste precious seconds fumbling with buttons, braces and cuffs. 'Please suck my titties, sir,' she said softly as my head sank down to her snowy white breasts. I was more than pleased to comply with this request and I licked and sucked at an aroused tawny titty as I explored the silky tuft of hair between her thighs.

This divine creature opened her legs wider to let my finger slip further inside her juicy crack.

' "Now, Your Majesty, now, please stick your fat cock inside me, please do me the honour of fucking my pussey!' she whispered passionately in my ear. I pushed my prick towards those glistening red lips but in my hurried frenzy could not effect an entrance. So the kind girl took hold of my throbbing tool and guided it herself, inserting the uncapped purple dome into the wet folds of her cunney. Sally possessed a remarkable gift of contracting her pussey so that it took hold of my prick, like a delicate soft hand frigging the shaft, and she wriggled away happily as I pumped my raging prick in and out of her sodden cunt, her vaginal muscles caressing my cock as we went faster and faster and she bucked and she twisted, urging me to thrust even deeper as she raised her legs and wrapped them round my shoulders. How tightly her cunt enclasped and sucked upon my prick and I felt her love juices drip upon my bollocks as they banged against her bum. Cupped now in my palms, her tight bottom cheeks rotated almost savagely as my tool slid in and out between her lips in a most sensuous way. I tried to make it last but soon there was just no way that I could hold back. So when I felt that warm, tingling feeling develop, I arched my body upwards and then plunged down hard, crushing those magnificently-proportioned breasts beneath me as her legs flexed and my frothy seed poured into her pulsating pussey. I pushed in, pushed away and pushed in again as her clever cunney milked my prick of every last drop of frothy jism. She clung to me like a leech and she shuddered to a grand spend herself as I let my shrinking shaft soak in my spunk inside her until she finished.'

'What a splendid story,' enthused Vazelina Volpe. 'Look, your royal prick is standing high again and my own cunney is aching to be filled. Won't you give me the same satisfaction that you gave that little serving wench?'

'Of course I will, my dear lady,' said the Prince gallantly, rubbing his hands against her not inconsiderable bosoms. And this set the party off again on a further final orgy of sexual games. At one time Count Gewirtz's cock was lodged in Susannah's cunney whilst with one hand, Patti was plying her bottom-hole with a dildoe and with the other was masturbating the thick shaft of Sir Ronnie Dunn who was finger-fucking the sopping cunney of Bella whose bottom cheeks were being speared by Sir Paul Arkley who was sucking the titties of Vazelina Volpe just as the Prince of Wales was presenting the red-headed knob of his cock to her pussey whilst he darted his tongue in and out of Lily's pussey which she pressed up towards his face as Bernado Rubeno engorged her bum-hole with his throbbing tool and Arthur McCann presented his stiff shaft for her to suck, which she did until Arthur's cock was ready to be plunged into Martina's waiting, wet pussey.'

Mr Formbey put his head round the door for a moment and hastily withdrew after taking in this extraordinary spectacle. 'Blimey, what I could earn for a photograph of that lot!' he muttered as he made his way downstairs. To his amusement he found Tim Fletcher on the floor of the servants hall busy working on the eager young maids Lizzie and Estelle, his cock forcing apart Estelle's cunney lips as he thrust his stiff truncheon between them whilst at the same time sliding a huge cucumber in and out of Lizzie's willing little pussey.

'He's learned more than he bargained for this evening,' muttered the butler, pushing open the door of the kitchen. 'Christ, not you as well, Hetty!' he cried as he saw the plump cook was down her knees, lustily sucking the stiff naked prick of Inspector Rogers who was leaning against the wall with his trousers round his ankles.

'Blow me, I thought you were supposed to be guarding the house!' complained the butler.

'I have three men patrolling the street,' panted Inspector Rogers, clutching hold of Mrs Beaconsfield's head as she circled her hands round his thick prick which already had a blob of sticky fluid at the end of the knob. She jammed down his foreskin and lashed her tongue round the huge pole as she sucked noisily upon the twitching tool, moving her head to and fro so that one moment the shaft was almost out of her mouth and the next it was all but totally engulfed between her wet lips up to his pubic hairs. Mrs Beaconsfield sucked greedily on the Inspector's ramrod-stiff truncheon until, with a hoarse cry, the police officer began to buck forwards and backwards as he spouted his jets of juicy spunk into her mouth and she swallowed the copious emission that came bubbling out of the 'eye' of his massive knob.

This erotic sight was too much for the butler to bear and Mr Formbey fumbled his fly buttons open and began to massage his stiff prick.

'Don't waste it, George, I'll come over and relieve your feelings,' called out the cook who dropped to her knees in front of him and began lewdly to play with his erect shaft, hugging it, pressing it to her ample breasts, squeezing it between them, pressing it against her cheeks, gently rubbing it with her hands and taking the uncapped head between her lips, softly biting it and tickling his knob with the end of her tongue. Then she suddenly thrust the shaft into her mouth and by her exquisite palating proudly erected his thick staff until even her wide mouth could hardly accommodate it.

But Mrs Beaconsfield was made of stern stuff and was determined to finish the job she had started. She rolled down the butler's foreskin and sucked greedily on his immense cock. She clasped his bottom cheeks in her hands to draw even more of his shaft into her mouth and somehow managed to take in practically all of his tool without gagging, until his hairy ballsack dangled in front of her straining lips. His climax arrived pretty soon and he hoarsely cried out through clenched teeth: 'Here comes the liquor!' as he felt the liquid fire boiling up from his balls into his shaft to ejaculate in a fierce hot tidal gush of white juice into her eager throat. She swallowed his creamy spend with great relish and he pulled her head even closer as his cock, milked by her delicious sucking, began to lose its stiffness to shrink back into its normal dangling state.

'You certainly know how to suck cocks, Hetty,' said Inspector Rogers admiringly as he pulled on his trousers.

'Yes, and I'm not ashamed of it neither,' she replied. 'I love sucking a good stiff prick but all the men I know spunk so quickly. I'd like to suck for at least ten minutes for I do so enjoy caressing the uncapped tip with my lips. But no one I know can last out more than five minutes. Mind, it's lovely to suck out the love juice as I'm very

257

partial to the taste and it's so exciting when the first squirt shoots into my mouth!'

'It's a natural gift you have, love, and I'm sure the Inspector will agree that there aren't many girls who could suck us off so well as you,' said Mr Formbey emphatically.

'Thank you, George, it's kind of you to say so. Actually I've always enjoyed it and even more so since Count Gewirtz gave me a little book from his secret library, *An Introduction To The Eastern Arts of Fucking* by A Lady Much Experienced In Those Parts.' You two boys should read it one day – I'll lend it to you with pleasure!

'Gad, you're all woman, Hetty,' growled the Inspector. 'Now is a little fuck out of the question?'

'Delete the word little from your question and I'm delighted that you can raise interest so quickly, Glenton,' she laughed, taking off her skirt and pulling her drawers down. She walked over to the kitchen table and leaned over it, pushing out her plump, proud backside as the police officer sidled up behind her, his rigid rod in hand, ready to wriggle his knob into her bumhole. He presented his cockhead to the puckered little orifice but the cook stopped him with a cry.

'I'd far rather you didn't push your cock into my arse, Glenton. My cunney is aching for a nice thick prick so I'd prefer you to slip it inside my pussey. You don't mind, do you?'

'Of course not, my love,' replied the Inspector graciously. 'After all, I'm not dedicated to bottoms like your guvnor's friend, Mr Oscar Wilde.'

He pulled her thighs apart until he had fair view of the pouting pink lips of her juicy cunney. He struggled at first to insert his knob but Mr Formbey kindly took hold of the Inspector's corpulent cock and guided it in gently between the lips of Hetty Beaconsfield's oily channel. Effecting a safe lodgement for the head, with one vigorous thrust he buried the shaft to the hilt and his heavy balls flopped wildly against the table. With his cock fully embedded in her, the cook was now galvanised into wriggling her rounded bum cheeks lasciviously as she whispered hoarsely: 'Oh, do it to me, do it to me, Glenton – empty your balls, you randy rascal!'

They were as one, a single, perfectly synchronised fucking machine – thrust and counterthrust, action and reaction! Inspector Rogers thrust again and again and he wrapped his arms around her, clasping the cook to him as, with a convulsive thrill, he poured out a flood of luscious love juice in an ecstasy of enjoyment.

In the meantime, Estelle and Lizzie were engaged in a heated discussion in the hallway just outside the dining room.

'I still say he might be very offended,' said Estelle, shaking her head.

'No, no, not the Prince, he likes a girl that has a bit of cheek – and I'm sure Count Gewirtz wouldn't mind,' argued her friend.

'Suppose he did? We'd lose all that lovely money Mr Formbey said we'd get at the end of the job.'

'Trust me, it won't happen. Look, Estelle, do you want to be fucked by the Prince of Wales or not?'

'Of course I do but I don't want to get into any trouble either.'

'Believe me, you won't,' said Lizzie firmly. 'Come on in, I'll do the talking and take all the blame if he or Count

Gewirtz gets cross. But I just know that no one will be annoyed, not after what they have all been up to this evening!'

Reluctantly, Estelle allowed herself to be pulled into the dining-room where Prince Edward was polishing off a bowl of fresh fruit salad. He and the guests were still all naked but no frenetic activity was currently taking place, both the men and the women were talking and laughing in little groups as happens at the close of most dinner parties.

'Excuse me, Your Majesty,' said Lizzie boldly. 'My friend and I would like to ask you a great favour which we sincerely hope you will see fit to grant.'

The Prince raised his eyes and looked benignly on the two pretty serving wenches who curtsied in front of him. 'Yes, my dears, what can I do for you?' he said.

'We would love you to fuck us,' said Lizzie with a shy smile. 'We swear that we would never tell a soul but we would be so honoured if we could have the future king of England's cock inserted in our cunnies.'

They looked anxiously at each other as the Prince considered their request. 'I think it's a splendid idea, girls,' he said after a moment's consideration. 'But I've been well-looked after already this evening and I don't know whether I'm up to very much just now. Still you are welcome to try and make my royal rod rise again!'

'There! I told you he wouldn't mind,' said Lizzie triumphantly, slipping off her blouse immediately the words left the Prince's mouth, joyously shaking her head so that the pert mass of blonde hair fell all around her pretty face. Estelle unbuttoned her skirt and let it fall to the floor. She pulled down her drawers and quickly shucked off her blouse and slip so that she stood naked except for her suspender belt and stockings. Lizzie drew up a chair and sat down upon it. 'You were wrong, Estelle and now you must take your punishment.' Estelle approached her and as quick as a flash Lizzie proceeded straight to business by bending her gorgeous friend over her knees, exposing her tight little nude arse cheeks to general view.

Lizzie then began to smack Estelle's beautiful bottom with the palm of her hand, lightly but in rapid succession until the poor girl cried out: 'Oooh! Oooh! That's enough, Lizzie, enough, enough, Oooh! Finish me off, there's a love!'

'Quiet now, you bad girl. You've been naughty and all naughty girls get slapped on the bum. Besides the Prince and I want to see your lovely bottom change colour and anyway your cheeks look divine as they jiggle as they get slapped.'

This scene certainly excited the Prince whose cock had stiffened up to a rock-hard erection as he watched this stimulating exhibition. In no time he was on his knees huddled up to Lizzie who, without missing one beat of her rhythmic swishing of Estelle's bum, clamped her full red lips around the purple knob of the princely prick.

Although this also excited Lizzie, mercifully for Estelle's poor bottom, the blonde girl ceased her spanking and circled her hands round the stately shaft which already had a blob of milky jism around the 'eye' of its head. She eased down the foreskin and, bending low, whipped her tongue round the noble pole as Estelle wriggled off Lizzie's knees to kneel before her, opening her thighs to place her head between her legs and nuzzle her mouth around Lizzie's silky golden bush which was already wet with love juice.

The Prince licked his lips and pulled his prick away from Lizzie's mouth and positioned himself behind Estelle who placed her hands on Lizzie's thighs to give herself enough leverage to stand with her legs wide open and at an angle so that her firm young bum was high in the air as she continued to slip her little pink tongue in and out of Lizzie's pussey.

Estelle then reached behind her and took hold of the Prince's sturdy member, directing its ruby bulb between the glorious cheeks of her delicious bottom and to the puckered little hole that lay between them. The Prince wet his cock with some butter thoughtfully offered to him by Sir Ronnie Dunn and then attacked Estelle's fortress with vigour.

'Aaah! You're there, sir! That's enough!' cried Estelle as the princely prong forced its way within the sphincter muscle and so he rested a moment or two and then slowly began to pull in and out and Estelle's wriggling of her delightful bum showed how well she was enjoying the experience, especially when the Prince moved his hand round to tickle and play with her cunney. Slow in, slow out, he eased his long, thick tool, probing her bottom hole with liquid fire, both trembling in an agony of bliss.

'Pump faster, pump, oh, spunk into me, sire!' she yelled and they both screamed loudly in the frenzy of emission as the Prince deluged her arse with his copious spendings. His cock was still stiff as with an audible 'pop' he uncorked it from her well-lubricated bum-hole.

'Don't forget that I have yet to come, sir. Please finish me off,' cried out Lizzie and the Prince gallantly gave

Estelle a little kiss on the cheek before murmuring: 'I must pay homage to Lizzie's sopping pussey.' He took Estelle's place in front of Lizzie and parted her soft, lightly-scented pubic hair with his fingertips to reveal her swollen clitoris. As he worked his face into the cleft between her thighs he breathed in the exquisite *odor di feminina* that so often causes the male nostrils to flare.

The Prince pulled the trembling girl gently off the chair onto the floor so that he was down on his stomach, with one hand under her bum for better elevation and the other playfully frigging her pussey, spreading the pouting lips with his thumb and middle finger.

He placed his lips over her clitty and sucked it into his mouth where the tip of his tongue began to explore it from all directions. He could feel it swell even further as her legs drummed up and down on the carpet, twitching uncontrollably along the sides of his body.

'Aaah!' she groaned as he found the little button at the base of her clitty and began twirling his tongue around it. As he moved it up and down rapidly, Lizzie became delirious with excitement. And the faster he vibrated his tongue the more reaction he got out of her. She gyrated her pelvis as he increased the pressure and he tasted the sweet juices that were flowing freely from her cunt. 'You are quite delicious,' said the Prince in a muffled voice as, pushing his mouth hard up against her, he began to move his entire head back and forth until they were both fast approaching the summit of sensual delight.

With surprising agility for such a heavily-built man, the Prince sprung up and placed his arms on Lizzie's shoulders. 'Shall I fuck you now, would you like my fat cock to slip between your cunney lips?' he asked somewhat rhetorically, his eyes twinkling as he took hold of his monster shaft, ready to place it fairly to the mark.

'Oh, yes please!' she gasped.

'So you want my prick inside your cunt?'

'Yes, I said, yes, I said yes!'

Lizzie reached out and pressed her breasts together as the Prince slowly moved on top of her and she opened her legs wide and clamped her feet around his back as he guided his throbbing shaft into her soaking little pussey.

'What a marvellously thick cock, Your Majesty,' she squealed. 'But do push harder now, further in, further in!'

She raised her legs and wrapped them round his waist as his enormous shaft stuffed her cunney to the very portal of its womb, their blonde and brown pubic hairs entangling as, with the Prince's cock fully inserted, they ground their bodies together in deliciously sensuous circles. The royal balls slapped in slow cadence against her bottom and her thighs as Lizzie thrilled to his long, smooth strokes.

Now the Prince moved up slightly and Lizzie wriggled her hips as he increased the pace. Supported just on his fingertips and toes, his cock entered at a high angle and he thrust home with pile-driving intensity against the soft, resilient flesh of her warm, wet cunney from which her juices were already flowing down her thighs. As they approached the coming climax, he changed the tempo to one of short, sharp jabs and she rotated her buttocks while he pulsed in and out until Lizzie almost fainted away with the exquisite sensations from his maddened thrusts. The contractions of her cunt sucked the boiling seed from his raging prick as the Prince spurted jet after jet of frothy white juice into her eager slit, her hands gripping his ample bum cheeks until they collapsed, utterly exhausted, into a tangle of naked limbs on the carpet which was now noticably stained from their joint spendings.

'Oh dear, I hope we will be able to clean this beautiful carpet,' said Estelle anxiously to Count Gewirtz who had come over with Vazelina Volpe and Martina Motkalowski to see the show.

'Don't worry, child, it only cost a couple of thousand pounds at trade price from Kleimans,' said the Count off-handedly.

'But in any case I gave Mr Formbey a bottle of a cleaning liquid Max Dalmain had especially made up for members of the Cremorne Club which is guaranteed to shift such stains so I am sure that there is little cause for concern,' he added.

'So you won't dock her wages, Johnny, or send a bill to Buckingham Palace?' laughed the Prince and the company laughed with him as Count Gewirtz shook his head.

This last erotic spectacle fired the guests into forming one further final fucking chain, with Sir Paul Arkley fucking Lizzie whilst having Bella work her dildo into Lizzie's bottom as she sucked the gigantic shaft of Count Gewirtz who in turn finger-fucked Vazelina Volpe who lapped at the juicy pussey of Martina Motkalowski who enjoyed the favour of having Arthur McCann insert his cock into her tight little bum-hole. Could there be a finer climax to an evening's entertainment? But before the party broke up, Count Gewirtz presented all his guests with a little memento of the occasion – a superbly

calligraphed piece of parchment upon which the Count
had inscribed the latest ironic verses by his old friend Sir
Lionel Trapes:*

> *Let those who never tried, believe*
> > *In women's chastity!*
> *Let Her who ne'er was asked, receive*
> > *The praise of modesty!*
>
> *Tho' woman's virtue's true as steel*
> > *Before you touch her soul;*
> *Still let it once the magnet feel*
> > *T'will flutter towards the Pole!*

*Sir Lionel Trapes [1826–1908] was a senior Civil Servant and noted
collector of gallant literature and art. Unfortunately his collection was
destroyed by fire during the London Blitz in 1941.

CHAPTER SEVEN

Back in the family mansion in Hyde Park Gardens, the two daughters of Sir Paul Arkley were entertaining their beaux in the privacy of their respective bedrooms.

Katie and Walter were lying in their underclothes on Katie's bed while the modern central heating radiators installed by Fagans were dispensing a generous warmth throughout the house. Walter was leafing through the *Morning Chronicle* when he suddenly noticed with interest on the letters' page, a missive from Professor Nicholas Webb [*Another well-known and extremely active member of the Cremornites – L.L.*] about the foolishness of the Government in continuing to deny women the right to vote.

'You must look at this letter my old tutor Professor Webb has written to the newspaper, darling,' called out Walter.

'Oh, I can't be bothered, sweetheart, you read it out to me,' said Katie lazily, twirling her fingers around the hairs on his chest.

'All right, I will. The letter is all about how nonsensical it is to fight against the inexorable march towards female suffrage. The Professor writes: ''We simply cannot afford as a nation to allow such a potent moral influ-

ence as that of women to lie fallow. The time has come
when that moral influence must be organised and put
into action. In olden times, when the population was
scattered and manners were patriarchal, individual charity and personal influence could work wonders. With
our vast cities and ever-increasing complication of interests and industries, a combination of influence and co-
operation in all good works have become absolutely
necessary, unless the feminine element is to be entirely
eliminated. Men are going forward so fast that the rift
between the sexes will become wider if women are to
continue working on the old lines and never take a step in
advance. The choice is not between going on and standing still, it is between advancing or retreating."

'Professor Webb is absolutely right – I mean, why
should a girl like you help plan some new scheme, for
example, that will turn our most wretchedly poor people
into valuable breadwinners yet have no influence with
Parliament to get that scheme carried into effect? It is all
most immoral.'

'I'm sure you are right, darling,' murmured Katie,
'though I must admit that just now I feel rather immoral
myself.'

'Do you now?' grinned Walter, laying down his newspaper. 'Well, that makes two of us!'

Before meeting Walter Stanton, Katie was very shy in
matters of *amour* but *experientia docet* and she turned
her pretty face to his, closing her liquid blue eyes and
began to kiss him passionately, putting her tongue deep
inside his mouth. Her hand wandered to the slit in his
drawers and pressed hard against his fast-swelling cock.
He pulled her even closer to him and returned the kiss,

his hands kneading the full softness of her bum cheeks and his tongue entwining with hers, sucking and licking as they exchanged the most delightful of embraces.

The scamp unbuttoned her flimsy negligee and released into view the most exquisite pair of naked young breasts, lusciously rounded, white as alabaster and crowned with superbly-fashioned hard, tawny nipples surrounded by large round aureoles. The adorable girl whispered: 'Kiss my breasts, Walter, I do so love the way you kiss my titties.'

He duly obliged, kissing and gently sucking the erect nipples, biting gently as she sighed, breathless with pleasure. He wriggled out of his drawers and they lay naked, entwined on the bed. He licked and sucked the lovely titties, running his hands along her thighs and Katie turned sideways so that he could insert his hands between her legs and stroke the golden silky hair of her bush before sliding a finger into her dampening crack. She moved across and over him so that her pussey was above his face as she lowered her head to kiss his pulsating prick. Her soft hands caressed his hairy ballsack as, with delicious slowness, she lapped up and around the length of his thick shaft, taking ages to reach the uncapped crown.

'Suck my knob, Katie,' he gasped and the willing girl smiled as she kissed his domed bell-end, encircling it and eagerly swallowing the pre-cum which had started to flow. Then she suddenly engulfed the throbbing knob, sliding down the foreskin and gobbling greedily on her hot lollipop.

His tongue was now pressed against her pussey and he licked at the dripping crack, moving around the outer lips and gently slipping his tongue inside the rolled lips until the juices ran into his open mouth.

'Let's change positions, for I want to fuck you before I spend in your mouth!' murmured Walter and Katie somehow managed to keep her lips clamped around his cock as she scrambled back to lie beside him. He lifted her head gently and, to her puzzlement, turned her over, but she obediently presented her back to him as he squeezed the curvaceous cheeks of her lovely bottom. Walter slid off the bed and padded round to Katie's side, his prick standing high and huge against his belly.

'Come off the bed and stand in front of me facing the bed, Katie with your legs wide apart – that's right, darling, and now I want you to bend over the bed.'

She did as she was bidden and Walter enjoyed a gorgeous view of her open bottom and pouting pussey as the lips of her cunney stretched to expose the flushed inner flesh.

He leaned over her and she gasped as she felt the hot shaft of his cock wedged between her bum cheeks. He did not try to cork her arse-hole but pushed his knob through to find the glistening crack of her cunt and he thrust forward deeply as she whimpered with joy. Fiercely he pushed, burying his thick shaft to the very hilt so that his heavy balls banged against her bum cheeks. He held her round the waist until his prick was completely embedded and then he shifted his hands to fondle those superb uptilted breasts, rubbing the pink little rosebuds till they were as hard as his prick which was nestling so nicely in her juicy crack.

He began to thrust backwards and forwards and he felt Katie explode into a series of little peaks of pleasure as he continued to fuck her 'doggie-style'. Her cunt felt incredibly tight and wet, the walls of her love-channel clinging to his prick so deliciously that it almost prevented him from driving in and out of this sweet prison.

They were lost in time as he rode against her, filling her pussey with his rock-hard shaft, pulling back for a moment and then surging forward again. He could sense Katie experiencing orgasm after orgasm and shortly afterwards he felt his staff quiver and he poured spasm after spasm of hot white spunk inside her willing pussey. His cock remained stiff as he withdrew and Katie turned round, her eyes shining, saying: 'Oh that was marvellous, Walter. Do let's continue and do it again.' She grasped his prick and rubbed it eagerly in her two hands until it rose majestically back up to its full length and strength, as hard as iron against his flat belly.

They clambered back onto the bed and this time Katie said that it was her turn to take charge.

'Let me do the work now, Walter – just lie back and let me play with your lovely cock,' she said sweetly. 'I want to fill my mouth until it bulges with your strong staff.'

The lucky lad lay back as Katie tossed back her mane of golden hair and knelt down between his legs. In a flash her tousled blonde hair was all over his groin as she fervently kissed his now rampant rod and began licking and sucking and squeezing it while his heavy balls jounced up and down in front of her face. Her little pink tongue circled his knob and her teeth scraped the tender flesh as she drew him in between her luscious lips, letting her tongue travel all the way up the length of his hard shaft, scrubbing her tongue under the plump, purple crown.

Now Katie sat astride him and leaned forward, trailing

those delicious breasts up and down his torso so that her rubbery nipples flicked exquisitely against his skin. She then lifted her hips and crouched over his stiff-standing prick, her cunney directly overhead, poised above the uncapped red dome. Then, positioning his cock, she managed to press it directly over her clitty and, rotating her body, she edged slightly forward, allowing his rigid prick to enter her. Ever so slowly she lifted and lowered her sopping pussey, moving her bottom around the fulcrum of his rigid penis, her cunney lips grasping him firmly and each time the crown of his cock went higher and deeper into her craving cunt until the couple thought their bodies would melt away in sheer delight. Their sense were at fever pitch as Walter drove upwards to meet her downward plunges, driving his sturdy cock even deeper into her up to the very hilt. She wiggled her bum wildly as they pushed and heaved, jerking their bodies into a further series of sensual excitement. As Katie thrust down to meet him it was impossible for Walter to hold back and he jerked upwards to cram every last inch of his hardness inside her.

'I'm in you, Katie, every inch of me,' he panted.

'Yes, Walter, darling and it's glorious! I'm filled with you! I could burst for joy!'

With Walter's stiff, throbbing cock fully buried, they ground their bodies together in a madness of passion. Each voluptuous shove was accompanied by joint wails of ecstasy. His hairy ballsack caressed the cheeks of her whirling bottom while Katie thrilled to a huge spend and his proud prick spurted jets of white love juice up her crack as waves of pleasure coursed through their bodies. Together they had climbed to and reached the summit of love and they sank back sated on the soft mattress. What joyous recollections of this time would Katie note in her diary the next morning – of the delights of lying naked next to her lover on the crushed and crumpled sheets after the adours of coition, listening to the muted sounds outside the boudoir.

Across the hallway the younger Arkley girl, Penny, was voraciously sucking the monster tool of Bob Goggin, her very own gardener's boy who also lay lazily on his back, his long cock bobbing with excitement whilst Penny gorged lustily on his uncapped red helmet, her hands encircling the base that was covered by a growth of mossy dark hair. The clever girl realised that Bob would spend too quickly so she gave a final friendly kiss to his cock before lying back herself on the bed, her long legs apart with her hands provocatively rubbing her dark, hairy pubis. Bob rolled himself over and their bodies crashed together as they exchanged a burning kiss and he slid a finger into her already soaking pussey, rubbing harder and harder until her little clitty turned as erect as a miniature little cock to his touch.

'Finger–fuck me, please, dear Bob,' she whispered in his ear. She placed her hands on her inner thighs and pulled her legs apart, revealing her fleshy, pink outer lips, so that Bob could see into the furthest recesses of her cunney. She was so wet and swollen that three of Bob's fingers went into her hot crack without meeting any resistance.

'Oooh! That's lovely, Bob! More, please, I must have more!' she begged.

Bob set up a well-paced rhythm, working his fingers in and out, slowly at first then faster and faster as her pussey became wetter and wetter. With the other hand he tweaked her tawny nipples and he felt his head being drawn irresistibly down towards her pulsating pussey. He removed his fingers and replaced them with his tongue and soon he was sucking away at her soaking cunney with all his might, inhaling and swallowing her tangy juices as he rubbed her nipples up' to the fullest erection against the palms of his hands.

Penny's body began to jerk up and down which made it even more exciting for Bob as his face rubbed against her curly, black bush. 'Aaaah!' screamed Penny as he worked his tongue until his jaw fairly ached, but it was well worth the effort for the trembling girl achieved a tremendous spend, grabbing hold of Bob's big cock and rubbing the shaft violently up and down until his spending followed almost immediately.

They sucked and tickled each other, changing their positions and exploring every inch of each other's bodies until, exhausted, they threw themselves down upon the bed to rest.

The noise of the front door slamming shut made Penny suddenly sit up. 'Oh God, one of my parents has come home! If it's Mama, she may come in to see if Katie and I are still awake. Bob, dear, you'd better take over immediately!'

Next door Katie was issuing a similarly urgent instruction to Walter Stanton so that when Lady Arkley (for indeed it was she) reached the top of the stairs both her daughters had naked young men crouching inside their wardrobes.

She first slowly opened the door of Katie's room and saw only the pretty blonde tousled head of hair above the covers. 'T'sk, T'sk,' muttered her mother, 'The silly girl has gone to sleep leaving the electric light on.' She switched it off and tip-toed out of the room, closing the door firmly behind her. Inside the wardrobe Walter Stanton grinned before stepping out and running to join Katie, whose naked body was exposed on the bed in all its glory as she lifted the covers to welcome him back, first with a passionate kiss on the lips followed by an equally delicious kiss on the ruby head of his fast-swelling cock.

Lady Arkley then quietly opened the door of Penny's bedroom where, after seeing that the room was in darkness and that her younger daughter was apparently fast asleep, she was satisfied that all was well. She was about to leave the room when, alas, just at that moment Bob Goggin moved his foot and trod on a shoe buckle. He let out a muffled gurgle of pain which caused Lady Arkley to draw her breath in sharply. 'Who's there?' she whispered fiercely. With commendable quickness of mind Penny opened her eyes and mumbled: 'Oh, hallo, Mother, is that you?'

'Quiet, Penny, I think I heard an intruder,' came back a fierce whisper.

'No, no, Mama, not if you mean that little noise just now. I am sure that this came from me. I was having a remarkable dream about taking part in a tug of war contest and I was pulling away with all my strength. Why, I could really hear myself grunt with the effort of it all and then I woke up,' said Penny, sitting up and stretching out her arms. Fortunately, she had had time to slip on a nightdress so there was nothing unusual about her appearance that might cause her mother to suspect the veracity of the glib explanation offered.

Lady Arkley frowned. 'Well, maybe you were responsible for that strange sound but I thought the noise emanated from elsewhere in the room, probably from the area near your wardrobe.'

'Oh, don't be silly, Mama, there's nobody here. Look, the window is shut and old Hutchinson downstairs would have heard any would-be intruder. There is no-one under my bed, is there?

'And I doubt that you will find anyone in my wardrobe either!' she added gaily although when he heard her utter these words Bob Goggin had the greatest difficulty in controlling his bladder.

'Go, on, have a look if you like,' said Penny, pressing her luck to the limit.

Lady Arkley hesitated and then turned on her heel as she wished Penny a very good night. When she heard the footsteps fall away and her Mama's bedroom door open and close, the cheeky girl burst into a fit of giggling. Bob opened the wardrobe door and in a strangled little voice said to Penny: 'My God, what on earth were you up to just now telling your mother to search the room? Suppose she had taken up your invitation?'

'Bob, dear, I had to calculate the odds. I find with Mama that the best way to get her to do something is quite simply to suggest she does so – for if I say white she will say black, if I say fast, she will say slow. I regret that she is one of those incorrigible people who can never admit that other people's opinions are worth the price of a box of matches.'

'Well, you may be right as I've had experience of Lady Arkley laying down the law in the servants' hall. Still, you took the devil of a chance,' said Bob with no little relief in his voice as he slipped back into bed.

'Never mind the servants' hall, it sounded more like a sketch from the music hall, didn't it? Bob, you really must take me to the Holborn Empire. I adore music hall but Mama does not really approve.'

'I never knew you'd ever been to such a show,' said Bob.

'Oh yes, I went to the Alhambra last month with my cousin the Reverend Stanley Radlett. The great juggler Cinquevalli was top of the bill but I'm afraid I shocked cousin Stanley when I laughed out loud at a saucy story told by the crosstalk comedians. One said to the other: "Bill, I went boating on the river last Sunday with two ladies."

' "Garn," said the other. "I saw them two females, they weren't real ladies." "Oh, yes they were, right out of high society." – "No they weren't, mate, not them two." – "They were, I tell you, and we had a lovely row until we came to Putney when I stood up and one of the oars went overboard." – "There, I told you they weren't ladies!" came the swift retort.'

This set them both a-giggling and Bob said: 'Ah, well, it was Mr Kipling, I think who said that there were only nine humorous stories in the world and eight of them cannot be told to a lady!'

But before Penny could answer him they heard a noise from downstairs and a second closure of the front door. 'That will be Papa!' exclaimed Penny whose words were being uttered almost simultaneously in the next room where Walter Stanton was on top of Katie, sliding his huge, throbbing shaft in and out of her quivering pussey.

'Damn!' said Walter, rolling off the soft body of the beautiful girl as Katie cocked her ears to hear whether

her father was coming up the stairs. 'He must have gone into the study for a night-cap,' said Katie after a few moments and Walter heaved himself back into position and guided the head of his glistening shaft back between her pouting cunney lips. Penny and Bob also breathed sighs of relief as they concluded that Sir Paul was imbibing a last cognac before retiring.

However, it was not a final measure from the crystal decanter that had caused Sir Paul to postpone his rendez-vous with his bed, but the sight of Charlotte, the plump maid who he had been fucking for the previous six months, gesticulating wildly behind Hutchinson, the old family retainer, for Sir Paul to join her in the library.

The baronet sighed but, after ascertaining that Lady Arkley had returned home, he gave orders for Hutchinson to lock up before joining Charlotte in the library.

'What is it, Charlotte? Why are you up at this ungodly hour?' he said, a trace of irritation noticeable in his voice, for he was concerned that she might be becoming too possessive, a state that he could not allow to grow out of hand. As had happened in the past with other female members of staff, he would have to find a pretext to dismiss her with suitable monetary compensation to ensure secrecy about his indiscretions.

'Oh, sir, I just couldn't sleep. Won't you please come up to the attic and fuck me before going to bed? I've tried playing with the dildoe you bought me but it isn't a patch on your lovely thick prick,' she said cunningly.

'Look, I'll come up with you for a moment but I've had a very demanding evening with Count Gewirtz and his friends. In all honesty, m'dear, I don't think I'm up to stiffening the sinews, so to speak.'

'Well, you come up and let's see what we can do,' said Charlotte with some satisfaction.

They climbed the stairs quietly to the maid's small room on the top floor and Sir Paul sat down heavily on the bed. 'I really am most awfully tired, Charlotte,' he said as she pulled her dress over her head to stand naked in front of him before kneeling down to undo his fly buttons.

'Goodness, so you are,' she exclaimed, taking out his flaccid cock which lay limply, in the palm of her hand. 'Now what can I do to perk up your prick?'

She contemplated the question for a moment and then said brightly: 'I know, would you like to hear of my rather interesting experience with a tribade this evening? I'm sure that my recounting the tale will stiffen poor little cocky here up to his usual imitation of a flagpole?'

Sir Paul's raised his eyebrows. 'I didn't know you were keen on that sort of thing,' he said with interest.

'Oh, well I do prefer a juicy thick cock but as you yourself once told me, variety is the spice of life and there aren't many men who can gamahuche my pussey as nicely as Maudie Littlehampton.'

'Maudie Littlehampton, Maudie Littlehampton – I've never come across the girl, Charlotte, who on earth is she?'

'Maudie is governess to the young children of our neighbours, Lord and Lady Hammond. Perhaps you have seen her when you've gone over to their house to play billiards. She is a pretty girl, tall and slim with long, curly auburn hair and she hadn't been in her present situation more than three weeks before Lord Antony started paying regular visits to her bedroom.'

'Ah, she does like men as well?'

'Only very occasionally, for she really prefers to play

around with girls. I had heard this information from old Hutchinson downstairs and his warning did cross my mind when I met her in the street this afternoon. She asked me if I were free to take a stroll in the park and I said that I would be happy to do so as I did not have to be back until seven o'clock.

'We enjoyed a pleasant walk and talked of this and that, nothing of real importance though she did ask me if I had any men friends. I said that at the moment I was unattached and asked her if she had any followers. She shuddered and told me that she was really not too keen on men. So old Hutchinson was right, I mused to myself but I accepted her offer to come up to her room and have a cup of tea.

'The Hammonds and the servants were all out so we had the house to ourselves although I noticed with some surprise that Maudie locked the door of her room behind us. "Do you want some tea, Charlotte, or perhaps I can offer you something a little more lively? I have a bottle of brandy here which I asked Lord Antony to buy for me – strictly for medicinal purposes, of course!' she laughed.

'To cut a long story short we sipped a glass or two of Lord Hammond's expensive cognac and before you could say Jill Robinson, Maudie stepped forward and kissed me really passionately. Still kissing, our mouths glued together, we fell back on the bed and she soon had her hand up between my legs, kneading my pussey through my best lacy knickers. This made me quite wet and I wriggled against her fingers so I could send her the message to finger my cunney. My body tensed with expectation when she slipped her hand inside my drawers and started stroking my pussey and I knew that I would soon travel the entire journey to bliss with my new female friend.

' "Ah, Charlotte, what a charming crack I see poking out its lips in the midst of that curly little bush," she said, finding my clitty almost immediately with her nail and sending the most divine sensations throughout my body.

'I opened my legs wider and held them apart as Maudie knelt on the floor and started to lick my cunt, working her fingernail delightfully over the clitty as she did so. Her tongue was spreading all the wetness round my cunney lips. Her fluttering tongue curled into a tensile tool, an oral prick that fucked me slowly . . . then more and more rapidly as rivulets of my love juices ran down my thighs and I squirmed my way to a first quick climax.

'Maudie scrambled up from the floor and stepped out of her dress. "Now I want you to make me spend, darling," she cooed, pulling down her knickers as she sprawled down besides me. She lifted her slip and showed me her cunt which I looked at with a rising lust coursing through my blood for Maudie had a lovely long crack set in a silky thicket of auburn hair. I rolled down the top of her slip to expose her firm, pointed breasts and she moaned a little as I stroked her nipples round my forefinger and thumb. She pulled my head down to one of these ripe beauties as I straddled her.

' "Suck my titty," she groaned as I took hold of the hardening little nipple in my mouth. I nibbled all round her titties, swirling my tongue first across one and then the other as the naughty girl frigged herself, jerking her hips up and down as I leaned over her. She wrapped her legs around my waist and pulled me right on top of her. "Finish me off!" she panted, guiding my hand down to her sopping pussey. I parted her lips with my fingers and dipped my digits in and out of her sweet honeypot. I couldn't wait to bury my face between her lovely thighs and taste her tangy love juices. I kissed her sweet pussey and then thrust my questing tongue into her hot, wet crack, teasingly licking and lapping all round the hole before slipping it all the way in. I closed my eyes and grasped her plump bum cheeks as my tongue flashed unerringly around the grooves of her clitty. Maudie's pussey gushed love juice and each time I tongued her, her cunney seemed to open wider as she lifted her bum high off the bed. Her clitty stiffened, ever more eager and pulsating, just bursting to explode into a marvellous all-embracing climax. I rubbed harder and harder until her clitty was a hard a little cock to my touch and her body jerked up and down, which made the experience even more exciting for me as the lovely girl writhed in delight while my face rubbed against her silky bush.

' "Oooh! Oooh!" she screamed as she pulled my head in further to her sopping slit. I moved my tongue delicately along the grooves of her pussey, sucking her tasty juices and I could tell by the spasms that racked her beautiful young body that she was about to enjoy the greatest of all pleasures. "I'm going to come!" she yelled unashamedly and with a final huge shudder Maudie achieved a most glorious spend that had her practically screaming the house down. It was as well indeed that we were alone in the house or without doubt we would have been discovered in a somewhat embarrassing position to say the least!

' "That was love at first lick!' joked Maudie as we lay back on the bed, exhausted after our fervent love-making. I smiled and kissed her again and we continued to play with each other, engaging in all kinds of intimacies for another full hour. I could not stay longer as I had to be back here by seven o'clock but I have made an arrangement to see Maudie again and she has promised me that she has a pretty friend who likes to take part in games with other girls – so we shall have a real frolic with three of tonguing each other's pussies at the same time!'

Charlotte paused for breath and her eyes brightened as she saw that this lewd confession had achieved the desired effect and that Sir Paul's prick was now standing smartly to attention. She rubbed her hands suggestively over her nipples and licked her lips to prepare for the feast to follow.

Then she swooped down and clamped her luscious lips round his domed knob. She grasped the hot, blue-veined shaft at its rigid base and rubbed the massive rod as she sucked happily away at the uncapped ruby helmet. He moaned and pressed her head downwards until her lips enclosed almost all his stiff staff and her head rose and fell in a regular rhythm that sent the baronet into sheer paroxysms of delight. She continued to suck lustily on his throbbing tool as his hand snaked out and reached for her dampening crack and Charlotte squealed while he nudged his fingers against her cunney lips, parting them gently to push first one and then two deeper inside her cunt. She raised her hips up, panting breathlessly as he began to move them in and out, matching his rhythm with hers while she continued to bob her head up and down over his twitching cock. Sir Paul gasped as he shot a stream of spunk into her receptive mouth whilst a pulse of sheer ecstasy coursed through every vein in his body.

At the very same time, in the bedrooms below, Katie and Walter were coupled together, the lusty young student pounding his prick in and out of the happy blonde girl's eager pussey and Bob Goggin was sliding his long tool between Penny's gorgeous bum cheeks to reach her yearning crack from behind as his clever fingers frigged her stiff, engorged nipples up to a fine erection. And what of Lady Arkley? Was she excluded from this *tableau vivant* of lustful excitement? Far from it – for in Sir Paul's absence, she too found solace in other arms, those of old Hutchinson the faithful family retainer who, as Sir Paul was shooting his seed, was lying flat on his back whilst Lady Arkley straddled him and guided his gnarled old truncheon into her hairy pussey.

And just over a mile away in Green Street, only Count Gewirtz and Vazelina Volpe were deep in the arms of Morpheus. Elsewhere in the house Connie Chumbley was being initiated into new delights by the always eager Lizzie and the happy young Tim who that evening had crossed the boundary into manhood. Mr Formbey, Estelle and Mrs Beaconsfield were enjoying a romp in the cook's bedroom with the butler's cock being substituted by the top of a bottle of champagne when necessary and even Inspector Glenton Rogers and P C Fulham, standing in lonely vigil outside in the street, were enjoying having their pricks sucked by two ladies of the night in exchange for looking in the other direction whilst the girls looked for late night custom in the still busy Mayfair street . . .